The Moonshine Shack Murder

Berkley Titles by Diane Kelly

THE MOONSHINE SHACK MURDER

The Moonshine Shack Murder

A Southern Homebrew Mystery

DIANE KELLY

BERKLEY PRIME CRIME
New York

BERKLEY PRIME CRIME
Published by Berkley
An imprint of Penguin Random House LLC
penguinrandomhouse.com

ISBN: 9780593333228

First Edition: July 2021

Printed in the United States of America
1   3   5   7   9   10   8   6   4   2

Book design by George Towne

To Carole Helm Pickett, my moonshine drinking
buddy and a lady who always shines bright.
Bottoms up!

Chapter One

The machinery sloshed, whirred, jangled, and clinked as I stood in breathless anticipation at the end of the conveyer belt on the factory floor. *Where is it? Come on!* After another jangle and clink, the rubber safety strips that hung over the machine's exit hatch swung outward, and there it was—the first jar of my Firefly brand moonshine, the mason jar's aluminum lid sparkling in the light from the fixtures overhead.

"Woo-hoo!" I threw my fists in the air and snatched the jar from the belt, planting a big kiss on the label before hugging it to my chest. Melodramatic maybe, but this jar had been years in the making. I'd invested my heart, soul, blood, sweat, and tears into my new moonshine business, not to mention every last cent I'd saved and then some. The first payment on my bank loan would be due in two short weeks. Good thing my Moonshine Shack would be ready to open for business first thing Monday morning, only three days from now.

I slipped the inaugural jar of shine in my tote bag and readied a cardboard box. Another jar exited the hatch and began its journey down the metal rollers, shimmying like one of Beyoncé's backup dancers. I grabbed the jar and tucked it into a corner of the box, adding eleven more as they jiggled their way toward me over the next two minutes. The ancient bottling machine wasn't fast, but it was efficient enough for my small-batch operation, and the factory manager had charged me a fair price to use it.

A quick *zip-zip* with the strapping tape dispenser and the box was sealed and ready to be loaded into my second-hand cargo van for transport to my shop. I'd had the van painted Day-Glo green and affixed magnetic signs with my Firefly moonshine logo to both sides. *Might as well advertise my wares while I drive around town, right?* My good friend Kiki, a freelance artist, had designed the whimsical logo for me. The graphic featured two flirty cartoon fireflies writing in fluorescent green against a midnight-blue background. The first firefly used his bright behind to spell *FIREFLY*. The other used her dazzling derrière to spell *MOONSHINE*. The image was cute and eye-catching, perfect for my products.

The floor supervisor circled around to check on things. "Everything all right over here, Miss Hayes?"

My dark curls bobbed as I turned to him. "Looking good!" I pointed to the carton at my feet. "My first case. Isn't it marvelous?"

He chuckled. "Never seen anyone get so excited about their products."

I shrugged. "What can I say? Moonshine's in my blood."

It was true, figuratively and, sometimes, literally. Back

in the days of Prohibition, my great-granddaddy was the number-one bootlegger in the region, the primary supplier of hooch all the way from his hometown of Chattanooga, Tennessee, south to the Chattahoochee River in Georgia. He'd made a small fortune before the sheriff arrested him. While my great-grandfather lost the fortune to revenuers, homestead laws allowed him to hang on to his rustic cabin in the Smoky Mountains and the rusty still hidden among the pine trees at the back of his property. He'd passed the cabin, the still, and the secrets of making shine along to my granddaddy, who'd passed them down to me when he'd moved into the Singing River Retirement Home a few years ago.

Yep, making moonshine was a family tradition, and it was high time the Hayes family started making money at it again.

With moneymaking in mind, I drove my van to the Moonshine Shack late Friday afternoon. The place was adorable, if I do say so myself. I'd hired a carpenter to create a front façade that resembled a hillbilly house. He'd fashioned an awning of spare boards that appeared haphazardly nailed together for effect but was completely up to code and had easily passed inspection. The words *MOONSHINE SHACK* were spelled out in neon-green glow-in-the-dark letters over the awning. I'd situated a couple of wooden rockers and a porch swing out front to entice tourists to sit a spell. Shamelessly stealing an idea from the Cracker Barrel restaurants, I'd also set out a small table and two stools so customers could challenge each other to a game of checkers, chess, or cards. I wanted the 'Shine Shack to be a comfortable, inviting place with a casual country charm. But even more, I wanted it to be a smashing success. I'd left a secure job with Chattanooga Bakery, Inc., maker of the world-famous MoonPie, and sacrificed a regular paycheck and the promise of a pension. I'd hate for it to have been for naught.

I circled around to the alley, parked, and hopped out to unlock the back door that led to the storeroom. My gray cat, Smoky, named for the nearby mountains, lay atop the wooden desk in the corner, watching me with his firefly-green eyes as he lazily licked a paw. The cat weighed upward of sixteen pounds and, unless food was in the offing, rarely moved, more cinder block than companion. I greeted him, as always, with an affectionate scratch under the chin and a "Hey, boy. Did you miss me?" His yawn told me that my absence had not affected him in the least. Hurtful, sure, but I'd long since accepted that ours would be a one-sided relationship.

Even with help from a dolly, moving the cases from the van to the storeroom proved to be backbreaking work. The muscles in my arms strained and shook, unused to being punished so severely. Smoky cast me a look of disdain each time I groaned or grunted. Next batch, I'd box the moonshine in smaller cases of six jars rather than twelve.

As I rolled the dolly outside to round up more moonshine, my ears picked up an unexpected sound. *Clop-clop-clop.* I turned to discover a mounted police officer riding up the alleyway on a beautiful chestnut mare. The horse's reddish-brown coat gleamed in the sunshine as she tossed her flaxen mane. The officer wore his uniform with black riding boots, a helmet, and mirrored sunglasses. Despite being built like a sculpted boulder, he rode with a graceful athleticism, at one with his steed.

Clop-clop. When they reached me, the officer pulled

back on the reins and spoke to his horse. "Whoa, Charlotte. Let's find out what this little filly is up to."

It took me a moment to realize I was the "little filly" he spoke of. Standing a mere five feet, I was undeniably small. But I made up for my stature in tenacity and sass. I looked up at the officer to see a set of broad shoulders, a strong jaw, and myself looking back, reflected in his sunglasses. I angled my head to indicate his horse. "I see you've got a thing for leggy blondes."

He sat silent and unmoving for a few beats before his lips spread in a slow smile. He ducked his chin and reached up to ease his sunglasses down, gazing at me over the rims, his amber eyes lit up like lightning bugs in amusement. His focus shifted to the logo on my van and the cartons of liquor before returning to my face. "A bootlegger, huh? I suspect you'll cause me no end of trouble."

"I can't make any promises, Officer."

In a swift, smooth move, he slid down from his horse to stand directly in front of me. He towered over me by a foot and then some, putting him around six feet, two inches tall and putting me on eye level with his rock-hard pecs and his name badge. *M. LANDERS. Why does that name sound vaguely familiar?*

Officer Landers removed his glasses and tucked them into the collar of his uniform. "I'll give you a hand. Charlotte needs a rest, anyway."

With my back and biceps screaming for mercy, I wasn't about to turn him down. "Thanks."

He tied his horse's reins to a water pipe before reaching up to remove his helmet. When he did, he released a cascade of loose, short curls the color of buckskin. He ran his hand through his hair and it settled into a contemporary pompadour, short on the sides, longer on top. He resembled a rockabilly artist, or a blond version of Elvis from his early years. I felt the heat of a blush warm my cheeks.

He grabbed a case from the back of the van and tucked it under one arm before grabbing another. As he turned to carry them through the back door of my shop, he spotted Smoky standing sentinel in the doorway. "Is your guard cat going to attack?"

"Smoky?" I stepped over and scooped my precious pet up in my arms. "He's harmless." Smoky stiff-armed me, pushing his paw against my chest, playing hard to get. Three years into our relationship and I was still trying to win the furry guy over. *Maybe someday.*

The cop eyed my cat and shook his head. "That there is why I prefer horses. They show some affection now and then."

Smoky issued a hiss, as if he understood he'd been insulted. As if she'd understood she'd been praised, Charlotte issued a nicker.

The officer stepped past me and my cat and into my storeroom, glancing around. "Where should I put these boxes?"

Returning Smoky to the floor, I gestured to an empty shelf. "Right there is fine."

After he'd placed the cases of moonshine, the guy crouched and reached out to run a hand over Smoky's head. "No hard feelings, buddy. I'll forgive you that hiss."

Smoky responded with a guttural growl. The cop countered with a chuckle.

With the brawny officer's help, my van was unloaded in no time. As he set the last case in the storeroom, I fished a jar out of a box. "Here. Take some moonshine on the house." I held the jar out to him, an expression of my gratitude.

He raised his palms. "Can't. If the captain catches me on duty with liquor in my saddlebags, Charlotte and I will end up on the unemployment line."

"Oh. Okay." Though his reason for refusing my moonshine was valid, I couldn't help but feel rejected.

My feelings must have been written on my face, because he tilted his head and said, "I'll come back to collect sometime when I'm off the clock. How's that sound?"

"How about Sunday evening?" I asked, hoping I didn't appear overeager. "You free then?"

"Sure am."

I set the jar of moonshine on my desk and picked up an envelope, holding it out to him. "Take this. It's an invitation to my private grand opening celebration."

"A private party? Well, now. This makes me feel special." He took the envelope, removed the invitation, and read it over before returning his gaze to my face. "Count me in."

"You can bring a plus-one if you'd like." Okay, so I was fishing to find out whether this attractive officer was attached. But unless you counted movie nights on the sofa with Smoky, I hadn't had a date in months. Could you really blame me?

Much to my delight, he said, "It'll just be yours truly. Charlotte's the only girl for me."

Good to know.

I followed him back into the alley, where he donned his helmet, untied his horse, and murmured sweet nothings to her, giving her a soft peck on the muzzle before remounting. He looked down at me a final time. "Be extra careful when you're out here and keep your back door locked," he warned. "Thieves sometimes come down these alleys looking for stuff to steal. A tiny thing like you would look like an easy target."

"I'm tougher than I look." I raised two fists and shadow-boxed the air before lowering my arms to my sides.

Judging from the quirk of his upper lip, Officer Landers was not impressed. "If anybody gives you trouble, sic Smoky on them and call 911 right away. You hear me?"

"Loud and clear, sir."

With that, he tipped his helmet in goodbye, gave his horse a light squeeze with his muscular thighs, and headed off.

As the officer and his horse *clop-clop-clopped* away from my shop, I issued a sigh and rolled the dolly into the corner of the storeroom, where it would be out of the way. I opened the door to Smoky's extra-large plastic carrier and walked over to the desk to round him up. A twinge puckered the muscles across my lower back as I lifted the hefty cat. "That's it, boy. I'm putting you on a diet."

I carried him out to the van and locked up my store, being extra careful and double-checking to make sure the deadbolt had hit home. Twenty minutes later, Smoky and I wound our way up the curved gravel drive that led to the two-bedroom, one-bath cabin the two of us called home. The place measured a paltry eight hundred square feet, but it had nonetheless hosted many a Hayes family holiday over the years. My mind held fond memories of summer evenings spent catching lightning bugs in mason jars with my siblings and cousins while our grandfather worked the still.

I parked next to the cabin and slid out of the van, greeted by the slow chirp of crickets. A trio of fireflies sketched secret symbols in the evening sky as I carried Smoky up the creaky steps to the porch. It was late April, but the air remained cool at the upper altitudes once the sun went down. *A little moonshine would warm me up, wouldn't it?*

I stepped into the cabin. While the interior walls bore standard drywall with soft green paint, the exterior walls were formed from reddish Douglas fir logs, looking the same on the inside as they did on the outside, as if the house had invited nature in. Though I'd kept many of my grand-parents' furnishings—the antique trestle table, the steamer trunks, the rolltop desk—I'd replaced their early-American velveteen couch with a more stylish faux-leather sectional. I'd also added bookshelves, a flat-screen television, and a carpet-covered cat tree for Smoky. The place was a won-derful mix of old and new, of mountain traditions and mod-ern comforts.

I released Smoky, who made a beeline for his food bowl. I followed after him, pulling the jar of shine from my tote bag and placing it on the counter. While I planned to save my first jar of Firefly moonshine as a cherished memento, I had plenty of my granddaddy's rotgut in the pantry. I grabbed a jug, splashed an ounce or two into a glass, and topped it off with lemonade. Other than condiments, a jar of pickles, and the pitcher of lemonade, my refrigerator was bare. Having devoted every spare second over the last few months to getting my business off the ground, I'd had little time to grocery shop. Luckily, I found a frozen pizza in the freezer that could serve as my supper.

Twenty minutes later, I was stretched out on the couch with a plate of pizza on my lap and the glass of spiked lemonade in my hand. After polishing off every last morsel in his food bowl and washing his whiskers with his paw, Smoky wandered up, stopping for a moment to sharpen his claws on the braided rug. I looked down at him. "Another Friday night at home, just me and you," I said. "I need to get a life, don't I?"

He hopped up onto the couch and curled up next to me, letting me know he was perfectly content with me having no life whatsoever. *Selfish cat.*

* * *

I rose bright and early Saturday morning, groaning as I sat up in bed. Every muscle in my arms, back, and legs let me know I'd overdone it yesterday. I'd been disappointed that the local liquor stores had placed no orders for my moonshine, citing insufficient shelf space to carry a local homebrew, but maybe it was just as well. I could only imagine the agony I'd be in if I'd made deliveries to liquor stores yesterday, as well. Still, I hoped they'd eventually come around. I could reach only a limited market with my Moonshine Shack and, while I was satisfied to start small, my long-term aspirations were much bigger than a single outlet in the riverfront district.

After feeding Smoky, I donned a pair of tennis shoes, jeans, and a T-shirt imprinted with my Firefly moonshine logo. I climbed into my van and rolled down the mountain, aiming for the Singing River Retirement Home. The place was named for its sweeping views of the picturesque Tennessee River, nicknamed the Singing River back in the day by the Yuchie tribe, who said its flowing waters sounded like a woman singing. Of course, you could hear lots of women singing up the road in Nashville, including Dolly Parton, who was born and raised not far from here.

Granddaddy was already out front waiting for me, sitting on his metallic red scooter near the double doors of the single-story stone structure. He'd dressed in his fanciest overalls, his least-scuffed boots, and the black felt Stetson cowboy hat my granny had given him the last Christmas she'd still been with us. *Hard to believe more than a decade has passed since then.*

With nothing much else to do with his time, my grandfather had appointed himself my unofficial, unpaid partner and insisted I take him with me today. It was only fair. After all, he was the one who'd taught me how to make moonshine.

He raised a gnarled hand in greeting and beeped his horn as I approached. *Beep-beep!*

I raised a hand in return and rolled to a stop at the curb in front of him. I hopped down to the pavement and circled around the van, giving him a kiss on his weathered cheek. "Good morning, Granddaddy."

"Good mornin' to you, too, Hattie."

After opening the passenger door, I held out a hand to help steady him as he raised himself off the scooter, grabbed his cane from the front basket, and ambled to the van. Once he was seated inside, I went to the back, opened the cargo bay, and lowered the ramp. Returning to his scooter, I plopped myself down on the seat and took off at full speed, fighting the urge to shout "Vroom-vroom!" I rounded the van, motored up the ramp, and parked the scooter in the now-empty cargo bay. All set, we headed to my shop.

After parking the van behind the Moonshine Shack, the two of us spent the day traipsing up and down Market Street, the main thoroughfare in the touristy riverfront district. I passed out invitations to my fellow business owners in the area, inviting them to the launch party the following evening. Granddaddy followed me on his scooter, his basket full of promotional T-shirts that he passed out willy-nilly to all takers. Couldn't hurt to turn folks into walking advertisements for the Shack, and passing out freebies would build buzz and goodwill. I made a mental note to set aside an extra-large tee for Officer Landers.

I held the door for Granddaddy as he scootered into the Smoky Mountains Smokehouse, a popular barbecue joint.

We'd eaten here many times over the years. The place made a mean potato salad, and their coleslaw was the creamiest and crunchiest in town. Though the place held a liquor license, it had no bar and offered only bottled beer, no hard liquor or wine. In other words, the restaurant wouldn't buy moonshine from me to serve to its customers. Still, that didn't mean we couldn't find other ways to be of benefit to each other.

We made our way up to the counter, where a fortyish man with dark skin and a bright smile stood behind the register, wiping down the countertop with a dish towel. I recognized him from our previous visits to the restaurant. As he always seemed to be on site and directing the staff, logic said he was either the owner, the manager, or both. I inquired and learned he was part owner of the place along with his two brothers, who were silent partners.

"Name's Mack Clayton," he said.

"Nice to meet you, Mack. I'm Hattie Hayes, owner of the Moonshine Shack." I hiked a thumb over my shoulder. "That's my granddaddy, Ben."

"Moonshine Shack?" He tossed the towel into a bin behind the counter and took the hand I'd offered him. "The new place down the block?"

"That's the one."

Our introductions and handshakes complete, I got down to business. "Your customer base and mine will likely have some overlap. We might could help each other out, send customers each other's way. Maybe offer a reciprocal discount?"

"Not a bad idea." His head bobbed as he seemed to mull over the prospect. "Let's touch base next week, work out the particulars."

"Great! Got a business card so I can get in touch with you?"

He punched a button on the cash register and the drawer opened with a *ding!* He fished a business card out of the till and held it out to me.

I took his card and, in return, handed him both my business card and an invitation. "If you come to the pre-opening party tomorrow evening, you'll go home with a free jar or jug of shine, your choice of flavor." While my Firefly brand featured fruity flavors such as wild blackberry, apple pie, and Georgia peach, the Shack would also sell earthenware jugs of Granddaddy's Ole-Timey Corn Liquor, the pure, high-proof stuff that a man could use to forget his troubles or clean his carburetor.

"Get a jug of my ole-timey moonshine," Granddaddy suggested. "If you add a dash to your barbecue sauce, it'll give it a nice kick."

Mack arched a brow. "Shine sauce. I like the sound of that."

"You'll like the taste of it, too," Granddaddy said. Of course, my grandfather thought everything tasted better with a dash of moonshine. He'd pour shine over his morning oatmeal if the staff at the retirement home would let him.

We continued down the block before circling back to hit the smaller establishments on the side streets. While most of the spaces were filled with restaurants or retail stores, a small accounting firm and a law office were tucked in among the businesses, occupying the second-floor space over a souvenir shop. With it being Saturday, neither office was open to the public, but I could see people working overtime inside. I slipped invitations under their doors.

The immediate area covered, we swung farther out, hitting the hotels along Chestnut Street. By the end of the afternoon, I'd passed out nearly a hundred invitations and logged over seventeen thousand steps according to my fitness tracker. *No wonder my feet are throbbing.*

"You're plumb tuckered out." My grandfather angled his head to indicate the seat behind him. "Climb on, Hattie."

He didn't have to ask me twice. I squeezed in behind him and we motored our way down Market Street, garnering several grins and a chuckle or two before we reached the Moonshine Shack. A glance to my right told me that Limericks, the Irish pub that sat directly across the street, had opened for its daily business.

"Wait here," I told Granddaddy as I climbed off the scooter. "I'll be right back."

My last invitation in hand, I scurried across the street. A three-foot-tall statue of a leprechaun greeted me outside the door. With his top hat, knee pants, and buckled shoes, the little man shared the fashion sense of the Pilgrims, though he'd gone his own way with the green fabric. Unlike the stoic and pious Pilgrims, the fun-loving fairy bore a broad, mischievous smile and held up a gold coin, presumably taken from a pot he'd found at the end of a rainbow.

I stepped past the little leprechaun to open the door and go inside. It took a moment for my eyes to adjust to the dimly lit interior, but when they did I saw a barely legal young woman with honey-blond hair, skintight jeans, and a low-cut top circling the floor, pulling chairs down from atop the round tables where they'd been placed, probably by the cleaning crew after the bar closed the night before. A pool table sat in a space to the side, separated from the rest of the bar by a half wall. A dartboard hung on a wall in the gaming area, the colorful darts standing in a rack beside it. Two male customers sat side by side at the bar with glass mugs of dark ale in front of them. A ginger-haired bartender stood behind the bar, using a remote control to change channels on the TV mounted in the corner. A green bar towel was draped over his shoulder.

I bellied up to the bar and gave the bartender my best smile. After all, if I made a good impression, maybe the bar would add my moonshine to their offerings. "Hi there. May I speak to the owner or manager?"

"You got 'em both in front of you."

I stuck out my hand. "I'm Hattie. I own the Moonshine Shack across the street."

"Oh, yeah?" The guy scowled and refused my hand, crossing his arms over his chest. "Just what I need. Another bar stealing my customers."

I retracted my hand. "We won't be competitors," I pointed out, trying to smooth things over with the grouchy barkeep. "I'm only permitted to offer samples. Patrons won't be drinking on the premises. They'll be taking the moonshine home."

"If they're drinking at home," he countered, "they won't be drinking *here*." He jabbed an index finger on the bar for emphasis.

Cheese and grits. This guy really needed to lighten up. "My location could be good for both of us. It's an opportunity to create synergy."

"Synergy?" He snorted. "Where'd you learn that term? Business school?"

"As a matter of fact, yes. That's exactly where I learned it." The University of Tennessee at Chattanooga, to be exact. I'd spent four years cheering on our sports teams at the behest of Scrappy, the mockingbird mascot, while earning a degree in business management, with honors, no less. *Go Mocs!* This guy, on the other hand, seemed to have scraped his business skills off the bottom of his shoe. His interpersonal communications sure could use an overhaul, too. "Given that I'm right across the street and can't serve liquor, I could send lots of thirsty customers your way." *Or not.* I could just as easily send them down the street to one bar and grill or another. "Of course, I'd be more inclined to send them your way if you offer my moonshine here." Hey, if he could play hardball, so could I.

He stood straighter and lowered his arms from his chest. *Finally, we're communicating.* All I'd had to do was stoop to his level.

"Yeah, I could maybe see that," he acquiesced. "I'd need to try your shine for myself first, see if my customers are even interested in the stuff."

"It's pretty clear your patrons like moonshine." I pointed to a nearly empty bottle on a shelf behind the bar, an unflavored variety manufactured by Backwoods Bootleggers, one of the big brands. But the fact that Limericks stocked another company's moonshine didn't mean he couldn't buy some from me, too. After all, bars normally carried several brands of any type of liquor. Each customer had his or her own taste. For instance, when it came to Tennessee whiskey, many people preferred Jack Daniel's. Others were fans of George Dickel. Some people even thought Irish whiskey was superior to that produced in my home state. It goes without saying that those folks were downright crazy.

He shrugged. "Bikers and college boys like the stuff. It's cheap and high proof. That's what appeals to them."

"You know what else appeals to men and college boys?" I didn't wait for an answer. "*The ladies.* You carry my fruit-flavored shine and you'll draw a larger female clientele. The more ladies you get in here, the more men will follow them. It's the reason bars hold ladies' nights. You could do it, too. Maybe call it 'lasses' night' since Limericks is an Irish pub."

My crafty persuasion seemed to be wearing him down. The guy glanced back at the bottle of Backwoods Bootleggers before turning an intent stare on me. "Some free product might convince me to stock your moonshine."

I'm two steps ahead of you, buddy. "Come to my party tomorrow night and you'll leave with a free jar." I laid the invitation on the bar and pushed it toward him.

He picked the card up and quickly perused it, issuing a grunt. "I might swing by."

"Then I might see you there." Raising a hand in goodbye, I backed away from the bar. "Take care now."

Chapter Two

Sunday afternoon, Smoky lay in the front window of my shop, lazily lounging while I rushed about like a woman on fire, unpacking the cases and stocking the store displays with mason jars of fruity Firefly moonshine and jugs of Granddaddy's Ole-Timey Corn Liquor. I positioned small replicas of early automobiles on the shelves and checkout counter, too, a nod to NASCAR's origins in the illegal moonshine trade. During Prohibition, booze "runners" would modify otherwise ordinary-looking cars by removing the back and passenger seats to provide more cargo space, installing extra suspension springs to handle the weight of the liquor, and adding protective plates to keep dirt out of the radiators. These expert drivers could maneuver at top speed along curvy single-lane dirt and gravel roads in the mountains and in the dark, their headlights off to evade law enforcement. Racing the souped-up cars became a popular pastime even before the end of Prohibition.

In fact, NASCAR Hall of Famer Junior Johnson learned to drive running corn mash hooch. My great-granddaddy had himself bought one of Ford's first flathead V8s for use in his bootlegging business. The car sat in a shed behind my cabin. Maybe one of these days I'd look into having it restored.

Hanging over the shelves of shine was a gallery of framed family photographs. There was a photo of me at eight years old, mason jar in hand as I ran after a firefly in the woods. A photo of Granddaddy filling a jug at his still. My great-grandfather's mug shot after he was arrested for bootlegging. I'd also framed the newspaper clipping announcing his arrest. *BIG WIN FOR PROHIBITION! CHATTANOOGA'S NOTORIOUS BOOTLEGGER NABBED BY SHERIFF.* The article included a grainy photo of my great-grandfather in handcuffs, scowling as he stood beside the smug sheriff.

In addition to the family photos, I'd decorated the walls with spare boards on which I'd stenciled other names for moonshine. There seemed to be no end of synonyms. *Bootleg. Rotgut. Homebrew. Radiator whiskey. White whiskey. White lightning. Firewater. Corn liquor. Corn squeezin'. Hooch. Hillbilly pop. Red eye.* Even *mountain dew*, though that term had long since been appropriated for the trademarked soft drink.

Once I'd filled the display shelves, I built a pyramid of jars in the front window, hoping Smoky wouldn't knock them over. I set out two tables, covered them with red-and-white-checkered tablecloths, and lined up shot glasses for the samples to be poured later.

Rap-rap-rap! The sound of someone knocking at the back door grabbed my attention. I scurried into the stockroom and peered out the peephole. *Kiki and Kate. Right on time.*

I opened the door to let my best friends inside. "Hey, you two!"

I went for Kate first, hugging her as best I could taking into account that she carried a platter of finger sandwiches and was thirteen months pregnant. Okay, so maybe the latter was an exaggeration. But it felt like she'd been pregnant forever. She'd had a difficult time and had been too sick or tired to spend much time with me over the past few months. Kate Pardue was the yin to my yang, with rail-straight blond hair rather than dark curls like me, blue eyes to my brown, and tall and voluptuous to my short and scrawny. Where I was unfailingly feisty, she was unswervingly sweet. We'd met back in high school, bonding over the shared trauma of a fire we'd accidentally set as lab partners in chemistry class. Thank goodness the sprinkler system had kicked on. Getting everyone out of class for an hour had resulted in a major, if short-lived, boost in our popularity.

Kiki Nakamura and I went even further back, all the way to second grade. We'd met while waiting in line for a turn on the monkey bars at recess. Her family had just moved to Chattanooga from Tokyo. *Talk about a culture clash.* I'd taught her the hand motions and words to "Miss Mary Had a Steamboat," which she'd mastered remarkably well considering she was just learning English at the time. In return, she'd shared her Hello Kitty stickers with me. We'd remained close friends ever since. During college, Kiki had spent a semester in London in a study-abroad program. She'd left for England dressing much like the rest of us, in jeans, sneakers, and casual tops, hair pulled back in a ponytail. She returned in clunky black boots, ripped jeans and shirts, and a studded leather dog collar, having fully embraced London's punk culture. She'd pierced each ear seven times and even shaved one side of her head, leaving her silky black hair long on the other. But while her look was frightening, she was still the same fun-loving, carefree Kiki we'd always known.

I took the platter of sandwiches from Kate and carried it to one of the tables. Kiki followed along with a tray of artistically arranged sushi. Once she'd set it down, I gave her a hug, too, and thanked them both for bringing the food. "What would I do without you two?"

"Happy to help," Kiki said.

"Me, too." Kate glanced around the shop. "This place is downright darling!"

"It is, isn't it? Of course, I couldn't have done it without Kiki's input on the design and décor."

Kiki performed a gracious curtsy. "So glad milady is pleased."

I took a place beside Kate as she looked over the photo gallery. "Stinks that you can't try my moonshine tonight."

She put her hands on her hips. "Your moonshine is exactly why I'm in this predicament."

Some predicament. Kate and her husband, Parker, had been thrilled to learn they'd have a child. But I'd play along.

"That was homemade hooch." I held up a jar of my Firefly apple pie moonshine. "This stuff is the real deal. See? It's even got a bar code on the label. That makes it official."

"La-di-da." She took the jar from me. "I'll save this for after the baby comes." She slid it into the purse hanging from her arm and glanced around again. "What else can we help with?"

I checked my to-do list and raised a finger. "The porch decorations, food table, and music."

After locking their purses in the desk drawer, Kiki held the small stepladder while I strung green Christmas lights

along the awning out front. The flashing LED lights were
the closest thing to actual fireflies I could come up with.
Kiki and I wound more strands around the support posts.
Meanwhile, Kate set out the chess set in case anyone might
want to play, arranged the rest of the food I'd picked up
earlier, and got the music going. To cut corners, I'd forgone
having speakers installed in the store. Instead, I'd bought a
cheap speaker system for my phone and downloaded a
playlist of songs that would mesh with the moonshine
theme. Jug band music from the 1920s and '30s. Bluegrass
classics. I'd even included "The Ballad of Jed Clampett," by
Lester Flatt and Earl Scruggs. After all, who didn't love the
theme song from *The Beverly Hillbillies*?

Though my sister and brother had wished me luck,
they'd both moved out of the area years ago and wouldn't
be able to attend the event. My parents arrived a half hour
early, bringing Granddaddy with them. He took up resi-
dence on a rocker out front, a chunk of wood and a small,
sharp carving tool in hand, whittling away.

Mom put a hand on my shoulder. "I hope this works out
for you, Hattie."

I'd have felt more encouraged if she hadn't been shaking
her head skeptically as she spoke. *Ugh!* I fought to keep
from rolling my eyes. My mother hadn't taken a single risk
in all her life, and she couldn't understand why I'd leave a
good job to venture out on my own, especially when there
was, in her words, "plenty of professionally produced
moonshine already on the market." She seemed to think
moonshining was merely a hobby for me. She was wrong.
Bootleg booze was both my business and my birthright. Of
course, I encouraged my customers to drink with discre-
tion. My logo included the phrase "Shine Smart."

My father, on the other hand, was far more supportive

than my mom. He raised his hand for a high five. "I knew you could do it, Hattie. Your moonshine will make a killing!"

"I sure hope so."

Over the next couple of hours, dozens of the business owners I'd invited to the party circled by to get a gander at the Moonshine Shack, sample the flavors, and collect their free jar or jug of moonshine. Every time the bells on the door jingled, my heart skipped a beat and I looked over to see if it might be Officer Landers arriving. But every time it was someone else. *Has he forgotten about my invitation?*

I tapped jar after jar, filling shot glasses so everyone could try as many types as they cared to. The apple pie flavor seemed to garner the most interest, while Grand-daddy's Ole-Timey Corn Liquor came in a close second. The younger women liked the blackberry flavor, while the older ladies seemed to have a taste for the cherry variety.

I tucked a jar of the Georgia peach moonshine into a gift bag, along with a copy of drink recipes I'd concocted. "This peach shine tastes great in iced tea," I told the woman who'd selected it. "You can add it to cobbler or preserves, too."

"What a fun idea!" She thanked me and headed on her way.

Mack Clayton stepped up to the table, smelling faintly of barbecue. No doubt he'd come directly from the Smoky Mountains Smokehouse. After we'd exchanged friendly greetings, he said, "I'll take a jug of your grandfather's corn liquor. I'm going to make some shine sauce, see how people like it."

Maybe Mack would become a customer of the Shack after all. I pulled a jug from the supply behind me and handed it over the table to him. "Would you like to try any of the Firefly flavors? Be a shame to miss out."

"Can't have that, can we?" He ran his gaze over the choices. "Let me try the blueberry."

I poured a sample into a shot glass and handed it to him.
"Cheers."

He tossed the shot back and raised his glass in tribute.
"Hoo-ee! That's some good stuff."

I beamed with pride.

The crowd grew, jars and jugs of moonshine flying off
the shelves. I hadn't expected such a turnout. By my best
estimate, I'd given away more than a thousand dollars'
worth of moonshine and we were only halfway through the
party. I hoped I hadn't been foolish to invite such a large
crowd, to offer a full jar for free. But as they say, you've got
to spend money to make money.

Although I'd invited the local media, both television stations and newspapers, all of the news outlets had declined.
I'd tried to spin the opening of the Moonshine Shack as a
human-interest story, as well as one involving the region's
moonshining history, but they seemed to know what I was
really after—free publicity. Only my university's alumni
magazine had taken up the story. They'd sent over a jour-
nalism major in her junior year who wrote for the mag. She
asked me some quick questions, snapped several photos,
and sampled some shine, leaving with details to distill into
an article as well as an already distilled jar of peach shine.

Jingle-jingle. The door opened again, and again it wasn't
Officer Landers. Instead, in walked a thirtyish guy with
short, sandy hair and stylish eyeglasses. He wore a slate-
blue dress shirt that perfectly matched the color of his
frames, but the fact that he wore the shirt with jeans and
loafers kept him from looking too fussy. A white, wireless
Bluetooth headset curled over his left ear. He glanced
around, assessing the people and place, before his gaze
circled around to me. His brows rose slightly in question. I
gave him a nod of acknowledgment, and he headed my way.

He stepped up to my table. "You're the proprietor?"

"Yep. That's me. Hattie Hayes, moonshine mogul."

"We didn't get a chance to meet when you delivered the invitation to my office. I'm Heath Delaney."

"From Delaney and Sullivan? The law firm on Fifth Street?"

He dipped his chin in confirmation. "Welcome to the neighborhood. It's a great place to run a business. Lots of tourist traffic."

"That's what I'm counting on."

"Do you have legal representation?"

"No." My lease for the Moonshine Shack and my contract with the bottling company had been standard boilerplate, and I'd done my due diligence to make sure my landlord and the bottler had good reputations among their tenants and clients. With my budget stretched tight, I'd taken a chance and signed the agreements without having them reviewed by an attorney.

"My firm represents many of the small-business owners in the area," Heath said. "If you need a contract reviewed or somebody sued, I'm your guy." He whipped a business card from his breast pocket and handed it to me.

"I'll keep that in mind." I tucked the card into my back pocket. Turning to the matter at hand, I swept my arm to indicate the selections of moonshine in front of me. "Anything in particular you'd like to sample? Or should I set you up with a shot of each flavor?"

"What the heck. I'll try them all."

"You got it." As I set about filling shot glasses for Heath, the ginger-haired owner of Limericks sauntered through the front door, the honey-haired cocktail waitress on his arm. He looked around at the crowded place and frowned. It wasn't like I'd stolen any of his customers. These folks were all fellow businesspeople here to get a jar of moon-shine and take a look at my place, that's all.

Mack Clayton was chatting with a woman from the toy train store when he spotted the barkeep over her shoulder. His eyes narrowed ever so slightly. If I hadn't been looking right at him at the time, I probably wouldn't have noticed. *I wonder what that's about.*

The owner of Limericks made his way over, stepping up next to Heath. He slid the attorney a steely look and a grunt before ignoring the man as if he weren't there.

"Welcome!" I repeated my earlier gesture, sweeping my arm to indicate the options. "What's your pleasure?"

He noted the seven shot glasses in front of Heath and angled his head to indicate the attorney. "Give me what you gave him."

The honey-haired girl stepped up on the other side of her boss. She curled her French-tipped fingers over his shoulder in a familiar, affectionate gesture that said the relationship between the two of them went beyond business. "Me too, please."

"All righty." I set up two lines of shot glasses on the ta-ble and eyed the man. "I didn't catch your name when I was in Limericks yesterday."

"I'm Cormac O'Keefe."

An Irish name if ever there was one. "Glad you could swing by, Cormac."

He offered another grunt in reply. Apparently, he spoke fluid caveman. What the blonde saw in him was anyone's guess.

She gave me a smile and stuck out her hand. "I'm Mi-randa."

"Nice to meet you, Miranda."

As I poured shots for Cormac and Miranda, Heath sipped at his samples. He nodded when he found them enjoyable but grimaced as the cinnamon sample went down. He banged a fist on his chest to fight the burn. "That'll put hair on your chest."

Cormac snorted. "You could use some."

Heath stood stock-still, staring at the side of Cormac's face. While Cormac had been brave enough to mock the attorney, he didn't seem quite brave enough to look directly his way. I deduced from the exchange that the two had a history. But what, exactly, did that history entail?

When I finished pouring the samples for Cormac, he tossed each of them back in quick succession, not bothering to stop and savor each flavor. Miranda, on the other hand, hadn't forgotten her manners. "Thanks!" she said before daintily sipping from her first sample cup.

A sixtyish woman with light gray hair tapped Heath on the shoulder, and he turned to address her. While Heath was conversing with the woman, I asked Cormac what he thought of the moonshine.

"It'll get the job done," he said.

Not exactly a rousing endorsement. I turned to Miranda. "What do you think?"

"Sooooo good!" she cooed. "I like them all, but the wild blackberry is my favorite."

I pulled a jar of the fruity shine from the shelf behind me and handed it to her. "On the house. Enjoy."

"Yum! Thank you so much! I can't wait to share this with my friends. They'll love it, too." She nudged Cormac gently in the ribs with her elbow. "You should buy some for the bar."

Miranda's enthusiastic affirmation seemed to convince

Cormac he should offer my moonshine in Limericks. He leaned in and lowered his voice. "Bring an assorted case over tomorrow. Two jugs of your grandpa's stuff, too."

My first sale! And fourteen jars, no less. *Woo-hoo!*

Before I could respond, Heath turned back around, cutting a scathing glance at Cormac before addressing me with a pointed look. "I couldn't help but overhear. Here's some free advice for you. Get that order in writing. Make sure the terms are clearly defined and the order is signed and dated."

Cormac scoffed but still didn't quite look Heath in the eye. "Quit mansplaining. She can run her own business." Cormac returned his attention to me. He lifted his chin and raised his brows, silently communicating *See you tomorrow with that moonshine?* I gave him a small nod.

As Cormac and Miranda walked off, Heath frowned at their backs. "Keep my card close at hand. If you're going to deal with Cormac O'Keefe, you're going to need me. That man is as cutthroat as they come."

Chapter Three

I watched Heath's back as he, too, headed out the door. My thoughts were all over the place. Had the lawyer been toying with me in the hopes of landing a new client? Or did he know something I didn't? Cormac wasn't exactly a nice guy, but he'd been straightforward in our limited interactions. Maybe he was the one I should listen to. Maybe Heath had overstepped by insinuating himself in our transaction, implying I couldn't handle my business on my own.

I was on the fence, unsure whom to trust, until Mack Clayton walked back over. He seemed as steamed as the green beans he served at his barbecue joint. "If you sell any moonshine to Cormac O'Keefe," the restaurateur snapped, "get the cash up front."

"You speaking from experience, Mack?"

"Unfortunately, yes."

Thanks to Mack, I was no longer on the fence about O'Keefe. "I appreciate the heads-up."

As Mack and I broke our little huddle, the bells jingle-jangled once more. I looked up to see Officer Landers coming through the door. I felt myself heat up, like a boiler full of corn mash. He wore cowboy boots and jeans, along with a blue western shirt embroidered with silver horseshoes on the yoke. He stopped to give Smoky a scratch behind the ears.

Kiki and Kate sidled up to me. Apparently, the officer's entrance hadn't gone unnoticed by the two of them, either. The three of us stared at him across the room.

"Giddy-up," Kiki purred. "Who's the hot cowboy?"

"He's a cop," I whispered. "He came by late Friday and helped me unload my van."

Kate asked, "What's his name?"

"His last name is Landers," I said. "I got that from his badge. The only thing I know about his first name is that it starts with the letter *M*."

"Maybe the *M* is for *manly*," Kate said.

"Or *magnificent*," Kiki said.

"Or maybe it's just a bunch of *M*s in a row," I murmured. *"Mmmmm."*

When the three of us broke into giggles, Officer Landers looked our way. Instantly, my friends turned their attention to the table in front of us, rounding up used shot glasses and wiping away drips. I wanted to do the same but found myself unable to look away. The cop and I locked eyes and a warm sensation spread through me, as if I'd taken a generous sip of shine.

He stepped over to the table and stopped in front of me, somehow both too close and not close enough at the same time. "Good evening, Miss Hayes," he drawled with a charming formality.

"Hello, Officer Landers."

"Call me Marlon," he said, solving the mystery of the *M*.

"And you can call me Hattie."

His focus shifted from me, to Kiki, to Kate. He took in Kate's big belly and the glass of water in her hand. "I suppose every party needs a pooper." His friendly grin let her know he was only teasing.

I introduced Marlon to my girls. "These are my friends, Kiki and Kate."

He dipped his head. "Nice to meet you, ladies."

Kiki lifted her tray of shot glasses. "I'm going to run these back to the sink and wash them. It was nice to meet you, Marlon."

Kate, too, begged off, giving the officer and me a chance to speak privately. "I'll check on your grandfather. See if he needs anything."

As Kate headed toward the front door, Marlon gestured to the window. "That's your grandfather out front? He's a hoot."

"Uh-oh," I said. "What did he do?" There was no telling. Granddaddy wasn't exactly what you'd call conventional.

"Challenged me to a game of chess," Marlon said. "Every time he got himself in a bad spot, he'd trick me into looking away and move the pieces around while my head was turned."

"Sounds about right. He can be a handful. When my granny was alive, she had to take her wooden spoon to him regularly."

Marlon looked around. "You've got a nice establishment here." He wandered over to the photo gallery and stopped in front of the photo of me chasing fireflies. "Is that you?"

"Sure is."

"You were a cute kid."

"Were?" I puffed out my lower lip in a mock pout. "You don't think I'm cute anymore?"

"You're still cute," he said. "But you're certainly not a kid anymore." He slid me a look that caused my toes to curl inside my tennis shoes. Turning his attention to the newspaper clipping, he pointed at the grainy picture. "What a coincidence. That's my great-grandfather."

Before I could stop it, a horrified "Ew!" burst from my lips. "We're related?"

"Only if your great-grandfather was the Hamilton County Sheriff in the 1930s."

"No." *Thank the stars.* "My great-grandfather is the one getting arrested in that photo." Now I remembered why the name Landers had sounded familiar. Sheriff Landers was the one who'd taken my predecessor to the pokey. Good thing my granddad hadn't heard our conversation. He'd hit the roof if he learned Marlon was kin to the man who'd put his father in the slammer.

"Ew?" Marlon referred back to my outburst as he eyed me intently. "Do I disgust you, Hattie?"

Quite the opposite. "No, it's just that . . ." I couldn't think of any way to end the sentence without revealing the fact that I found him attractive.

He bent his head down and whispered, "You've taken a shine to me. Haven't you?"

My cheeks flaming, I said, "Don't flatter yourself."

"I don't have to." A cocky grin played about his lips. "You already did with that 'ew.'"

Two could play the cocky game. "Then I suppose it's your turn to flatter me, isn't it?"

"All right." He ran his gaze over my face and hair. "Your curls are adorable."

So are yours. "And?"

"You've got gumption."

So he found a woman with gumption attractive rather than emasculating. That said something about him. "And?"

"You're pushing your luck, little filly. Now serve a man some moonshine."

I raised a jug of Granddaddy's Ole-Timey Corn Liquor in one hand and a jar of my peach moonshine in the other. "Pick your poison."

He pointed to the jar of my moonshine. "Let me try that one first."

I poured him a sample of the peach. While he savored the sample, the bells rang again and in slipped a thirtyish man I didn't recognize. He was tall with dark hair and sported both a five-o'clock shadow and a bright red shirt bearing the logo of Backwoods Bootleggers. His cap bore the same logo, telling me he was in uniform. He'd paired the shirt with loose-fitting, multipocketed cargo pants. Besides the hillbilly aesthetic, the ample on-person storage was the same reason I wore overalls to work. The man kept his head down and attempted to blend into the crowd, but with most of the guests having already come and gone, he didn't succeed. He stopped at a shelf and picked up a jar of my moonshine to peruse the label.

"Excuse me just a moment, Marlon." Leaving Officer Heartthrob at the sample table, I headed over to the man. "Hello, there. I don't believe we've met."

The man's eyes flashed in alarm. He'd been caught trespassing, and he was waiting to see how I'd react.

Though I was a bit miffed that he'd ignored the sign on the door that read *PRIVATE EVENT BY INVITATION ONLY*, there was no reason for me to be uncivil. Heck, if I noticed an event involving moonshine, I'd want to check things out, too. I smiled and gestured to the logo on his breast pocket. "I see you work for the big boys."

"I do." He offered me a smile in return. "I was calling on customers in the area and spotted your shop. Figured I'd come over and check out the competition."

"Competition?" I repeated, pleased that he considered me such. "Not hardly. I'm just a local, small-batch operation." *For now.* "Besides, there's room enough for both of us in this business." It was true. Moonshine was a growing market. There were plenty of customers to go around. Even if we were competitors, we didn't have to be enemies. I offered my hand and introduced myself. "Hattie Hayes."

He gave my hand a firm but friendly shake. "Gage Tilley."

"Would you like to sample our flavors, Gage?"

He declined, offering me the same excuse Marlon had given me on Friday, that he was on the job. "Better not. I've got some deliveries to make."

Even though the man had crashed my party, I offered him some complimentary shine. "Take a jar or jug with you. Wouldn't want you leaving empty-handed." Unlike the police captain, Tilley's boss couldn't complain if he had alcohol in his possession. After all, selling and delivering liquor was his job, and scoping out the competition said he took that job seriously.

"That's very generous of you." He snagged one of Granddaddy's jugs, bade me goodbye, and headed out the door.

I watched Tilley out the window. He strode across the street and opened the door to Limericks, holding it for a curvy woman in jeans and a form-fitting periwinkle-blue T-shirt. Her wavy, golden-blond tresses hung clear down to her waist. I remembered seeing the bottle of Backwoods Bootleggers moonshine at the bar the day before. *Cormac O'Keefe must be one of the customers Tilley is calling on.*

I made my way back to Marlon and picked up a jar of the cherry-flavored shine in one hand, the apple pie flavor in the other. "Which one would you like to try next?"

"The apple pie."

I poured a shot of the apple pie moonshine for him. "Bottoms up."

Marlon raised the shot glass to his lips and tossed it back, letting the liquor sit on his tongue for a moment before he swallowed. "Not bad. Not bad at all."

As I poured him a shot of the cherry-flavored shine, a high-pitched shriek from outside caught our attention. Through the window, I saw Miranda ducking her head and flailing her arms in an attempt to ward off the golden blonde, who was scratching and clawing at Miranda like a feral feline.

"Catfight!" someone cried.

Smoky stood up in the front window to get a better view. Out front, Granddaddy rose from his stool, tottered to the curb, and hollered across the street, brandishing his cane in a valiant effort to stop the blonde-on-blonde brawl. While those in my shop gathered at the windows to gawk, Marlon leaped into action. He bolted out the door, past my grandfather, and across the street, raising a hand to stop an oncoming pickup. When the truck screeched to a stop, he dashed past it and deftly grabbed each of the women by the upper arm, yanking them apart. He held them at bay, his head turning from one to the other as he issued reprimands and orders.

Kiki slid up next to me and issued a low wolf whistle. "Officer Landers sure is—" She stopped herself, her face contorting as she appeared to search for the right word.

"Capable?" I suggested.

"Yeah," she said. "He's all kinds of capable."

I pointed out a pertinent fact my friend seemed to have forgotten. "You've already got a boyfriend."

"Exactly," Kiki said. "A boyfriend. Not a fiancé. Not a husband. Trading up is still an option."

So much for that strategy. "I already called dibs on Marlon."

"No, you didn't."

"Then I call it now," I said. "Dibs."

After a tongue-lashing from Marlon, Miranda and the other woman stormed off in opposite directions down the sidewalk. Marlon returned to the Moonshine Shack and stepped back over to my sample table, glancing down at the jars. "Where was I?"

Kiki wagged her brows. "About to tell us what happened over there."

Kate leaned in, eager to hear the gossip. I was curious, too. It wasn't every day you saw two women toss their pride and purses aside to scuffle on a sidewalk. They must have had a good reason.

Marlon pointed at the cinnamon-flavored moonshine, and I poured him a shot while he filled us in. "Those two ladies work at Limericks. They just learned the owner has been dating both of them. He scheduled them to work different shifts, told them to keep the relationship under wraps, and gave them strict orders not to come around while they were off duty."

Kiki scoffed. "He was trying to keep them apart so they wouldn't find out he's a bloody, two-timing, cheating chump."

"Yep," Marlon said. "Didn't quite work out for him."

Looked like I was wrong. The women hadn't had a good reason to fight. A prickly guy like Cormac O'Keefe didn't seem worth a second glance in my opinion, let alone worth the risk of an injury.

Putting the encounter behind him, Marlon downed the

cinnamon shine and raised his glass. "This here's my favorite. Matter of fact, you could mix this cinnamon flavor with the apple pie and call it 'candy apple.'"

"That's a fantastic idea." Mixing the two varieties would give me another option to offer my customers with little additional effort on my part.

"You'll have to get the ratio of apple to cinnamon just right," Marlon added. "If you need taste testers, count me in. I ate my weight in candy apples as a kid."

"I'll take you up on that."

The party wrapped up not long after. My parents and grandfather left together so they could give Granddaddy a ride back to his home. Kate offered to help clean up, but in her condition she needed rest so I gave her an appreciative hug and insisted she go home. Kiki and Marlon stuck around and helped me break down the folding tables and move them into the storage room. I stashed what little food remained in the mini fridge. I decided to leave the sweeping and mopping until morning. It had been a fun but exhausting event. I'd need a good night's sleep to tackle my grand opening day tomorrow.

After making sure Kiki got safely on her way, Marlon saw me to my van out back, carting Smoky's carrier for me. He lifted it up and down a few times, performing an improvised biceps curl. "Carrying this chubby cat is a good workout."

"He's not *chubby*," I insisted. "He's *fluffy*."

Marlon slid me some side-eye. "If you say so."

After Smoky was safely stashed in the cargo bay, I opened my door and turned to face the officer a final time. "Thanks for all your help, Marlon."

"Happy to be of service." With that, he pretended to tip a hat and headed off.

* * *

Late Monday morning, I picked up my grandfather from Singing River and we drove to the Moonshine Shack. Smoky promptly claimed his spot in the shop's front window, where he could watch the activity on the street between naps. While I finished cleaning the place, Granddaddy sat on a rocker out front, whittling and telling the few early tourists to be sure to come back when the Shack opened at noon. I knew from monitoring the comings and goings of foot traffic in the area that only a handful of people came around before lunchtime, so I'd decided my store hours would be noon to nine p.m. Monday through Saturday, and noon to five on Sunday. With my bank account nearly empty, I hadn't dared to hire any employees yet, unsure if I could make payroll. Kiki had offered to help out on weekends for the time being, and I took her up on her generous proposition. Granddaddy could hold down the fort when I took necessary breaks during the weekdays.

I readied the cash register, filling the plastic till with bills and coins to make change. I double-checked to make sure the card reader device was working properly and turned on the mood music. I packed up a case of assorted Firefly moonshine and two jugs of my granddaddy's hooch to take over to Limericks when it opened later today. When the preparations were complete, I stepped over to the newspaper clipping of my great-grandfather's arrest, closed my eyes, and sent up a silent plea to my bootlegging ancestor in the hereafter. *If you've got any sway up there, please ask the powers that be to make my moonshine shop a success*.

The instant my watch read 12:00, I pulled the front door open and set out the sandwich-board sign on which I'd written *GRAND OPENING SPECIAL—20% OFF ALL MOON-*

SHINE! I tied a trio of helium balloons to the sign to ensure that it grabbed people's attention. Once everything was in place, I took up a position next to a porch post out front and looked up and down the street, wondering who would be my first customer. Would it be the middle-aged lady window shopping at the boutique down the block? The older couple on the bench across the street eating donuts and drinking coffee? The leather-clad bikers rolling up the street on their raucously rhythmic Harley-Davidson motorcycles?

Spoiler alert, it was the bikers. The guy in the lead glanced over at the Shack as they rolled past, signaled his cohorts, and hooked an illegal U-turn, pulling to the curb in front of my shop, cutting his engine. The others did the same, lining up their bikes at an angle to fill two parking spots.

Once the last engine died down, I called out, "In the mood for some moonshine today?"

"I'm in the mood for moonshine *every* day." With that, their leader marched into my shop, his four friends on his heels. They left the scent of Old Spice aftershave in their wake, the same stuff my father and grandfather wore.

As I followed them in, I took in the name of their gang, which spanned the back of each of their vests. *DESPER-ADDOS.* That extra *D* had to be a typo, didn't it? Before I could stop myself, I blurted the word out loud, pronouncing it as it was spelled. "Desper*add*os?"

The men exchanged knowing looks and grins before their leader put a finger to his lips and, eyes twinkling with amusement, whispered, "*Shh.* Don't blow our cover. We're CPAs from Knoxville, out for our annual post-tax-day ride through the Smokies."

Accountants, out for some fun after the April 15 deadline. That explained their moniker. It also explained why there wasn't a single tattoo, earring, or unkempt beard among them. In fact, four were clean-shaven. The only one with facial hair sported a well-trimmed goatee. This was no outlaw biker gang. Rather, they were a motorcycle club, out for a leisurely ride, looking for fun, not trouble. Some might call them posers, but I hoped to call them customers.

"I was a business major," I said, hoping to establish a rapport and, perhaps, a repeat business relationship when they were back in town again. "I'm not certified, but I earned As in all of my accounting courses."

The jaw of the man nearest me dropped in jest. "Guys! She's one of us."

After sharing a chuckle, I offered to share my wares. "Samples, anyone?"

Their leader whooped. "Heck, yeah!"

They emerged from my shop ten minutes later, each bearing a jug of Granddaddy's Ole-Timey Corn Liquor for themselves and one of my fruity Firefly jars to take home to their wives or girlfriends back in Knoxville. They left behind a selfie I'd taken on my cell phone to celebrate my first sale. I stood beaming in the center with the bikers gathered around me, raising the jars and jugs they'd purchased.

I thanked them as they slid their purchases into their saddlebags. "Enjoy your ride back home! Be sure to come by next time you're in town!"

Chapter Four

Only a handful of customers wandered into my shop the rest of the afternoon, but while the lack of traffic was a disappointment it wasn't necessarily a surprise. After all, it was a weekday and not yet peak tourist season. At five o'clock, as I poured tasting samples for a group of retired ladies at the counter of my shop, the neon *OPEN* sign illuminated in the window of Limericks across the street. As soon as I was done serving my customers, I'd take Cormac's order over to him. Given the warnings from Heath Delaney and Mack Clayton, I'd insist on payment up front.

The ladies spent a few minutes sampling and savoring before deciding on their favorite flavors. Each of them purchased a jar and were delighted when I slipped a copy of my drink recipes into their bags. As soon as they'd gone, I put a hand on my grandfather's shoulder to rouse him from the nap he was taking in the rocker out front. "Can you cover for me?"

"Of course." Setting his whittling aside, he rounded up his cane, rose stiffly from the rocker, and ambled inside, circling around to the back of the checkout counter.

"You remember what to do?"

He picked up the handheld bar code reader and waved it about like Yosemite Sam waving his cartoon pistols. "I aim this magic doohickey at the stripes on the label and pull the trigger."

"Exactly," I told him. "When you hear the beep, you'll know it worked."

"Gotcha." He took a seat on the padded stool behind the counter.

I hustled to the storeroom, loaded Cormac O'Keefe's moonshine order onto a dolly, and rolled it through my shop and across the street under Smoky's watchful eye. As I approached the pub, a *HELP WANTED* sign in the window caught my attention. It hadn't been there the day before. My guess was that Miranda and the other server had quit their jobs after their sidewalk skirmish the preceding evening. *Who'd want to work for a man who'd cheated on her?* Or maybe Cormac had fired the two. Miranda had only appeared to be defending herself, but the other had launched an aggressive attack. Having someone like her on staff could pose a liability. Then again, if Cormac fired the golden blonde, he might be risking a sexual harassment lawsuit.

The leprechaun greeted me with his mischievous grin, holding up his coin as if to tell me there was money to be made here at Limericks. *I hope so.* I pulled the pub's door open and held it with my foot while I wrangled the dolly over the threshold. A wiry, dark-haired man walked up on the sidewalk. He had a tattoo on his neck of what was probably supposed to be a black bear roaring but looked more like a belching Labrador retriever. *I suppose even tattoo artists have to start somewhere.*

The tattooed man looked down at the cases of moonshine on my dolly and read the label aloud. "Firefly moonshine?" His focus shifted to my face. "Never heard of it."

"Maybe not yet," I said with a smile, "but you will!" I removed a hand from the dolly and pointed to my shop across the street. "That's my new moonshine store. Stop by sometime. We offer free samples."

"Oh, yeah?" His eyes brightened. "Is that just a onetime thing or what?"

I hadn't considered that someone might try to take advantage of my free samples on a regular basis without making a purchase. I supposed I'd have to come up with a policy. I replied with "Reasonable limits apply." *How's that for the fine print?*

The man followed me as I rolled the cases inside. Cormac was pouring drinks at the far end of the bar. To my surprise, the curvy golden blonde who'd been whaling on Miranda the night before stood in a back corner, a round tray tucked under her arm as she looked up at the television, taking in the early news. I was surprised she'd come back to work for Cormac after learning he'd cheated on her. Either she was very forgiving or she couldn't afford to quit her job. She wore jeans and a cute peasant blouse in a colorful print with elastic around the neckline, waist, and wrists.

Cormac pushed the drinks he'd poured to the front edge of the bar and barked, "Ashlynn! Order up!"

On hearing her name, the woman turned around. Her lips looked full and luscious in a shimmery shade of pretty pink lipstick. *I wonder how my lips would look in that color.* With my pale skin, most lipsticks looked clownish on me, but the shade she wore just might work with my complexion. I was tempted to ask her for the name of the makeup line and the color of the lipstick, but I was here to conduct business and I didn't want to appear unprofessional. I also didn't want to risk getting walloped if she somehow found my question offensive. I'd seen what this woman could do.

As she walked up and retrieved the drinks from the counter, I rolled my boxes over and parked my dolly in front of the bar.

"Hi, Cormac." I dipped my chin to indicate the case of liquor below. "I've brought your moonshine."

He put down the glass he'd been drying, flipped the bar towel over his shoulder, and pointed a finger in my direction. "Get out!"

"Excuse me?"

It wasn't until a voice came from behind me that I realized Cormac was speaking to the guy who'd followed me in. "Be cool, dude." The man raised his palms. "I only want to get a beer."

My impulse was to shrink back and cower behind my dolly. Ashlynn, on the other hand, seemed unfazed. Having delivered the drinks, she circled around to the back of the bar. She reached up to straighten a bottle on a nearby shelf before calmly making change at the cash register. I supposed people who work in bars are used to dealing with a rowdy crowd.

The elastic band on her sleeve must've ridden up, because she tugged it back down into place at her wrist before closing the cash drawer. *Wait . . . did she just tuck some bills into her sleeve?* Her movements had been so smooth and swift, I couldn't be certain. Add in the dim lighting and the reflections off the bottles and mirror behind the bar, and I was even less sure. *No one would have the audacity to steal from the till right under their boss's nose, would they?*

"Out!" Cormac shouted again, moving his arm so that he pointed to the door. "Now!"

My attention shifted from Ashlynn back to the tattooed guy. When the man made no move to leave, Cormac yanked the towel from his shoulder, slung it onto the bar, and raised the hinged part of the counter to come around to our side.

"All right! All right!" Palms still up, the guy backed toward the door. "Relax. I'm going."

Cormac stormed after him. The guy turned, shoved the door open, and left, but not before raising a middle finger at the barkeep. Cormac stood in the open doorway, making sure the man had headed off, before stalking back through the bar, muttering under his breath.

"Not your favorite customer, I take it?"

Cormac scowled. "He's nothing but trouble. Hits on my waitresses, hustles my customers at pool and darts, skipped out on a sixty-dollar bar tab. I'd bet he's the one who broke my front window a few months back, too."

Running a bar was more difficult than I realized. No wonder Cormac was such a sourpuss. Getting back to the matter at hand, I gestured to the moonshine again. "I've got your order here."

"Cancel it."

"Excuse me?"

"Cancel it," he repeated. "I don't need it after all." He went around to the back of the bar and dropped the flap back into place with a *bang*.

Fury flared, heating me from the inside out, and my hands grasped the dolly in a death grip. "But we had a deal!"

He shrugged. "I got a better one."

"From who?"

His answer was evasive. "Another moonshine company."

My mind flashed back to the distributor from Backwoods Bootleggers who'd crashed my party the night before. "It was that man from last night, wasn't it? Gage something-or-other."

"Not that it's any of your business," Cormac said, "but when I told him you'd offered me a discount, he offered an even better one if I'd go exclusive with Backwoods."

"So you're breaking our contract? That's a lousy way to treat a fellow small-business owner."

He snorted. "What are you getting worked up about? I won't be selling jars of moonshine over here. I'll just be making drinks with it. Like you said, you and I aren't competitors."

My own rationalizations coming back to bite me. Heated and humiliated, I grabbed my dolly and rolled it out of the pub without another word. Rather than promising me riches, the leprechaun outside the door seemed to be taunting me now, holding up his gold coin as if poised to snatch it away, just as Cormac had done. *Insolent Irish imp!*

As I pushed the handcart back into my shop, my grandfather took one look at my face and his own puckered in concern. "What happened over there? You brought the moonshine back, and you got a burr in your britches now, too."

"Cormac O'Keefe refused his order."

"On what grounds?"

"Remember the guy from Backwoods Bootleggers who snuck into our grand opening uninvited last night?"

"I do." Granddaddy's eyes narrowed. "What about him?"

"After he crashed our party, he marched right over to Limericks and offered O'Keefe a big discount if he'd agree to stock Backwoods moonshine exclusively."

"You mean to tell me that sorry snake across the street took the deal?"

"He did." Cormac had made the business equivalent of a bootleg turn, heading one way at high speed before executing a controlled skid to end up going in another.

Granddaddy threw up his gnarled hands. "But the Hayes family hooch is the best in all of Appalachia!"

"Without a doubt. Everyone will learn that soon enough, whether Limericks serves our shine or not. I'll make sure of it."

As enraged as I was that Cormac O'Keefe had reneged on our agreement, at least I hadn't parted with any product. Better to learn now that the guy was an unscrupulous shyster than later down the line. I returned the moonshine to the storeroom and unpacked the case. It helped a little to know that the guy with the neck tattoo had introduced a little misery into Cormac's life. *What goes around comes around.*

When I went back into the store, Granddaddy said, "Maybe this will cheer you up. It's Smoky." He held out a small wood carving in the shape of a sleeping cat.

I took the whittled wood from him and gave it a closer look. As always, my grandfather had made a miniature masterpiece with intricate detail—curved indentations for the cat's closed eyes, smooth rounded cheeks, distinct tiny toes. He'd sanded it smooth, not a rough edge anywhere. He'd whittled his initials, *BJH* for Benjamin Joseph Hayes, on the underside. "It's perfect, Granddaddy. It deserves a special spot in the store." I glanced around and decided to display the cat next to the register, where customers could admire it.

I sold a few jars of moonshine that evening thanks to my

grandfather suggesting to passersby that their life would not be complete until they came inside and sampled our shine. Fortunately, the customers found him charming rather than pushy. If I thought his arthritic hands would be up to it, I'd give him one of those signs to spin.

When we wrapped up at the end of the night, I was thrilled to discover that, even after deducting the cost of the products sold and the day's proportion of overhead and rent, we'd earned a small profit. A whopping sixty-four cents, in fact. The Hayes family was once again making money with moonshine.

Over the next few days, thanks to the free jars I'd offered, my grandfather enticing passersby into the shop, and my incessant social media posts, word spread and business picked up at the Moonshine Shack.

Another group of bikers came in, though these guys weren't a well-groomed, well-mannered club. Their faces bore burly beards and battle scars. They laughed on seeing the displays of my Firefly shine.

"Apple pie?" one of them barked. "Peach? Wild blackberry? This fruity stuff is for chicks and sissies. You got any real moonshine?"

I bristled at the sexist remark, but him saying that my Firefly flavors weren't real moonshine was what really got my goat. My shine *was* real and, what's more, it was *mine*. I'd continued the family business and expanded on it, taken it in a new direction. I was proud of what I'd accomplished. But no sense arguing with these men. They were entitled to their opinions—even if they were wrong. I gestured to the jugs of Ole-Timey Corn Liquor. "Try the jugs. It's for purists."

They might have insulted me, but at least they bought

several jugs of Granddaddy's shine. They slid the jugs into the saddlebags on their bikes and motored across the street to Limericks.

On Thursday night, traffic picked up on Market Street, mainly college kids getting a jump start on the weekend. Groups wandered by wearing gear with Greek letters on it designating various sororities and fraternities. Alpha. Beta. Chi. It was like watching a live version of a Mediterranean *Sesame Street. Tonight's episode brought to you by the letter epsilon!* Several groups wandered into the store and purchased moonshine. *Maybe I should offer a student discount . . .*

Marlon rode by on Charlotte several times, stopping once to chat with me and my grandfather. Fortunately, my grandfather hadn't noticed Marlon's badge when I'd introduced them, and I'd used first names only. If Granddaddy realized the officer was related to the sheriff who'd arrested his father, he was bound to blow a gasket, and any chance I might have of getting to know Marlon better could be ruined.

A few minutes shy of eight o'clock Friday evening, Cormac O'Keefe stormed toward my store, his face purple with rage. I suppose my face had looked much the same when I'd left Limericks four days earlier after he'd refused to accept his moonshine order. Smoky stood in the window as Granddaddy rose from his rocker out front. As my grandfather and Cormac exchanged words, I rushed outside to learn what the ruckus was all about.

"You can't say I wasn't telling the truth!" Granddaddy brandished his small whittling tool for emphasis. "You're not to be trusted."

"You crazy old coot!" Cormac barked. "I should sue you for slander."

"I'd sue you right back!" Granddaddy hollered. "I might be an old coot, but I ain't crazy!"

That's debatable.

Several people stopped on the sidewalks nearby to watch the exchange. My cheeks blazed in embarrassment.

As if realizing that an argument with my grandfather wasn't likely to be productive, the barkeep turned to me. "Did you know your grandfather's been telling people not to come to my bar? He's called me a crook."

"No. I wasn't aware." Though I could hardly blame him. My grandfather was fiercely protective of his family, and he'd been insulted by O'Keefe choosing another brand of moonshine over ours. Still, antagonizing O'Keefe wouldn't help anything. Better to keep the peace. "I'll talk to him."

"You'd better," O'Keefe snapped.

"Git!" Granddaddy motioned with his tiny tool. "Go back to your watering hole."

O'Keefe issued another of his signature derisive snorts and strode back to his pub. I raised a hand and smiled at the crowd that had gathered, hoping to make light of the uncomfortable situation. "Everything's okay!" I called out as I took my grandfather by the arm. I lowered my voice to a whisper. "Why don't you come inside for a bit? Cool down?"

He resisted. "I'm not afraid of that whippersnapper."

"I know, Granddaddy. But the best thing you can do for our business is keep your mouth shut. You want the Moonshine Shack to be a success, don't you?"

He scowled. "You know I do."

"Then come inside. I'll fix you some iced tea with a dash of peach shine."

His mouth spread in a broad smile. "Now you're talkin'."

I'd wrangled a rocker inside and settled my grandfather in it with a glass of spiked tea when a telltale *clop-clop-clop* sounded out front. I looked out the window to see Marlon dismount at the curb. He stepped forward and tied Charlotte's reins to one of the front porch posts. Removing his helmet, he came inside, stopping to give Smoky a scratch under the chin.

"Hi, Marlon," I said, moving forward to meet him. "You're working late today."

"Drew the short stick and got assigned the swing shift. I'll be on duty most of the night." He looked from me to my grandfather and back again. "Received a report of a man in overalls brandishing a knife and making threats in front of your store. You two wouldn't happen to know anything about that, would you?"

I rolled my eyes. "Cormac O'Keefe called you?"

"Couldn't say. The caller hung up before dispatch could get his name."

It had to be Cormac who called. He probably knew he'd look like a wimp for reporting an octogenarian with a harmless whittling tool. Still, that didn't keep him from wanting to give us a hassle. I turned to my grandfather. "Show Marlon your knife."

Granddaddy raised the tiny blade he'd been holding during his argument with O'Keefe. "If that man feared this itty-bitty tool, he's as yellow as he is crooked."

"I'm inclined to agree with you." Marlon exhaled a sharp breath and scrubbed a hand over his face. "That said, do me a favor, Ben. Don't wave those tools around when you're arguing with someone. They might take it the wrong way. Okay?"

Granddaddy raised his right hand to his forehead and gave Marlon a salute. "Yes, sir, Officer—" He squinted at Marlon's chest, trying to read his badge. "Landers."

I went rigid, hoping my grandfather wouldn't make the connection. *No such luck.*

His squinty gaze went from Marlon's badge to his face.

"You're not kin to Sheriff Daniel Landers, are you?" He pointed his whittling tool at the newspaper clipping on the wall before directing it accusingly at Marlon.

Marlon's gaze cut my way. What could I do but shrug and sigh? The truth was bound to come out sooner or later, though later would have given Marlon more of a chance to win Granddaddy over first.

Marlon returned his focus to my grandfather. "Matter of fact, we are kin. Sheriff Daniel Landers was my great-grandpa."

My grandfather's face puckered and his hands fisted. "Well, I'll be a son of a—"

"Granddaddy!" I cried, cutting him off. "That's all water under the bridge."

"No, it ain't!" he snarled. "I'll never forget when my father was taken away. I remember it like it was yesterday."

"You don't remember it at all," I pointed out as gently as I could. "Your father was arrested in 1933. You were only a baby."

My grandfather's scowl deepened. "Well, I remember visiting him in the clink. Mama cried every time we left."

Prohibition ended in December 1933. Mere weeks after my ancestor's arrest, liquor production and sales became legal again. But by that time, Eustatius Hayes had been convicted and given the maximum sentence: a ten-thousand-dollar fine and five years in the Tennessee state penitentiary. Despite the change in the law, those convicted of making or selling liquor during the period when it had been illegal were forced to serve out their full terms. So while my granddad hadn't actually seen his father arrested, he had lived without his father for the formative years of his childhood.

"For what it's worth," Marlon said, "your father evaded arrest for years and made a fool of my great-grandfather before he finally caught him." He lowered both his voice and his head. "I'll let you in on a little-known secret. If your daddy's tire hadn't blown out that night, he'd have gotten away again."

On learning that his father had made a formidable rival, my grandfather's tight face and fists loosened, but only a little. His eyes took on a distant look. "A flat would explain why Daddy was always checking the tires after he was released."

Marlon straightened up. "I hope you won't hold our families' history against me. I do my best to be fair, and I hope you'll give me a fair shake, too. Let's let bygones be bygones. What do you say?" Marlon extended a hand to my grandfather.

"I say no sir, no way, nohow." Granddaddy glared up at Marlon and crossed his arms over his chest, refusing to take his hand. For an octogenarian, he sure was acting childish.

"Grandaddy!" I snapped, using the same tone my granny had used to keep him in line. "Every man should be judged for himself. You've said so yourself."

He merely harrumphed in reply. He knew I was right, but he wasn't willing to admit it.

I sent the point home. "If Marlon held a grudge against you the way you're holding one against him, you'd be in handcuffs right now and on your way to the police station for booking. He has grounds to arrest you. You've confessed to brandishing your tool at Cormac."

Granddaddy's eyes slid to the handcuffs on Marlon's belt, but he remained silent, refusing to budge.

Marlon, being the bigger man both literally and figuratively, said, "Come on now, Ben. Give me a chance to prove myself. Who knows? Maybe one day you and I can even be friends."

Granddaddy still pouted, but at least he uncrossed his arms and gave a grunt of agreement. It was better than nothing, and the best we were going to get. A provisional peace made, I exhaled in relief and gave Marlon an apologetic smile.

Marlon glanced out front, where Charlotte waited for him. "I better get back out on patrol. You two take care."

I saw him to the door, closing it behind him. I hoped my grandfather's bad behavior wouldn't scare Marlon off. I'd begun to look forward to his occasional stops by the shop. It would be a shame if my curmudgeonly granddad put an end to those visits.

Chapter Five

A few minutes later, the sounds of hooting, hollering, and general mayhem met my ears. Five rambunctious frat boys approached on the sidewalk. All were white with various shades of brown hair. Two wore hoodies, two wore long-sleeved T-shirts, and one wore a short-sleeved tee, all of which were emblazoned with the Greek letters Mu Sigma.

The tallest one in the front threw out an arm, stopping his buddies in their tracks. "Look! Moonshine!"

Another gaped. "The sign says free samples!"

Granddaddy groaned from his seat in the rocker as he eyed the boys through the window. "These hooligans look like trouble."

I clucked my tongue at him. "You think anyone under the age of fifty is a hooligan who looks like trouble."

"Sometimes I'm right."

"You got me there."

The bells on the door jangled as the boys came inside.

"Hi there!" I called. "How are y'all doing tonight?"

The tallest of the five had brown hair generously gelled into a stiff Ken doll style. He picked up a jug of my grandfather's shine in each hand and raised them high. "It's time to party!"

It looked to me like they'd already been partying. Smelled like it, too. The scent of beer had wafted into my shop along with them. But even though they'd downed some beers, their boisterous behavior seemed born more of immaturity and excitement than intoxication. When I'd been in college, I'd lived for Friday nights, too, the chance to put away the books for a few hours and have some fun.

The shortest and stockiest pointed a finger and swung his arm to indicate the entire sales floor. "Give us a sample of everything you've got."

"I'd be happy to," I said, "once I see some ID." I circled around the back of my sample table. "You boys aren't driving, are you?"

"Nah," said Short-'n'-Stocky. "We walked over from the frat house."

At least they'd had the sense to come to the area on foot.

After checking their IDs to make sure they were all of age, I reached behind the sample table to the cabinet where I kept the clean shot glasses. The glasses clinked as I lined up a set of seven in front of each boy so they could sample all six of my flavors, as well as my grandfather's shine. "Let's start with the apple pie." I splashed a tiny dash in each shot glass, not more than a few drops, just enough that they could taste the flavor.

While most of them remarked that it tasted good, the Ken doll cringed. "Too sweet!"

While I loved my fruity flavors, I realized they wouldn't be for everyone. What product was? "You might prefer the cinnamon." I served them each a small sample of the cinnamon flavor next.

After tilting the shot glass back and letting the drops run onto his tongue, the Ken doll said, "That's more like it." When we'd exhausted the Firefly flavors and he savored a sample of Granddaddy's Ole-Timey Corn Liquor, he let loose with a wolflike howl. "Moonshine, baby!"

I scanned the faces in front of me. "Interested in purchasing some jars or jugs tonight?"

"No, thanks," said Short-'n'-Stocky. "We're gonna hit the bars. We can't be lugging jugs around with us all night."

Though I was frustrated not to make a sale after spending the last quarter hour serving them samples, I didn't let my feelings show. After all, maybe they'd come back another time. "No problem," I said with a smile. "Be sure to come back again sometime when you can take some home with you. Maybe bring your girlfriends in for a tasting." I had no idea whether these guys had girlfriends, but odds were at least one or two of them did.

They jostled one another on their way to reach the door first. When one of others shoved him, Short-'n'-Stocky lost his footing and veered into a pyramid display of wild blackberry shine. I scrambled over and managed to wrap my arms around the base of the display before all the jars could topple over. The jar that had been on top performed somersaults on its way down to the floor, shattering in a spray of shine and glass shards, wetting my sneakers and the legs of my overalls.

"Oops." The boy looked down at the mess he'd made. "My bad." He backed up from the rapidly spreading pool of purple liquid, his rear end aiming for the door. "You've got insurance for that, right?"

I didn't bother explaining about deductibles and simply

circled around the puddle to escort him out. My grandfather used his cane to lift himself from his chair and joined
me. The boy's friends were already on the move outside,
looking back over their shoulders and snickering as they
walked away from my shop. The Ken doll was hunched
over suspiciously, as if he might have something hidden in
the pouch of his sweatshirt—something like a jar of moonshine he'd swiped when I'd been distracted by the mess his
friend had made. As they skittered off down the sidewalk,
I stepped outside. My grandfather followed me. Half a
block down, the boy yanked a jar of shine from the pouch
of his sweatshirt and held it up as if in victory, raising the
other fist as well and hollering "Woot-woot!" I couldn't be
sure from this distance, but from the color it appeared to be
a jar of cherry shine.

Granddaddy raised his cane and shook it in the air. "You
boys ever come back here," he hollered, "I'll give you a
whooping!"

They merely laughed and ran off.

I turned to my grandfather. "Did Marlon's warning
mean nothing to you?"

He waved a dismissive, arthritic hand. "He only told me
not to threaten people with my whittling tools. He said
nothing about my cane."

I sighed. "You've got me there, again." I supposed I
could have called the police on the boys, but it seemed unlikely they'd return to the Moonshine Shack, and they'd
probably have swallowed the evidence of their crime and
ditched the jar by the time the police could catch up with
them. Besides, it was closing time. All I wanted to do was
mop up the mess, go home, and get a good night's sleep. I
let the theft slide. A person has to choose their battles and,
after facing off with Cormac, I had no more fight left in me.

After cleaning up and closing the store, I drove my grandfather back to the Singing River Retirement Home. Though I appreciated him keeping me company at work, after the confrontation he'd caused today, I was glad it would be Kiki working alongside me over the weekend. I drove back to the cabin and was fast asleep in minutes, the stress and excitement of my first week in business having zapped every ounce of my energy.

M y eyes popped open, but as dark as it was in the mountainside cabin I could see nothing. My heart raced in my chest like a bootlegger being chased by the law. *Had I locked the front door of the Moonshine Shack and set the alarm?*

I couldn't be certain. My grandfather's run-in with Cormac O'Keefe and the subsequent visit from Marlon Landers had thrown me for a loop. The punks who'd made a mess in my shop and stolen the jar of shine certainly hadn't helped, either. While I'd made a closing checklist earlier in the week, I hadn't used it tonight, figuring after four nights I had the routine down. Maybe I'd overestimated myself.

I fumbled for my cell phone and consulted the screen when it lit up. 2:28. *Ugh.* As exhausted as I was, I'd never be able to go back to sleep until I returned to the Moonshine Shack and checked on things. For all I knew, some one could have made off with my entire inventory.

I slid my feet into a pair of rubber-soled slippers and tied a fluffy white robe over my pajamas, a custom-made pair with Smoky's face printed on them. Kiki had given the PJ's to me as a gift on my most recent birthday. Truly, you can order anything on the Internet these days. When I grabbed my purse and keys, Smoky took that as his cue to accompany me to the door. I scooped him up in my arms and carried him with me. There was no time for his carrier, but as lazy and docile as he was there was little risk he'd escape. I set him on the floor of the cargo bay, climbed in, and motored down the mountain.

While the riverfront area was normally lit up and busy, this late at night many of the lights in the businesses had been turned off and the people had returned home or to their hotels. Even the neon lights at Limericks were off, the pub having closed at two o'clock. Hardly a soul was in sight as I made my way down Market Street and turned down the alley behind my shop.

Grabbing Smoky once again, I carried him from the van to the back door and cradled him in my arms as I unlocked it. I set him down and he sauntered inside with a saucy swish of his tail. The space was dimly lit by an automatic night light plugged into an outlet next to the powder room, but the device provided enough illumination for me to see without turning on the harsh overhead lights and frying my tired eyeballs. I eyed the security system keypad. The lack of a red flashing light told me I had indeed forgotten to set the alarm earlier. From now on, I'd always use my checklist when I closed up.

Smoky mewed and pawed at the door that led from the stockroom into the store. I opened it and he slipped through, making his way to his favorite spot in the front window and hopping up to take a look outside. I didn't bother turning on a light in the store, either. The glow-in-the-dark labels on my Firefly moonshine told me that the everything was as we'd left it. *Thank goodness.* I checked the front door and found the deadbolt locked. *Good.* At least I hadn't forgotten to lock the entrance. I would've felt really stupid.

As long as I'd come all this way in the middle of the

night, I figured it couldn't hurt to make sure the cash was still securely stashed. Leaving Smoky for the moment, I returned to the stockroom and lifted the cardboard box I'd used to disguise the small floor-mounted safe. Setting the box aside, I knelt down and spun the dial on the combination lock to open it: 33 for the year my great-grandfather had been arrested, 92 for the year I'd been born, and 21 for the year I'd begun my moonshine business.

I pulled the door of the safe open. A quick glimpse inside told me the cash was secure, too. As I closed the door and spun the lock, a series of odd noises came from out in front of my store. A thud, followed by a tinkling sound, followed by a cry, followed by two more thuds. *What in the world made those sounds? Is someone out there?*

My heart spun out of control as I grabbed the back of my desk chair to lever myself to a stand. I stood stock-still, listening, but heard nothing more. I tiptoed to the door and peeked into the shop. Smoky stood in the window, staring intently down the street, his bushy tail twitching in agitation. I had no idea what he'd seen, but he'd definitely seen something. Fortunately, my front door and windows were still intact.

My first impulse was to call the police, but I realized the sounds were similar to the ones I'd heard in my shop earlier when the frat boy had knocked over the display. It could merely be some rowdy young men who'd accidentally dropped a beer bottle on the pavement. Maybe there was no real cause for alarm. Law enforcement had already been summoned to my shop once today on specious grounds. No need to waste their time again if nothing serious was afoot.

To get a better view, I turned on the lights inside the shop and walked to the window to stand behind Smoky. Unfortunately, the interior lights reflected off the glass, turning it into a virtual mirror and making it impossible for me to see outside. I reached over to the light switch inside the front door and flipped on the outside lights, too. The exterior of my shop was visible now. A glance in the direction Smoky had been looking told me that whatever he'd been watching down the street was gone now, the sidewalks and roadway deserted. But when I lowered my eyes to my cat, they spied a red smudge along the outside of the glass. *What is that?*

My gaze moved down to see a crumpled human form lying on the pavement in front of my shop. *Oh!* I sucked air, shocked, my hand reflexively moving to my chest as if to slow my racing heart. *Could the smudge be . . . blood?*

Once I was able to gather my wits, I rapped on the inside of the glass and called out to the person below. "Are you okay? Hello? Are you all right?"

No response. The person lay eerily still. Had they passed out, hit their head on the shop window, and collapsed? I had no idea what had happened, but I knew I had to find out. I unlocked the door, yanked it open, and looked down.

Cormac O'Keefe lay on the concrete, his neck spurting blood in rhythmic pulses, his head surrounded by a fresh and flowing pool. My stomach seized, my mind whirled, and my legs buckled, my world thrown a-kilter. Bright spots of light zigzagged in my peripheral vision, like a swarm of frenzied fireflies. I put a hand on the doorframe to steady myself and held my breath to slow its pace. My mind finally stopped spinning enough that I could process what I was seeing. Cormac had been attacked, and his life was in serious jeopardy. Next to Cormac lay the weapon that had been used to slash his throat—a broken jar of my Firefly cherry-flavored moonshine.

Chapter Six

My legs moved of their own accord, backing away from the open front door of my shop until my rear end butted against the checkout counter. My brain kicked in on auto-pilot. *Call for help, Hattie!* I pulled my phone from my pocket, but my hands shook so hard I couldn't seem to push the right buttons. Realizing I had a better chance of dialing 911 with one shaking hand rather than with two that seemed to be at odds with each other, I dropped my phone onto the checkout counter and stabbed at the screen with my index finger, finally managing to dial emergency dispatch. I picked up the phone and held it to my ear, the device slapping against my cheek as my hand trembled.

A male voice came over the line. "Chattanooga 911. What's your emergency?"

"There's a man lying in front of my shop! He's hurt!" *Probably dying as we speak.* But I didn't want to think it. I was no fan of Cormac O'Keefe, but I wouldn't wish death on him.

The dispatcher asked for my address and I was so discombobulated I couldn't remember. Luckily, the shop's address was printed on the business cards on the counter in front of me. I recited the address. He told me he'd send both police and an ambulance right away. "Stay on the line until they arrive."

"Okay." I felt fairly certain Cormac's soul was already on its way to the hereafter, but what kind of person would I be if I didn't do whatever I could to save his life? Jabbing the speaker button on my phone, I tucked it into the pocket of my robe, grabbed one of my promotional T-shirts, and stepped outside, closing the door behind me to keep Smoky from wandering out to investigate. Curiosity might not kill the cat in this instance, but a curious cat could contaminate the crime scene.

Cormac lay at an angle, not quite on his side but not flat on his back, either. His legs were curved slightly and his right arm was draped over his torso. His eyes were at half mast, staring down the street in the same direction Smoky had been looking. The dull look in them, as well as the fact that he wasn't blinking, told me he was likely a goner. If the blank stare hadn't convinced me, the amount of blood he'd spilled should have. While the cut no longer gushed blood, it produced a steady, heavy ooze. Still, I was no medical professional and was wholly unqualified to make a death determination. Moreover, it was difficult to tell precisely how much of the liquid surrounding him was blood and how much was cherry-flavored moonshine. Judging from the dark color and viscosity, though, most of it was blood. Regardless, I'd never forgive myself if I didn't try to my best to save him.

Steeling myself with a deep breath, I pulled back the

sleeves on my robe and bent down next to Cormac, careful to avoid the pool of blood. I pressed the rolled-up T-shirt against the ragged, gaping gash. I murmured positive notions like a mantra, as much to calm myself as to reassure Cormac . . . *if he could even hear me*. "You'll be all right, Cormac. It's not so bad. You'll be okay. It's not so bad." *All lies*. It was highly unlikely he'd be all right, and the situation was well beyond bad. Even Smoky seemed to realize the gravity of the situation. He stood inside the window, watching with his head cocked and ears back, his tail swishing in concern.

The dispatcher stayed on the line until the ambulance arrived. As the EMTs opened the back bay and hopped down to the asphalt, I stood to get out of their way but left the T-shirt in place at Cormac's neck. A black-and-white Chattanooga Police Department cruiser eased to the curb a dozen feet behind them, allowing ample room for a gurney.

I retreated into my shop, remaining just inside the now-open door. With Cormac's body blocking the way and the large pool of blood on the stoop, I'd have a hard time exiting. Besides, it was best if I didn't disturb things any more than I already had. Despite my efforts to stay out of the blood, the expanding puddle had reached the toes of my slippers as I'd crouched next to Cormac, and I'd tracked some of the fluid into the store. Horrified by the discovery, I kicked off my slippers, leaving my footwear lying haphazardly next to the rain mat.

I scooped up Smoky and clutched him to my chest like a furry security blanket. To the cat's credit, he didn't fight me this time. He, too, seemed in need of comfort. *What exactly had he seen? And whom?*

The uniformed EMTs, one male and one female, stepped

forward, their feet crunching on the glass. They knelt down by Cormac. The woman felt for a pulse on the exposed side of his neck before putting a stethoscope to his chest. Her gaze met her partner's. "No pulse."

Despite my efforts, it appeared Cormac had lost his life. Emotion wrapped invisible hands around my throat, pressing on my neck like I'd just been pressing on Cormac's.

While the man began what were likely futile lifesaving measures, the woman looked up at me. "What happened?"

"I don't know," I squeaked. I forced a cough to clear my throat so I could speak without sounding like a dolphin. "I was in the back room of my shop, and I heard a thud, then the sound of glass breaking, then a cry, then two more thuds. When I came out to see what was going on, I found him lying here. It looked like he'd been attacked."

"How long since you heard the cry and thuds?"

It seemed like it had taken the first responders a lifetime to arrive, but I knew that wasn't actually the case and it only seemed that way because I'd been totally freaked out. "Maybe three minutes? I called for help immediately."

The woman stood as two police officers, both men, climbed out of their cruiser and walked up. One of the cops was a solidly built, olive-skinned man who appeared to be approaching forty. The younger one was taller and thinner, with fair skin and brown hair. He looked to be a fresh-faced recruit just out of the academy.

As the female EMT rushed to round up a gurney from the ambulance, the more seasoned officer looked down unflinchingly at Cormac. The rookie forced his head to turn toward the grisly scene, but his eyes were averted, his gaze off to the left. I wondered if this was his first encounter with a murder victim. If so, it was something the two of us had in common. To his credit, his partner didn't ridicule him for his squeamishness. Instead, he put a hand on the younger man's shoulder and gave it a supportive squeeze.

His partner mollified, the officer turned his attention to me. With a corpse and a medic between us, he couldn't come close enough for a handshake. He simply raised a hand in greeting. "I'm Officer Barboza."

"Hattie Hayes."

Niceties exchanged, Barboza asked, "What happened here?"

"I'm not sure." I repeated what I'd told the EMTs. Thud. Tinkling glass. Cry. Two more thuds. Body on the walkway in front of my shop.

The officer looked down at the prone figure at our feet before returning his attention to me. "Any idea who the victim is?"

"Cormac O'Keefe." My arms still wrapped around my cat, I lifted my chin to indicate the Irish pub across the street. "He owns Limericks." I turned my head in the direction Smoky had been looking earlier. "When I came out of the back room, Smoky was staring out the window that way. My guess is whoever hurt Cormac took off in that direction."

"Any idea who we're looking for? How many attackers?"

"I don't know," I said. "I didn't see anyone." It was possible, even likely, that the attacker or attackers had seen me, though. I would have been easily visible inside my shop after I'd turned on the inside lights. Even if they hadn't seen me inside, I'd unwittingly signaled my presence at my shop when I'd turned on the exterior lights. The thought sent ice through my veins. *Killers don't like witnesses.*

"Do you know whether the attacker or attackers left the scene in a vehicle?"

"I didn't hear car doors close or engine noise or tires squeal, so I assume whoever did this was on foot."

Addressing his partner, Barboza gestured to the cruiser. "Drive the area. See who's around. Call for backup if you come across anyone who looks suspicious."

A look of relief swept over the rookie's face. He wasted no time hopping back into the cruiser and taking off down the street, leaving Cormac's lifeless body behind.

Barboza pulled his radio from his belt and pressed the talk button. After identifying himself, he said, "I'm at the Moonshine Shack on Market Street. We've got a body here. Send crime scene out to collect evidence."

The fact that he referred to Cormac as "a body" told me he, too, thought Cormac's chances of survival were extremely slim to nonexistent.

He clipped the radio back onto his belt, ran his eyes over my robe and cat-print pajama bottoms, and asked, "What're you doing here this time of night?"

For the first time, it dawned on me that my presence at a murder scene could be suspicious. "I own this shop. I was home in bed when I woke up and worried that I'd forgotten to lock the door and set the alarm when I closed up. I came back to check."

He cocked his head and looked at Smoky, as if willing my cat to either confirm or deny my story. Though his head remained cocked, the officer's eyes returned to me. "Had you set the alarm?"

"No, but I'd locked the door." *At least I'd done one thing right.*

He cocked his head in the other direction, as if to examine my story from every angle. "Any particular reason you were concerned about the alarm?"

Ugh. I'm going to have to tell him, aren't I? "I was distracted when I closed up. It had been a difficult night. Some college boys came in right before I shut down and broke some of my stock and shoplifted from my store. Earlier, my grandfather had an argument with—" I gulped and pointed to the man at our feet. "Officer Landers stopped by, too."

Barboza snorted. "You girls love the cowboys and never outgrow your pony phase, do you?"

Girls? I was a grown businesswoman, an entrepreneur, and I didn't appreciate being reduced to a sexist stereotype . . . even if there might be a bit of truth behind it. My ire rose, but it was good to feel something other than terrified. "Officer Landers was responding to a complaint," I snapped. "I didn't make the call or request Officer Landers." *Not that I was disappointed he'd been the one to handle the matter.*

"Who made the call, then?"

Again, I pointed a feeble finger at the man lying between us. "He did." The call could well have been the last phone call Cormac had made. "He claimed my grandfather had threatened him with a knife." Smoky patiently complied as I performed some feline puppeteering, using his paw to point to the display of ole-timey corn liquor. "That's Grand-daddy's brand. He works here with me. He's the one who taught me how to make moonshine."

He arched a brow. "No kidding? All my pappy taught me was how to catch a fly ball."

The Hayes family weren't athletes. If anything, we were outlaws. "Cormac placed a big order with me last weekend, but he refused the moonshine when I tried to deliver it on Monday. My grandfather didn't like Cormac jerking me around. Granddaddy overheard some of my customers talking about getting a drink at Limericks, and he suggested they take their business to another bar. When Cormac found out, he stormed over and confronted my grandfather." I hated to speak ill of the dead, especially when "the dead" was at my feet, being lifted onto a gurney, but I had to defend my grandfather. Myself, too. "My grandfather gestured with his whittling tool, that's all. He wasn't threatening anyone with it. Besides, the blade is tiny. I could do more damage with a thumbtack."

"Where's your grandfather now?"

"At the Singing River Retirement Home. He lives there."

"No chance he attacked O'Keefe, then?"

"Absolutely not!" Granddaddy might be what my granny had called cantankerous, but he was all bark and no bite. Not to mention that he was nearly as old as the mountains. "He'd never try to end someone's life. Besides, he can't drive anymore. He'd have no way to get here on his own."

"There's always taxis or Uber."

"My granddad is too cheap to call a cab and he couldn't download an app if his life depended on it."

"What about *you*?"

Confusion overtook me. "I can download an app."

He skewered me with his pointed gaze. "That's not what I'm asking. I'm asking if you're the one who cut the guy's throat."

"Of course not!"

Barboza cocked his head again. He was beginning to look like a rooster. "You're here under dubious circumstances." His gaze shifted to the shattered glass on the sidewalk and the aluminum lid encircled by jagged, blood-smeared shards that had been used to slice Cormac's flesh. "Looks like the murder weapon was a jar of your moonshine, too."

"That doesn't mean I did it!"

The two EMTs exchanged a knowing look over the gurney as they raised it.

As the reality of the officer's words sank in, my body broke out in a cold sweat. In my panic I tightened my grip on Smoky, nearly squishing the poor beast. "If I'd killed Cormac O'Keefe, why would I use my own jar of moonshine to do it and then call the police to report it?"

Barboza raised a shoulder. "People do all kinds of things that don't make sense. That's why they call it 'senseless' violence. Maybe you thought calling it in would throw suspicion off you."

I stomped my foot in outrage, though the fact that I was in socks rendered the gesture ineffective. "I thought no such thing!"

Ignoring me, he turned to the medics. "Check his pockets for his keys, his wallet, and his phone. The detective's gonna need them."

The male EMT quickly patted Cormac's front pants pockets, shoved his hand into the right pocket, and pulled out a set of keys and a cell phone, handing them to the cop. Easing a hand underneath Cormac's lower back, he retrieved his wallet from a rear pocket, handing that over as well. The medics rolled the gurney over to the ambulance, slid Cormac into the bay, and climbed in after him. As soon as they'd shut the doors, the ambulance pulled away, lights flashing, siren wailing. Taking Cormac to a hospital was likely a hopeless endeavor, but given the short time frame since he'd been injured it was understandable that they'd give it a try, see if anything could be done for him.

Headlights flashed again as a large police department SUV came up the street, pulling a horse trailer behind it. The vehicle rolled to a stop at the curb where the ambulance had been only seconds before and the driver's window came down. Marlon's eyes locked on mine before closing for a couple of seconds. He exhaled a long, loud breath before opening them again and returning his gaze to me. "My swing shift just ended and I was loading Charlotte into her trailer when dispatch came on the radio and said a body was found here . . ." He drifted off, shaking his head. But his message was clear. When he'd heard a person had been killed at the Moonshine Shack, he'd assumed—maybe even feared—that it had been me.

I filled him in. "It was Cormac O'Keefe."

"O'Keefe? Really?" Several emotions played over his face. First, there was surprise. Then there was whatever was the opposite of surprise. *Expectation or understanding, maybe?* Cormac had been a thorn in the side of many of the area's businesspeople, myself included. The fact that someone had decided to do him in wasn't as shocking as it would be had he been a nice guy that everyone admired and respected.

Barboza looked from me to Marlon. "You two seem well acquainted."

"Of course," Marlon said. "I make it a point to meet the people on my beat." As if realizing his words might imply his fellow officer had fallen short in community relations, he added, "It's much easier when you patrol on horseback than in a cruiser."

"I imagine it would be." Barboza rocked back on his heels. "That still doesn't explain what you're doing here."

"I responded to a call here earlier tonight."

Although Barboza was responding to Marlon, he cut a glance my way. "So I've heard."

As Marlon climbed out of the SUV, headlights flashed a second time. The squad car returned, pulling up behind the horse trailer. A look inside told me it held only the rookie, no suspects.

"Long as you're here, Landers," Barboza said, "mind marking a perimeter?"

"Sure." Marlon reached back into his SUV and pulled a roll of bright yellow cordon tape from the map pocket. "Where do you want it?"

Barboza whipped his flashlight from his belt, turned it on, and used it like a laser pointer to outline the porch. "When you're done here, put some tape over the front and back doors of Limericks. If there's any cars in the bar's back lot, cordon them off, too. Crime scene and the detective will want to take a look around there."

As Marlon began to string the tape between the support posts on the front porch of the Moonshine Shack, the rookie climbed out of the cruiser and issued his report. "Didn't see anything out of the ordinary, only the usual late-night crowd heading for their cars or hotels. Nobody looked suspicious or seemed to be in a hurry to leave the area."

Officer Barboza turned to me with an accusing stare.

Before I could stop myself, I blurted, "I told you, it wasn't me! Besides, I'm not the only one who's had issues with Cormac O'Keefe."

"Oh, yeah?" He whipped out a pen and notepad. "Who else?"

Uh-oh. I've done it now. I'd have to snitch on Heath Delaney, Mack Clayton, Miranda, and Ashlynn. "He's cheated several small business owners in the area." Barboza made notes as I provided a quick rundown of what Heath and Mack had told me at my grand opening. "He cheated on his girlfriends, too. He was two-timing a couple of his servers. A woman named Miranda and another named Ashlynn."

"It's true," Marlon told his fellow officer. "I had to break up a fight between the two of them last Sunday."

Barboza held his pen aloft. "Did you file a report?"

"No," Marlon said. "Didn't seem to be any sense getting the ladies in trouble when it was O'Keefe's fault and neither of them was hurt. After I pulled them apart, they willingly went their separate ways."

I remembered the guy with the belching bear tattoo, the one who'd followed me into Limericks when I'd gone to deliver the moonshine. We'd engaged in a brief conversation about my moonshine, shop, and sample policy before Cormac had ordered the man out of his bar. *Could he be the killer?* "Cormac told me he's had repeated problems with a customer. He said the guy ran out on a tab and hustled some of his customers. Cormac thought the guy had broken a window in Limericks a while back, too."

"Oh, yeah?" Barboza said. "What's the customer's name?"

"I don't know," I said, "but I saw him myself. He came into the bar when I went to deliver the order. Cormac hollered at him to leave. He's got dark hair and a bad tattoo on his neck that is probably supposed to be a bear but looks more like a dog."

Another knowing look was exchanged, this time between Officer Barboza and Marlon. "Damien Sirakov," Barboza said with a grunt.

I looked from one of them to the other. "You know the guy?"

"We do." Marlon used his teeth to cut through the tape and tied it off on the final post. "Sirakov's got a rap sheet as long as an epic fantasy novel. You name it, he's done it. Misdemeanors, anyway. He's managed to avoid a felony charge so far. That's the only thing that's kept him out of prison."

Barboza whipped out his radio and contacted dispatch, asking them to send officers to Sirakov's address to keep an eye on it, to stop the man if he tried to leave. "He's a person of interest in a death investigation." The task completed, he turned back to me. "Show me your arms."

I was holding my cat in them. Couldn't he see them? "What do you mean?"

"Put the cat down," Barboza instructed, "and pull your sleeves back."

Marlon frowned slightly at the other officer, but he said nothing. He probably realized that Barboza was only following protocols and that insinuating himself too much in the situation wouldn't be good for either of us. I placed Smoky on the floor behind me. Relieved of my furry burden, I pulled back my sleeves and stretched out my arms.

Barboza leaned in to take a closer look. After examining the back of my arms, he made a circular motion with his finger. "Turn your wrists."

Again, I did as he'd instructed. He ran his gaze over my inner arms. There was nothing to see but a few freckles, a thin white scar from a minor summer camp injury that had healed two decades ago, and a couple of blue veins throbbing with panic at the thought that I could be a suspect in a murder investigation. I'd never survive prison. Heck, I'd barely survived the summer camp. I'd been horribly homesick.

He exhaled sharply. "No defensive wounds."

I couldn't help myself. "Told you I'm innocent."

"Maybe," Barboza said. "Or maybe you caught O'Keefe by surprise." As a police department crime scene van eased into a parking spot nearby, Barboza narrowed his gaze and asked, "Do your eyes always look so red and puffy?"

I fought the urge to roll my *red, puffy* eyes. "Only when it's three o'clock in the morning, I've had only four hours of sleep, and I'm being wrongfully accused of murder."

Officer Barboza offered a mirthless chuckle. "Stick around. Crime scene might have some questions for you.

They'll want to take your fingerprints, too, if you're willing to give them voluntarily. If not, we'll get a warrant."

I raised my hands, fingers splayed, as if about to perform a jazzy tap dance number. "Take my prints. I've got nothing to hide." *Other than my sheer terror, that is.*

Chapter Seven

While the cops stepped over to the evidence collection team and brought them up to date, I picked up Smoky, took a seat on the stool behind the counter, and stroked my cat over and over and over again, as much to calm myself as to pamper my pet.

A member of the crime scene team ventured over to Limericks and used the keys the EMT had retrieved from Cormac's pocket to open the place. Meanwhile, as Marlon and Officer Barboza lingered outside the open door, the lead tech donned blue paper booties, picked his way carefully around the pool of blood, and took one step into my shop, glancing around. After noting the blood I'd tracked in and my bloody slippers by the mat, his gaze moved upward, tracing a circle around the ceiling of my shop. "I'm not seeing your security cameras. Are they hidden?"

"I don't have any."

"No cameras?" Barboza barked a mirthless laugh. "That's mighty convenient."

Marlon, in turn, cut an irritated glance at his fellow officer before addressing me through the doorway. "Give some serious thought to installing a camera system. Maybe get a panic button for your alarm, one you can tuck into your pocket. Robbers would see a small shop like this as an easy target, especially if they realized a young woman was in charge, and a tiny one at that."

His concern was sweet and touching. "I'll have a system installed ASAP." While I'd balked at the cost before, there was no need to think twice about it now. A killer was on the loose, and there was a chance he'd targeted Cormac to rob him of the bar's cash. He could come back to try to steal my cash, too. "Do you think that's why Cormac was killed? That it was a robbery?"

"Who knows?" Marlon raised his palms. "It's not unusual for thieves to hit a place at closing time, when there aren't any customers around and the employees are leaving, often through a back door that isn't as visible as a main entrance. The later a place closes, the more likely it is to get hit, too."

"If that were the case," I mused aloud, "wouldn't Cormac have been killed inside Limericks? Or at the back door of the bar?"

"Not if he tried to get away."

My gut twisted tight as my mind entertained the horrifying mental image of Cormac fleeing a pursuer, running for his life to the stoop of my shop.

Even though the lights were on, the crime scene tech shined a flashlight about, as if looking for vestiges of blood or other footprints I might have attempted to clean up. When that got him nowhere, he extinguished the overhead lights and turned on a black light, hunkering down to look under the shelves and sample table for the telltale luminescence of bodily fluids. He aimed the light at my clothing but, despite my efforts to stanch Cormac's bleeding with the T-shirt, I'd miraculously managed not to get his blood on my robe or pajamas. *Thank goodness.* It would've totally freaked me out.

The man peeked into my trash cans, which I'd emptied at the end of the day into the larger bin in my stockroom. He checked that bin, too. Seemingly satisfied that the interior of my shop was not part of the crime scene, he said, "You've voluntarily offered your prints?"

"I have."

I set Smoky down on my stool while the man took my fingerprints. Once he was done, he instructed me to remain in the shop. By then, Smoky had endured enough of my affection and jumped down from the stool when I went to pick him up again. It was just as well. My fingers were covered in black ink. He followed me to the back room. While I washed my hands in the powder room sink, he curled up in his bed atop my desk, looking for some peace and quiet. My skin felt strangely prickly, my bones hollow. I'd never felt more alone.

Marlon stood in front of the Moonshine Shack with his fellow officers, presumably to appear neutral, though he cast an occasional, reassuring glance my way. Even so, he could have his doubts. After all, we'd spoken only four times before now—when he'd helped me unload my van, at my grand opening, when he'd stopped by my shop during the week while on patrol, and earlier tonight when responding to Cormac's call to the police. All of our interactions had been relatively brief. We hardly knew each other, really. Maybe he was simply sticking around out of curiosity,

to see what might develop, to see if I'd be hauled off in handcuffs. I could only hope the food in jail was better than it
had been in summer camp. The only good thing had been
the s'mores, and I doubted the Tennessee state penitentia-
ries allowed bonfires and pointy sticks.

I placed a call to Kiki. Despite the late hour, I knew
she'd be there for me. She always was and always would be.
I served the same role for her. We had an implicit pact.

Realizing a late-night call could only mean an emergency, Kiki answered on the third ring with a cry of "Hattie! What's wrong?"

"I found Cormac O'Keefe on the stoop of my shop."

She paused for a beat before shrieking, "You found *who*
on your *what*?!"

I gave her a quick rundown. Thud, tinkling glass, cry,
thud, thud, blood, moonshine, paramedics, cops. "I could
be a suspect."

"That's bollocks! I'm on my way." She hung up without
taking time to say goodbye.

Twenty minutes later, Kiki drove up on the street and unrolled the window of her bright red Mini Cooper. Evinc-
ing her status as a confirmed anglophile, she'd decorated
the roof and exterior mirrors with Union Jack decals. Her
hair was a mess. Well, the one side of her head on which
she had hair was a mess. The other sported a five-o'clock
shadow, though the time was actually nearing four a.m.

I stepped to the door and called to her over the heads of
the crime scene techs, who were using tweezers to pick up
shards of glass and place them in plastic bags. I circled a
finger in the air. "Drive around to the back!"

She revved her engine and looped around, careening down

the alley and leaping from her car. I met her at the back door. Like me, she was still dressed in her pajamas. But while mine featured images of Smoky, hers were covered in streaks of paint. Some of the streaks were intentional, part of the artsy cartoonish print. Others were actual paint stains. Her artistic muse sometimes struck in the wee hours of the night.

She grabbed me by the shoulders and looked into my eyes. "Are you okay?"

I choked out a sob. It was all I could do, and it told her everything she needed to know. I'd been strong up until then, but finding a body in front of my shop, one killed with a jar of my moonshine no less, was quite a shock.

She pulled me to her in a tight hug. Even Smoky walked over and reached up a paw, tapping her on the knee as if to say he'd like one of her hugs, too. After a few seconds, she released me and picked up the cat, treating him to a consoling squeeze before returning him to the floor. "What now?"

I blinked back the tears in my eyes. "I wait until they say I can go."

"No. That's unacceptable." Kiki had always been far bolder and more brazen than I. She took the bull by the horns and stepped to the front of my shop, calling out to Officer Barboza and the crime scene techs. "Hattie's exhausted. I'm taking her home."

Before Barboza could object, Marlon raised a hand to stop him. "Miss Hayes isn't a flight risk. Besides this shop, she's got family in town, too."

"All right," Barboza said to Marlon before turning to me. "Leave your van, though. We need to search it. Don't tell anyone what you saw here, and don't mention the victim's name to anyone until it's publicly released." He gestured to Kiki. "Same goes for your friend. We'd rather the next of kin heard the news from us first."

"Of course. We'll keep the details to ourselves." Heck, I didn't want anyone to know a man had been murdered right in front of my shop. I'd happily keep quiet.

He skewered me with a final, pointed look. "Expect a visit from a homicide detective later today."

I replied with a weary nod. Though I didn't look forward to going through all the disturbing details again, the more I cooperated with the investigation the sooner the police could determine who had put an end to Cormac's life, and my own life could get back to normal. *Who had killed him? And why?*

I rummaged in my purse for my van keys, as well as the spare key to my shop, and handed them over to Barboza, who passed them off to one of the technicians. Turning my attention to Marlon, I said, "Thanks for sticking around. It was nice to see a friendly face."

He gave me a soft smile and glanced behind him at the horse trailer. "I'd better get Charlotte back to the barn or she just might bite me."

"Tell her thanks for me, too."

"I will." Softly, he added, "Don't worry, Hattie. It's going to be okay."

I bit my lip. "I hope so."

At my ankles, Smoky offered a nervous mew. He, too, seemed to have his doubts.

Only Kiki seemed certain. She circled a supporting arm around my shoulders. "Come on. Let's get you home."

After Kiki dropped me and Smoky off at my place, I fell into bed only to toss and turn for the next few hours. No sweet dreams for me. Every time I closed my eyes, all I could see was Cormac's curled-up body lying on the concrete. Smoky, tired of being constantly jostled, chastised me with a growl, and hopped down from the bed to go sleep on the couch. When my alarm went off at eleven o'clock, I wasn't sure I had even slept at all. Still, weary or not, I had a store to run and I wasn't about to let my customers—or myself—down.

After a quick shower, I donned one of my promotional T-shirts, slipped into my overalls, and slapped on a little makeup. With my van still at the shop, Kiki swung by to get me. She sported her usual black studded boots along with a lacy white dress and a silver nose ring, a clash of fashions.

As I climbed into her car, she asked, "Any developments in the case?"

"If there were," I said, "nobody told me."

She whipped out her phone and used her thumbs to run an Internet search. "The news is out." She held her phone out to me.

I took the device from her and looked down at the screen. A local news report had spilled the beans, at least some of them anyway. They said a man had been found dead in the early-morning hours on Saturday on Market Street, that the death had been ruled suspicious, and that the man's name was Cormac O'Keefe. He was identified as the owner of Limericks. Anyone with information was asked to contact the Chattanooga PD. An image of an unsmiling Cormac against a pale gray background, most likely his driver's license photo, was included with the article. Given the news report, Kiki and I no longer had to keep Cormac's name secret, though I presumed we were to remain mum regarding the rest of the details, including the exact location of his body and his manner of death—murder by mason jar.

I returned her phone and we headed back down into town,

leaving Smoky behind this time. Even he had seemed worn out. Rather than following me to the door, he'd rolled over on the couch and turned his back on me when I'd asked if he wanted to come to the 'Shine Shack. The cat might not speak English, but he darn well knew how to communicate.

As Kiki turned down the alley, I was surprised to see a maroon Dodge pickup parked next to my van behind my shop.

Kiki must've seen it, too. "What's that truck doing here?"

"Beats me."

As we drew closer, the driver's door opened and Marlon slid out. He wore jeans and cowboy boots with a chocolate brown T-shirt, the sleeves of which were stretched tight over his bulging biceps. Whether he'd developed the muscle from working out at a gym or from wrangling his half-ton horse was left to be determined. Either way, his arms were nice to look at.

Kiki zipped her Mini up next to him and we climbed out.

Marlon greeted Kiki with a nod before eyeing me closely, his gaze locking on the dark circles under my eyes. He smelled clean, natural, and leathery, like saddle soap or boot polish.

"What are you doing here?" I asked. *Could he have some additional news? Had the killer been caught?*

"I was worried about you. Came by to check on you, see how you're holding up."

My heart warmed at his concern. "I'm really tired." The instant the words left my mouth, guilt puckered my gut. I might be tired, but at least I was intact. That was more than could be said for Cormac. "I tried to sleep, but I had awful dreams."

"Finding a murder victim can do that to you." He offered a sympathetic smile.

I winced. Cormac had lost his life, his throat slit by one of my moonshine jars. The fact that the killer had used a jar of my moonshine to kill Cormac told me the murderer had been in my store. The thought sent an involuntary shiver through me. My father's words from the grand opening came back to me. *Your moonshine will make a killing!* Dad had been right . . . just not in the way any of us had expected.

Marlon went on. "Detective Pearce rounded up my report from my visit here yesterday evening and took a look at it. She called me an hour ago, wanted to know my thoughts about you and your grandfather."

I looked up at him. "She's not the only one who wants to know." *Could Marlon consider me a suspect?* It would break my heart to hear that he would ponder the idea, even for an instant. Even so, the guy barely knew me. It wouldn't be unreasonable for him to toy with the thought.

He ducked his head so he could look me directly in the eye. "I know you had nothing to do with O'Keefe's death, Hattie, despite the murder weapon being a broken jar of your shine. I told her as much."

I sighed. "It's nice to know someone believes in me."

"Hello?" Kiki raised her palms and rolled her eyes. "I believe in you."

I reached out and gave her hand a squeeze. "I know. Thank you for that." I released her hand and turned back to Marlon. "Is Detective Pearce a good investigator?"

"Total crackerjack," he replied. "They don't call her 'Ace' for nothing. She'll believe in you, too, once she meets you in person."

"I hope so," I said on a sigh, still not completely convinced.

"Even if Ace weren't inclined to trust you," he said, "she trusts me and my judgment."

"Oh, yeah?" Kiki said. "Are you two close?"

Marlon's head dipped in a definitive nod. "We are. We worked an undercover case together a year or so ago, one involving horse theft. Found ourselves trapped in a barn at the wrong end of a double-barreled shotgun. We got ourselves out of the predicament. Guess that goes without saying. But you don't share an experience like that without forming a bond."

I hated to point out the obvious, but I did it anyway. "You hardly know me, though. How can you be so sure I'm innocent?"

"C'mon now." Marlon reached out and chucked my chin. "Who could possibly think a little thing like you could bring down that man?"

I wasn't sure whether to be relieved or insulted. Did he consider me an unviable suspect merely because of my size? "I could kill a full-grown man if I really wanted to. I'd find a way."

Marlon's brows knit. "Excuse me?"

Kiki, too, appeared confused, her forehead crinkled.

Groaning, I waved a hand. "No, no. Excuse *me*. My brain is fried, I'm running on zero sleep, and I'm not making sense. I'd never kill someone, no matter how much they deserved it." *Cheese and grits.* That wasn't much better. Kiki cut me a look that said maybe I should just shut my mouth and never open it again. Fortunately, Marlon seemed unfazed by my nonsense. I supposed police officers are used to dealing with people under stress saying odd things. "Have there been any developments?" I asked.

"There have." Marlon straightened up. "Damien Sirakov is in custody. He was apprehended just after three a.m. at a gas station a couple of miles from here. He tried to use a stolen credit card to fill his tank. He says he was at a bar shooting pool until it closed at two, and that when he returned to his car the battery was dead. He claims he hit up other people for a jump, but he didn't have jumper cables and the first several people he asked didn't have cables, either. He had to wait until somebody who had jumper cables in their car came to the lot."

"You think he's telling the truth?"

"Not for a minute," Marlon said. "That man isn't capable of honesty. He's got more stories than Mother Goose and Dr. Seuss put together. He tried to convince the arresting officer that the woman whose credit card he tried to use had given him the card. He claimed they were romantically involved."

"Any way that could be true?" I asked.

"She's eighty-two years old."

Kiki issued a scandalous *hmm*. "A cougar, then? One with a taste for bad boys?"

"Not at all," Marlon replied. "She's been happily married for over sixty years, and she's never heard of Damien Sirakov."

I mused aloud. "He could be lying about the car trouble, too."

"Yup," Marlon agreed. "He claims a man gave his battery a jump, but he can't recall what the guy looked like, what he was wearing, or what kind of car the guy was driving. He says he only remembers that the man spoke with a Spanish accent." He shook his head, as if disgusted by Sirakov's lame story. "The fact that he was taken into custody at the gas station puts him in this area last night. He could well have had the time and opportunity to attack O'Keefe beforehand. He certainly had the motive. O'Keefe filed multiple reports against him. Sirakov slipped out without paying his bill. Cheated some Limericks customers at darts. It was never proven, but it seems likely he's the one who tossed a manhole cover through the front window of the bar awhile back. He's been a general nuisance. He's never been convicted of a violent offense before, but there's always a first time. It wouldn't be surprising if the two got into an argument and things escalated, got out of hand."

At the risk of incriminating myself, I asked, "But where would Damien Sirakov have gotten the jar of cherry moonshine? I don't believe he's ever been in my shop."

Marlon's eyes narrowed ever so slightly. "Can you be certain?"

I bit my lip. "I guess not. I've stepped away from the Shack a few times this week and left my grandfather in charge. But it was never for more than a few minutes at time, just long enough for me to grab some dinner or run a deposit to the bank."

Kiki consulted the wristwatch she'd bought at the military surplus store. The gadget had an army green nylon band and a face that told both civilian and military time. "It's only three minutes until noon. We better get inside if we want the shop to open on time."

While Kiki wrangled her artist portfolio out of her cargo bay, I unlocked the back door to my shop. Kiki and Marlon followed me through it. After stashing my purse in the safe and retrieving some start-up cash for the register, I led the way to the sales floor, flipping light switches along the way. My slippers no longer sat by the doormat. No doubt they'd been taken into evidence. Someone had cleaned up my footprints and the blood on the window and stoop, too, thank goodness.

Kiki took a seat on one of the padded stools behind the

checkout counter and I readied the cash register, sliding the bills and coins into their correct slots, and pushing the drawer closed.

Marlon angled his head to indicate my computerized register. "Ace will want to take a look at your records, see who bought jars of cherry shine. You might as well get crackin'."

I grabbed a jar of cherry moonshine from a display and used the scanner to input the product code. A few keystrokes later and a report came up on the monitor. "I've sold twenty-three jars of cherry moonshine since my store opened on Monday. Twenty were paid for with debit or credit cards. Three were purchased with cash."

I maneuvered the mouse and clicked on the icon to print the report. Once it finished printing, I handed the pages to Marlon.

He ran his eyes over them. "This will give Ace a place to start." He handed the report back to me. "I'm gonna head out. Best if I'm not here when she shows up. Don't want her thinking I'm stepping on her turf, or that you and I have something unprofessional going on."

Shucks. I was actually kind of hoping something unprofessional was indeed going on, or at least developing, that Marlon might have a personal interest in me. Turned out Marlon was just a dedicated cop, using his private time to check on the people of his beat. I'd been a fool to think there could be more to it. Maybe I should take Kiki's advice and look into online dating. She'd already written up a bio for me. *Hattie is five feet of feisty fun and runs her own business. She can't wait to show you her jugs . . . of moonshine!*

I walked Marlon to the back door and bade him goodbye. He climbed into his truck. After starting his engine, he unrolled his window and stuck his head out, casting me a serious look. "Keep your eyes and ears open," he said. "Anything or anyone gives you pause, don't hesitate to call dispatch. Hear me?"

"I do."

"All righty, then." With that, he raised his fingers off the steering wheel in a goodbye wave and drove off.

Chapter Eight

When I returned to the checkout counter, I eyed Kiki and asked, "You think it's true what they say? That criminals always return to the scene of their crime?" With my shop being the crime scene, I certainly hoped that was not the case. Still, it seemed possible. Maybe even probable. The killer could return to gloat, to revel in their deadly misdeeds. Or they could come back for an update on the police investigation, to determine whether they were under scrutiny. Or they could come back to do away with the only person who might have witnessed their crime—*me*. That last thought made my stomach squirm.

"Don't worry. If the killer comes back, we'll be safe." Kiki reached into her purse and pulled out a spray can. "I brought protection."

I leaned forward to read the label. "Spray sealant?"

"It was left over from one of my craft projects."

"How is that going to protect us?"

She struck a wide stance and brandished the can in a
defensive pose. "One spritz of this adhesive in the killer's
face and their eyelids will be glued shut. We could pinch
their nostrils and lips shut and seal off their air supply, too.
While we're at it, we could spray their palms and glue their
hands together." She shook the can, the ball inside rattling.
Rat-a-tat-tat. "Who needs handcuffs or a gun when you've
got Mod Podge?"

It was a creative solution, if not likely to be a particu-
larly effective one. "What do you think will happen when
people learn a man was murdered at my shop? Killed by
one of my mason jars, no less?" I'd just opened the Moonshine Shack. *Could this tragedy close its doors?*

"No need to worry," Kiki said with a confidence that
was likely faked for my benefit. "Nobody watches TV news
anymore, and they only skim articles online. Besides, from
what you've told me, it doesn't sound like Cormac O'Keefe
will be missed."

"That's a tragedy, too."

"Yes, but it's a tragedy of his own making. It's not hard
to be a decent human being."

Kiki's words might have sounded harsh, but she wasn't
wrong. Maybe if Cormac had treated others better, he
wouldn't be dead now. In fact, I was pretty sure of it. There
was a chance he could have been the subject of a random
homicidal psychopath, but odds were he'd enraged the
wrong person for one reason or another. But what person?
And for what reason? I wish I knew.

It was probably a violation of labor law for Kiki to work
here for free, but when I'd offered to put her on the payroll
she'd been adamant. *"I won't take money from you. Only
moonshine and inspiration."* To that end, she pulled her
sketch pad and pencil case from the portfolio and placed them

on the countertop in front of her. After selecting a charcoal pencil from the case, she reached over for the jar of cherry moonshine I'd left on the counter and pulled it closer so she could sketch it. She drew often to keep her skills sharp.

I went to the door, unlocked it, and turned the *CLOSED* sign around so that it read *OPEN*. Circling around to the back of the counter, I grabbed the chessboard and carried it out front, along with a bin of chess pieces and another of checkers. I plunked a deck of cards and a box of dominoes on the table, too. Once I was back inside, I plugged in the twinkling lights. Though they'd be less visible during the daytime, the porch provided enough cover that they'd help catch the eye of potential customers strolling along the sidewalks.

A piece of yellow cordon tape flapping in the breeze drew my gaze from the porch to the pub across the street, where tape formed an X over the front door of Limericks. A piece of paper had been posted on the door, too, though from this distance I couldn't read it.

Curious, I told Kiki, "I'll be right back." Going outside again, I looked both ways for traffic before scurrying across the street to read the notice. It advised:

DO NOT ENTER BY ORDER OF THE
CHATTANOOGA POLICE DEPARTMENT.
FOR ACCESS CONTACT DETECTIVE PEARCE.

The detective's phone number was provided at the bottom. Looked like nobody would be getting into Limericks without going through her first.

An hour later, I was ringing up three women at the checkout counter in my shop when a white Chevy Impala pulled up out front. At the wheel sat a full-figured, fiftyish Black woman with copper-colored hair cut in a cute pixie.

She lifted a large gray bag from the passenger seat and climbed out of the car. She wore a flattering royal blue pantsuit with copper jewelry that complemented her hair, along with bold metallic-tone makeup.

Kiki met her at the door. "Welcome to the Moonshine Shack."

Judging from the woman's vehicle and her assessing stare, I surmised she was the homicide detective, though if I'd seen her elsewhere I might have pegged the fashionable woman as a real estate agent or the manager of an art gallery or upscale women's boutique.

She waited for my customers to exit the store before speaking. Once they'd gone, she stepped up to the counter and looked from Kiki to me. "Is one of you Hattie Hayes?"

Instinctively, I raised my hand like a schoolchild. "That's me. I'm Hattie."

She reached into the bag hanging from her shoulder. Judging from the bag's style and size, it served as her purse, briefcase, laptop tote, and possibly a second home. She retrieved a business card from an inside pocket and held it out to me. "I'm Detective Candace Pearce. I'll be heading up the homicide investigation."

I looked down at the card. "Candace," I mused aloud. "Is that where your nickname 'Ace' came from?"

Her head angled slightly. "How'd you know my nickname?"

Rather than revealing I'd heard it from Marlon, I said, "One of the officers referred to you as Ace."

Fortunately, she didn't ask which officer. "Ace might have originated as shorthand for Candace, but I've earned the name, too. I've closed more cases, and closed them quicker, than any other detective on the force."

Impressive. I set her card on the counter and handed her one of my own, along with the printout detailing the sales of cherry moonshine. "Officer Barboza told me a detective would be coming by. I thought you might need that information. It's a list of all the sales of cherry moonshine since my store opened on Monday."

"Well, aren't you the teacher's pet?"

I shrugged. "Just trying to be helpful. It scares me to think there's a killer out there."

The expression on her face said she thought there might be a killer *in here*. But surely I could disavow her of that notion, right? She took her eyes off me to peruse the printout, running her finger down the list. "I see three cash sales here. Any idea who these cash customers were?"

"No. Sorry."

"And you claim you don't have security cameras."

She'd made a statement, an accusatory one at that, rather than posing a question. Nevertheless, I responded with, "No. There are no cameras in my shop."

"No chance of identifying the cash customers from video footage, then." She exhaled sharply and gave me the same disappointed, disapproving gaze my mom used to give me before she'd ground me for one adolescent infraction or another.

"I plan to have cameras installed," I offered in my defense. "As soon as possible."

Ace held up the printout. "Does this list account for all of the cherry moonshine that has left your shop?"

Realization struck and I bit my lip. The list showed only the jars that had been purchased, not the ones I'd given away at my grand opening. "Unfortunately, no. I gave away jars of moonshine as party favors at my grand opening. I let the guests choose their flavors, and I didn't keep track of who picked the cherry moonshine." I'd had no idea the information might later be important. "But my grand opening was a private event. Only business owners from the area were invited."

She frowned. "That'll make tracing the jar more difficult, but at least it narrows down the list."

I cringed as another thought came to me. "There were some frat boys in my shop the night Cormac was killed. They came in around eight thirty. They're members of Mu Sigma. One of them stole a jar of shine. I can't swear to it, but I think it was the cherry flavor." I told her how the short and stocky one had knocked over a display, how I'd stepped outside onto the sidewalk and seen the tall one pull the shine from his sweatshirt pouch and hold it up.

"What did these boys look like?"

"They were all white with brown hair. The one who stole the shine was tall and had thick hair with lots of gel in it. The one who broke the jar was shorter and stockier."

"Did you report the theft?"

"No," I admitted. "It was nearly closing time and we'd already had the police at my shop once that night. I decided to let it go." I left out the part where my grandfather raised his cane and threatened to whoop the boys if they returned.

She exhaled sharply, clearly questioning my decision not to report the offense. "Did you happen to catch any of their names?"

"No. Sorry."

She eyed Kiki before returning her focus to me. "Is there somewhere we can speak in private, Miss Hayes?"

I gestured to the back of the shop. "We can talk in my office."

We stepped into the storeroom and strode to the corner that served as my administrative workspace. I offered her my desk and rolling chair. As for myself, I pulled two cases of moonshine from a shelf, stacked them, and sat down atop the boxes.

Ace set her bag on the desktop and proceeded to pull a notepad and pen from its cavernous depths before taking a seat. As she swiveled to face me, her jacket flapped open, revealing a handgun holstered at her waist and reminding me that despite her stylish and businesslike appearance, this woman was a law enforcement officer.

She clicked the top of the ballpoint pen as she locked her gaze on me once more. "Tell me about your interactions with Cormac O'Keefe. I understand he refused a moonshine order he had placed with you, and that he later called the department on your grandfather?"

"That's right." I told her the same things I'd told Marlon when he'd responded to Cormac's call last night, the same things I'd repeated to Officer Barboza in the wee hours this morning. Order placed. Order refused. Granddaddy mouthing off in my defense and waving his little whittling tool. "My grandfather is eighty-eight years old. He needs a cane or scooter to get around. Cormac could have easily walked away from him. He was never in any danger."

"I see." After mulling things over for a moment, she said, "Sounds like there was no love lost between you and O'Keefe."

"None," I admitted, "But I wouldn't wish him dead."

"Of course not," she said. "But given the circumstances, it would be understandable if you'd lost your temper. Happens to the best of us."

I suspected her expression of empathy was less about making me feel better and more about encouraging me to confess. "I was annoyed with Cormac, sure. But I didn't lose control. I'm more of a curse-them-under-my-breath kind of woman than a cut-their-carotid-artery type."

"Is that so?"

My head dipped in a definitive nod.

Her head tilted as she narrowed her eyes at me. "Your prints were on the broken jar that was used to slash Cormac's throat. All over it, as a matter of fact."

The police lab had certainly moved fast. "I boxed the jars as they came off the assembly line, and I stocked the shelves of my shop." I circled my finger to indicate the boxes of shine on the shelves behind me. "My prints would be on every jar of my shine. Every jug of my granddad's stuff, too. It's the other fingerprints that might tell you who killed Cormac." Too bad my cat couldn't speak. Smoky was the only one who'd seen the attack and could confirm the killer's identity. "There were other prints, weren't there?" There'd have to be. *Unless they'd been wiped off* . . . My throat constricted in concern. *What if my prints were the only ones on the jar? Could I end up in prison?*

Ignoring my question, the detective took a different tack. "It's awfully coincidental you just happened to be in your closed shop in the middle of the night at the exact time a man you'd had an altercation with only hours earlier was murdered."

I raised my palms in innocence and, trying to remain calm, squeaked, "Fully acknowledged. But that's exactly what it was! A coincidence. Nothing more."

"You got his blood on your shoes."

"When I was trying to help him! I tried to save his life, not end it."

She stared at me for a long moment before consulting her notepad. "You mentioned an attorney named Heath Delaney, a restaurant owner named Mack Clayton, and two waitresses as possible enemies of O'Keefe."

"'Enemies' is a strong term," I said, not liking the way

the word sounded. "But each of them had conflicts with Cormac."

"You mentioned a customer, too." She consulted her notes again. "A man by the name of Damien Sirakov."

"That's correct. The officers last night mentioned that they knew him, that he has a criminal record." The fact that Sirakov had been arrested before meant his fingerprints would be on file. If his prints had also been on the broken jar, this should be an open-and-shut case. The fact that Ace was grilling me said the man's prints had not appeared on the jar. *Could Sirakov have worn gloves? Or somehow wiped his prints off the jar without wiping away mine?*

I was considering these questions when Ace said, "You've given us quite a long list of potential suspects to look into."

"Cormac wasn't well liked," I said. "He didn't treat people right."

"You're not just deflecting, trying to get me to waste my time looking elsewhere when you're actually the one who killed O'Keefe?"

Whoa. She doesn't beat around the bush, does she? I couldn't blame her for suspecting me, though, not with so much circumstantial evidence pointing my way. Heck, I'd probably arrest me if I were in the detective's position. I leaned forward and looked her directly in the eye. "I'm not deflecting. I know how important a woman's time is. There's never enough of it. I wouldn't waste yours, and I certainly wouldn't waste mine."

She stared at me for a long moment before the tiniest of grins tugged at her lips.

I think I've won her over. "Have I convinced you of my innocence?"

She issued a derisive snort. "Not in the least. You might talk a clever line, Miss Hayes, but you were at the crime scene, got the victim's blood on your clothes, and had a motive to kill O'Keefe."

The thought that Ace could consider me a viable suspect made me queasy, and my back broke out in a cold sweat. *I have to convince her I didn't kill Cormac, but how?* I decided to take the same tack Marlon had taken earlier, to point out that it would be difficult, if not impossible, for a small woman like me to kill a man. "I'm like my grandfather's whittling tool, too tiny to pose a real threat to anyone. Even if I had been wielding a broken jar of shine, I would have had a hard time slashing Cormac's neck. He could have just pushed me away or run off."

"On the contrary," she said, "your size could be an advantage, give you the element of surprise. Cormac might have underestimated you and unwittingly have left himself vulnerable."

What?! My mind went round and round, like moonshine looping through the copper coils of a still. My mouth fell open and words spilled out, as incoherent as my thoughts. "But I . . . you . . . he . . . Aaargh!" I threw up my hands in frustration before burying my face in them in an attempt to shut out this madness.

The chair creaked as Ace relaxed back in it. "Tell me what you were doing here last night, and what you heard and saw."

For what felt like the millionth time, I ran through the events. The confrontation with Cormac, which threw me off my game. Waking up wondering if I'd forgotten to properly close up shop. The thuds, the tinkling glass, the cry, the smear of blood on the window, Smoky looking off down the street. When I finished, I sighed. "I wish I could tell you more."

She readied her pen. "Any chance you know the names

of the servers from Limericks? The ones that got into the fight?"

"I gave their names to Officer Barboza last night. Didn't he put them in his report?"

She gave me a wry look. "Barboza's a solid beat cop, but his reports leave much to be desired."

Looked like I'd have to go over the names again. "One of them is Miranda. I don't know her last name. I've never been introduced to the other one, but I heard Cormac call her Ashlynn. Their full names should be listed in his pay roll records." Assuming the guy paid his taxes, of course. Judging from the way he stiffed other businesses, he might have defrauded the IRS, too.

"You met Miranda, then?"

I thought back to the grand opening, how Miranda gushed over the blackberry moonshine. "Yes. She came to my grand opening party with Cormac. She left with a jar of my black-berry shine."

"What flavor did Cormac take?"

I racked my brain, but for the life of me I couldn't re-member what variety he'd selected. I'd been too busy won-dering about Heath and Mack, their warnings about O'Keefe. "I can't recall. Sorry."

After tucking her pen and notepad back into her bag, she pulled my van key and fob out of it and returned them to me. She rose from the chair, which I took as a sign her in-terrogation was concluded.

I stood from my boxes and worried my lip. "Are you go-ing to tell Heath Delaney and Mack Clayton that I snitched on them? And the servers?"

"No," she said. "Your secret's safe with me."

Thank goodness. I hoped to develop good working rela-tionships with my business neighbors, but if they knew I'd pointed the detective in their direction they weren't likely to have warm and fuzzy feelings toward me.

"Speaking of secrets," she added, "keep the details of Cormac's murder to yourself. Same goes for your friend. The media outlets have been notified of his death, but they were not told the exact manner in which he'd been killed or where his body was found."

"What do I say if someone asks me about it?"

She gave me a pointed look. "You tell them Detective Ace Pearce has ordered you to keep your mouth shut, or else."

Or else what, exactly? She didn't elaborate, leaving me to wonder. As she opened the door and we left the store-room, I asked, "Is there anything else I can do?"

"Yes," she said. "Don't leave town."

I gulped and said, "I meant is there anything I can do to help you solve this crime?"

"You can keep an eye on Limericks for me. If you see anyone trying to enter without a police escort, call me immediately."

"I will."

She stared intently at me, as if trying to look into my soul. "Officer Landers has vouched for you, Miss Hayes. Don't you dare make a fool of him—or me."

Heat rushed up my neck to set my face ablaze, partly due to indignation and partly due to learning that Marlon had defended me again, like a knight who'd exchanged his shining armor for a polyester police uniform. "I wouldn't dream of it." *Though I would dream of Marlon.*

Ace raised a hand in goodbye to Kiki as she left the shop, and Kiki returned the gesture.

As soon as the woman had backed her sedan out of the parking space, Kiki turned to me. "Spill the beans, Hattie."

I ran through my discussion with the detective. "She considers me a prime suspect."

Kiki scoffed. "That's ridiculous!"

"You and I know that, but Ace doesn't. What if the killer comes back while she's focusing on me?"

"Then we'll catch the killer on camera." Kiki turned to the computerized cash register. "Let's find you a system right now, one with a panic button like Marlon suggested."

I climbed onto the stool beside her and eyed the screen. "I suppose I could get in touch with the company that installed the alarm." The system had already been in place when I took over the shop, but a sticker on the keypad identified the company and listed its phone number and website. "Maybe they can put in cameras for me. They'd probably charge an arm and a leg, but what choice do I have?"

"If we find an affordable camera system," Kiki said, "I know someone who can install it."

"You do? Who?"

"Remember when I designed and painted the set for that production of *West Side Story* at the community theater? I worked closely with the lighting guy when we built the streetlamps. He's a whiz with electrical stuff. I bet he'd install the system in return for some shine."

"You'd ask him for me?"

"Sure."

I felt a twinge of guilt. "You've already designed my logo, helped me decorate my shop, and run the sales counter for me, all for free. How can I ever repay you?"

She affected her best British accent. "Fix me a spot of tea. Earl Grey if you've got it."

"That's all?"

"Heck, no," she teased. "That's only the start."

Chapter Nine

After I fixed Kiki a steaming cup of tea, we spent several minutes on the computer comparing the relative costs and features of various security camera systems. We eventually decided on a two-camera system with wide-angle lenses, heat-sensing motion detection, and internal built-in memory cards that could store footage for up to a week. The system would send alerts to my cell phone and allow me to access real-time footage remotely. The devices also sported a microphone so I could communicate with intruders. *Halt! Who goes there?* We'd have one of the cameras installed over the front entrance where it could oversee the shop. The other would go over the back door and keep a digital eye on my stockroom. We bought a separate wireless door chime system that would alert us to anyone entering the store. The device came with a panic button to activate an audible alarm. Fortunately, the door chime was a plug-in model that didn't have to be hard-wired, requiring only an electrical outlet and backup batteries. I'd be able to install it myself and wouldn't have to further impose on Kiki's buddy from the theater. Even more fortunately, the company offered two-day delivery at no extra charge. The devices would be dropped at my shop by ten o'clock Monday morning.

We were about to sign off the computer when an idea popped into my head. "The police will run a background check on the people who bought my cherry moonshine. Why don't we see what we can find, too?" If I could help Ace track down Cormac's killer, I'd be exonerated and wouldn't have to worry she'd return to arrest me. I also wouldn't have to worry that the killer would think I might have seen something and return to my shop to do away with me. I printed out another copy of the list of people who'd used a debit or credit card to buy cherry moonshine and handed it to Kiki. "Call out the names for me."

As she read off the first name, I typed it into the Internet browser along with the word *arrest*. I hit enter, and the two of us leaned in to peruse the resulting links. While there were links to the woman's social media accounts, as well as a listing and photo on her employer's website, none of the entries indicated she'd ever been arrested, let alone for a violent crime. The same went for the next fourteen customers. By all accounts, they were upstanding citizens.

Our next target was not so upstanding. "Bingo!" I cried. "This customer was arrested in an undercover sting for solicitation of prostitution." Fitting, given that the man's name was John.

On seeing the guy's photo in the online article, Kiki cringed. "Ew. He looks like he hasn't washed his hair in weeks. He's got a mustard stain on his shirt, too."

"This guy doesn't look familiar to me. Maybe he just has the same name as the customer."

"Could be," Kiki agreed. "But just in case, I'm going to grab the disinfectant and sanitize the store."

She proceeded to do just that as I ran through the remaining names with no luck. As far as I could tell, the list was a dead end. But not all violent crimes made the news. Ace would have access to more complete records. Maybe she'd find something I didn't.

Business was brisk that afternoon, people coming out to enjoy the beautiful weather and riverfront. Kiki and I scurried about, pouring samples, helping customers select their favorite flavors, and ringing up jugs and jars. The pace was a nice distraction from thoughts of Cormac's murder and my status as a suspect.

My cell phone erupted into song in the pocket of my overalls, blaring my ringtone, a version of "Good Old Mountain Dew" recorded in 1964 by an all-female band called The Womenfolk. I pulled it from my pocket to see that it was Kate calling. *Is the baby on its way?* After I accepted the call and greeted her, I put the call on speaker so Kiki could join in. "Are you in labor?" I asked.

"No!" she cried. "Haven't you heard? The owner of Limericks was found dead! I just saw a blurb about it on TV."

Kiki and I exchanged a glance. "We've heard," I said. "A detective came by my shop earlier to see if we knew anything."

Naturally, Kate assumed we were completely in the dark, and it seemed best not to disabuse her of that notion with her baby's arrival so close at hand. "I hope they figure out who did it," she said. "It worries me that something so awful happened so close to your store."

Closer than you know. I changed the subject, partly because I couldn't say much more without violating Ace's order to remain mum and partly because I wanted to focus on more positive things. "How are you feeling?"

"Like a soccer ball," she said. "The baby seems to be trying to kick its way out."

"That's a good sign," I said. "It means the baby is healthy."

"Look on the bright side," Kiki added. "At least it's not wearing cleats."

After a few minutes of chitchat, a customer came in and we ended the call.

Around four thirty, my stomach began to rumble. My first thought was to call in an order for barbecue, but then I realized maybe I could do a side order of sleuthing if I went for slaw in person.

"Can you hold down the fort for a few minutes on your own?" I asked Kiki.

"I can handle the customers." She reached under the counter and held up the can of her toxic adhesive spray. "If the killer comes back, I can handle them, too."

I hurried down the block to the Smoky Mountains Smokehouse. The smells of onions, baked beans, and spices met me at the door. Luckily, I'd beat the dinner rush. Even more luckily, Mack Clayton was working the register. I stepped up to the counter. "You're just the man I wanted to see. How's the chino sauce workin' out for ya?"

"The customers love it! I've nearly emptied the jug of Ole-Timey Corn Liquor you gave me."

"You'll need more, then. How many jugs should I put you down for? Five? Fifty? An even hundred?"

He chuckled. "Let's start with one."

"Make it two and I'll give you one of them at half price."

"You've got yourself a deal."

Our sales transaction concluded, we spent a few minutes

chatting and working out an arrangement to give each other's customers a mutual five percent discount if they showed a receipt dated the same day from the other establishment.

"My friend Kiki can work up a flyer to that effect," I said. "We can post it by our registers to let our customers know of the arrangement."

"You sure do have a mind for business, Hattie."

"I was born with it," I said, beaming. "I ran the most successful lemonade stand on my block as a kid." Granddaddy had helped me out then, too, and was likely the secret to my success. He'd sold my customers jugs of his homemade shine along with the lemonade. Though I'd been too young and naïve to know it at the time, it had been an entirely illegal operation. By this point, though, the statute of limitations had probably run on my grandfather's offenses. At least his moonshine sales were legit now, thanks to yours truly.

I recited my dinner order, and while Mack rang me up, I fished for information. I was curious whether the detective had been by to see him yet. It would've made sense that she'd stop by his restaurant after leaving my shop. His business was in the area, and he was more likely to be in his barbecue joint on a Saturday afternoon than Heath Delaney was to be in his law office. I was also curious whether he suspected I might have been the one to give his name to the police. I'd been told to remain mum about the specific circumstances of Cormac's murder, but I hadn't been told I couldn't raise the matter of his murder at all. By now, those in the area were likely aware of it. Bad news travels fast, after all. "Did you hear about Cormac O'Keefe?"

"I did," he said flatly. "Looks like what goes around finally came around."

"Speaking of coming around, a detective came by my shop earlier."

"Ace Pearce?"

"That's the one. She'd heard that my grandfather and Cormac had it out in front of my shop last night."

"Oh, yeah?" Mack said. "What was their argument about?"

I told him that Cormac had placed an order, then refused to accept it. "A sales rep from Backwoods Bootleggers crashed my grand opening party, then went right over to Limericks and convinced Cormac to go exclusive with the brand."

"That so?" Mack said. "There must've been something in it for Cormac, then."

"A nice discount, I suppose." I told Mack about Cormac calling the police on my granddad, that the detective had come by to ask about the incident.

Mack scoffed. "No offense to your grandfather, but he looks about as dangerous as a butterfly."

"That's what I told Ace. I'll be curious to see if she bothers going by his retirement home to interview him."

"She might," Mack said on a sigh. "She sure put me through the wringer."

"She did? About what?"

"About a demand letter I'd sent to Cormac. She must've found it at Limericks. I'd threatened to sue the guy if he didn't pony up what he owed me." Mack's face clouded, as if the matter had frustrated him all over again. "I catered a buffet dinner at Limericks for St. Patrick's Day. Cormac paid only half of what he owed me. The shyster claimed I'd shorted him on the food. I'd done no such thing. Couldn't prove it, though. By the time I realized he planned to pull a fast one, I'd already sent my staff back here with the empty food containers."

I handed Mack my credit card. "You'd mentioned at my grand opening that if I sold any shine to Cormac O'Keefe,

I should get the payment up front. You said you were speaking from experience. Is the catering gig what you were referring to?"

"It was. O'Keefe said he'd pay me on delivery. Then when I delivered the food, he said he was too busy to round up the cash right then and would settle with me at the end of the night." A vein in his temple pulsed as he flexed his jaw. "I never should've taken that man at his word." He ran my credit card through the machine as if slashing the device in two. Clearly, I'd struck a nerve. He handed me the card and a receipt and rounded up my order from the service window behind him.

Does Mack Clayton have a vengeful side? Does the fact that Detective Pearce had put Mack "through the wringer" mean she considers him to be a viable suspect, too? I carried these questions along with two bags of barbecue sides back to my shop. After seeing Cormac slaughtered on my shop's porch last night, I wasn't sure my stomach could handle anything other than vegetables. Fortunately, the baked beans would provide plenty of protein. Kiki took one bite and rubbed her belly in bliss.

As soon as I'd finished eating, I prepared an invoice for Mack Clayton and carried two jugs of my grandfather's shine down to the barbecue joint to fulfill the order. He issued me a check on the spot.

As the afternoon turned into evening, we saw several people walk up to the doors of Limericks only to turn their heads toward each other in surprise and walk away. Some of them came into my shop and inquired about the police tape and the posted note on the door.

I didn't want to scare them out of the area, but I didn't want to lie to them, either. "The owner of the bar was found dead last night." I neglected to say by whom. "After closing time."

Learning that the victim wasn't a customer like them and that he was killed very late at night seemed to bring them some relief, though enough worry remained that many decided they needed a jar or jug of moonshine to calm their nerves. I'd feared the murder would be bad for business, but so far it had only increased traffic into my shop. Guilt made my guts squirm. Profiting off Cormac's murder felt wrong.

At a quarter before the nine o'clock closing time, Marlon pulled to the curb out front in his police department SUV. After taking a look around in the twilight outside, he strode into the store.

"Hey, cowboy copper," Kiki called. "Where's your trusty steed?"

"It's Saturday night," Marlon said. "Pretty thing like Charlotte's out to pasture with a handsome palomino."

"Uh-oh. Are there ponies in her future?"

"Baby horses aren't ponies," Marlon said. "They're foals. But, that said, no. I would never let a stallion defile my sweet Charlotte. Only geldings are allowed near her."

I'd been sweeping when he arrived, and I carried the broom to the front of the shop. "Working another swing shift tonight?"

"No," he said. "I'm not on duty."

Kiki ran her gaze up and down him. "Then what's with the uniform? That very nice-fitting uniform that hugs your muscles in all the right places."

Marlon raised a brow while I apologized for my brash friend. "You'll have to forgive Kiki, she—"

"Tells it like it is," Kiki said, completing my sentence for me.

"Yep." I shrugged. "That."

Marlon looked her way, a gleam of mischief in his eyes. "I'm more than my muscles, you know. I have feelings and hopes and dreams."

"Tell me all about them." Kiki put her elbow on her knee and rested her chin in her hand. "Flex your triceps while you're doing it."

Despite just insisting he was more than beefcake, Marlon raised his arms, hands fisted, and flexed.

Kiki fanned herself with a hand. "Mercy me." She grabbed her charcoal pencil and sketch pad. "Hold that pose, copper."

Marlon continued to stand, arms flexed and brazenly objectified, while he told me the reason for his off-duty visit. "I was worried about you locking up alone. I came to make sure you were safe."

A full-body blush warmed me from the tips of my toes to the tips of my ears. "That's very thoughtful of you, Marlon." The thought that Marlon didn't have a date tonight warmed me, too. "Have there been any developments since Ace was here earlier?" Maybe Marlon would be more forthcoming than Ace. I figured it couldn't hurt to hazard a guess, either. If Cormac had been dating two of his own staff, he likely had other women on the string. "Maybe another woman who might have had reason to want Cormac dead?"

"He had dozens of women's names in his phone, and he'd exchanged texts with a bunch of them recently. Pics, too, but I won't disgust you with the details. None of the messages indicated he was at odds with any of them, though."

"Did Ace have any luck with the printout I gave her? The one listing the sales of cherry moonshine?"

"Nothing panned out."

Darn. Was it too much to hope that Damien Sirakov had confessed and this ugly, scary matter could be put behind us? I realized that was not likely the case, or Marlon wouldn't have bothered to come to my shop now. Still, it couldn't hurt to ask. "What about Sirakov?"

"He's maintaining his innocence," Marlon said. "Under Tennessee law, he can be kept in custody seventy-two hours before he has to be arraigned. There's enough evidence to charge him with credit card fraud, but not enough to pin a murder rap on him. Unless we come up with some real evidence that he killed O'Keefe, he'll likely be released on bail once the holding period expires."

"Which means he could kill again."

Would Sirakov piece together that I'd been the one to finger him for the murder? When he'd followed me into Limericks earlier in the week, I'd told him I owned the Moonshine Shack. He knew I'd witnessed his confrontation with Cormac. Cormac's killer might not have spotted Smoky in the window of my shop, but once I'd turned on the lights inside and outside the store, the killer would have seen me, or at least have been clued in to my presence. My body began to shake of its own accord. *Now I know how my jars of moonshine feel shimmying out of the bottling machine.*

Seeming to forget his role as Kiki's model, Marlon lowered his arms and took my chin in his warm hand. But rather than chuck my chin this time, he cupped it, gently forcing me to look up at him. "I've talked to the officers scheduled to work the holding cell the next couple of days. They'll notify me the second Damien is released, and I'll call you right away."

It was reassuring to know Marlon was looking out for me, doing what he could to keep me safe. But he had other duties. He couldn't keep watch 24/7, even if he wanted to.

As he let go of my chin, Kiki pointed her charcoal pencil in my direction. "You and Smoky can come stay with me."

"Don't you and Max have plans?" Saturday was normally date night for the two of them.

"We did," she said. "But I texted him earlier and canceled. In fact, you should live with me until the case is resolved. The killer will never know to look for you at my place."

My voice quavered when I spoke. "But he'll know to look for me *here*."

"Don't you worry," Marlon said. "I'll make sure a patrol comes by regularly while you're at the shop, and I'll be here every night at closing."

"I can't ask that of you, Marlon."

"You didn't ask," Marlon said. "I offered. I'm not taking no for an answer, either, so you might as well not waste any time arguing with me."

I looked up into his amber eyes. "How can I ever thank you?"

He shrugged. "I suppose you could cook me a nice dinner."

Kiki snickered. "No, she can't. Trust me on that."

I grimaced. "It's true. I'm a terrible cook."

"The worst," Kiki clarified. "Unless you're a fan of charred oatmeal."

"Yuck." Marlon cocked his head. "You can take me out for a nice dinner, then."

I couldn't help but smile. *He'd asked me on a date, hadn't he? Or asked me to take him on one?* "Dinner out it is."

Kiki raised her pencil again. "Point of order. Will this dinner have to wait until the murder case is solved?"

I was glad she'd asked. I'd been wondering the same thing.

"It will," Marlon said, much to my disappointment. "An officer spending personal time with a witness isn't a good idea. A criminal defense attorney could make it an issue, claim some type of undue influence or bias, especially since I responded to O'Keefe's complaint against Hattie's grandpa."

I admired Marlon's dedication to his job. At the same time, though, I found myself with a new reason for wanting Cormac's killer found quick. It had been a long time since I'd gone to dinner with a guy as attractive and engaging as Marlon. Heck, I'd *never* gone to dinner with a guy as attractive and engaging as Marlon. The thought set my toes wiggling inside my sneakers.

Marlon brought the cards and games inside for me and stood sentry at the front door as I set about my closing routine. Lock the front door. Turn off the outdoor lights. Turn the sign in the window from *OPEN* to *CLOSED*. Clear the cash from the register and lock it in the safe to be deposited later. Turn off the lights in the shop. Set the alarm.

Kiki, Marlon, and I slipped out the back door and I closed it behind us. The alarm armed with a reassuring *beep-beep-beep*. As Kiki climbed into her car, she raised a hand and called, "Bye, copper! See you at my place in a little bit, Hattie!"

"Thanks for helping out!" I called back.

Marlon circled around to the passenger side of my van and took hold of the handle. "How about you give me a ride around the building to my car?"

"Gladly."

I pressed the button on the fob to unlock the doors and we climbed in. As I closed my door, I realized that this was the first time Marlon and I had been alone since the first time we'd met.

Marlon looked up and down the alley as I backed up, his expression pensive. "It wouldn't be hard for a car to block each end of this alley and trap you back here. Or for someone to turn the garbage dumpsters crossways and create a roadblock."

My nerves, which had just settled, began to prickle again. "Great. Now I've got to something else to worry about. What would you suggest I do, replace my van with a Sherman tank?"

"Shoot, yeah, if it were possible. Short of that, I'd suggest you move your car from the back alley to a spot out front before sundown. You'll have to feed the meter, but I suspect that would be deductible as a business expense. Besides, a few dollars is a small price to pay for safety."

True, but a few dollars a day could add up over time into big money. If this murder investigation dragged on, my piggy bank could soon be empty. Heck, I rarely even sprang for fancy coffee due to the price. I settled for preparing my own coffee at home in my granny's ancient stainless-steel stovetop percolator circa 1948. The Moonshine Shack was doing okay for a brand-new business, but it wasn't yet bringing in anything close to a livable income.

I turned the corner, circled the end of the business strip, and drove up to Marlon's SUV, braking to a stop behind it. "Thanks again, Marlon. You're a dedicated cop."

"Maybe." He cocked his head, a roguish gleam in his gaze. "Or maybe I'm just a hopeless flirt."

My nose issued an amused yet involuntary snort. "If warning me that a killer might trap me in an alley is flirtation, then you're a really *bad* flirt."

"Point taken. Let's stick with 'dedicated cop' then." He sent me a soft, sideways smile and slid out of my van, leaving me feeling prickly once more, but this time in a good way.

Chapter Ten

I woke mid-Sunday morning on the fold-out couch in the spare bedroom of Kiki's condo. Her unit was on the fourth floor of a high-rise building that had been built a half century ago in the neighborhood now referred to as North Chattanooga. While the space had been updated multiple times over the years by its previous owners, none of the updates had encompassed the entire unit. Thus, while her master bedroom and bath sported pink-and-blue floral wallpaper and gold-plated light fixtures circa 1900, the shower in the guest bath was formed by the type of clear glass blocks popular a decade later. The kitchen had been updated in the mid-2000s with stainless-steel appliances and dark woods. On her balcony, which faced downtown and gave her a great view of the skyline, sat two vintage metal lawn chairs she'd rescued from a curb years ago. She'd hammered out the dents, sanded off the rust, and painted them an eye-catching turquoise color. Kiki didn't mind the clash of decades and décor styles in her place. In fact, she liked the idea that just by walking about her condo, she could essentially walk back and forth through time.

Seeing that my eyes were open, Smoky issued a whisker-twitching chirrup that told me I'd better get him his breakfast right away or he'd cough up a gooey hairball on my sneakers in retaliation.

I reached over and ruffled his ears. "Okay, boy. At your service." Smoky trotted along beside me as I padded to the kitchen to round up a can of food and a can opener.

Kiki sat at the dinette set. Her two rescue cats, Kahlo and van Gogh, lounged on the tabletop in front of her, lazily engaged in their morning ablutions. Kahlo, named after the famous artist Frida Kahlo, sported white fur and a black unibrow, much like her namesake. Van Gogh was an orange tabby with only one intact ear. Where the other ear had gone to was anyone's guess. It had already been lost in feral cat warfare or some type of accident before he'd been rounded up by animal control, carted to the city shelter, and put up for adoption.

Kiki raised her steaming mug of English breakfast tea in salute. "Fancy a cup?"

"I'd love one. Thanks. Just don't try to feed me beans on toast."

She tsked. "You don't know what you're missing."

While I set about feeding my cat, Kiki set about heating her teakettle. A few minutes later, we were seated at her table, sipping from dainty, delightfully mismatched teacups and eating toasted English muffins slathered with jam.

The two of us had been exhausted by the time I'd arrived at her condo the night before. We'd gone right to bed. Now that we'd had a full night's sleep and were feeling refreshed, she picked up where we left off. "So. Dinner with the copper, eh?" She wagged her brows.

"Once the killer is caught." All the more reason to help move things along. I'd be keeping my eyes and ears open for any opportunities to assist the authorities in the investigation.

Smoky finished his breakfast and sat back on the floor, licking his whiskers. He'd left a few bites in his bowl. Van Gogh noticed and hopped down from the dinette to see if he might sample the leftovers. Smoky froze mid-lick before issuing a warning hiss that said *Stay away from my bowl or risk your other ear!*

"Smoky!" I scolded, reaching down to grab him. "That's no way to treat your hosts."

Smoky wriggled in my arms, but I held on tight. Van Gogh flicked his tail in a manner that said *Nyaa-nyaa. Try to stop me now!* He helped himself to the rest of Smoky's food while Smoky struggled and spat.

Kiki stood and walked over to the easel that stood in front of the glass doors to her balcony. She rounded up two long oil painting brushes, one with a pointed tip, the other with a fan tip. She held them up. "Let's take these brushes with us today. They could be used as improvised weapons."

"How?" I said. "Are we going to tickle the killer to death with the bristles?"

"No." She shifted them in her hands, holding them like daggers. "The handle end could put an eye out."

I shuddered, envisioning an eyeball shish-kabobbed on a paintbrush and the disembodied eye envisioning me in return. As much as I disliked the thought of getting attacked by a would-be killer, the thought of poking someone's eye out held nearly as little appeal. "Why would we need to poke their eye out? Wouldn't we have already sealed their eyes shut with your adhesive spray?"

"It can't hurt to have options," Kiki replied. "Have you considered getting a gun?"

"Guns make me nervous. For it to be of any use, I'd have to keep it loaded and carry it on me. With as much as I move about the shop, I'm likely to shoot myself in the butt when I crouch down to stock a lower shelf."

"Get a stun gun, then. The worst you could do is accidentally perform electrolysis on yourself."

"I'll think about it." Problem was, I didn't want to think about it. I didn't want to think that I, or anyone else at my store, could be in so much danger that we'd need to defend ourselves with a deadly weapon. I preferred to focus on happy things like the launch of my own moonshine line and the positive feedback I'd received, not to mention a certain attractive copper.

"Maybe it's a moot point," Kiki said, a hopeful lilt in her voice. "Maybe they solved the case while we were sleeping." She bit into her English muffin and held it between her teeth as she picked up her phone and used her thumbs to type in a search. When she finished scrolling and skimming, she removed the muffin, less a large bite, from her mouth. After quickly chewing and swallowing, she said, "Nothing new is being reported."

I heaved a sigh. "Too bad Damien Sirakov didn't confess." I'd feel much better knowing for certain that the killer was in custody. So far, Sirakov was merely a person of interest. If they didn't find something more to link him to the crime, he could be released shortly.

After breakfast, Kiki and I got ready to head to my shop. With it being Sunday, the store would be open only from noon to five today, so it would be a short shift. After spending the day home alone yesterday, Smoky decided he wanted to come with me today. He followed me to Kiki's door as we prepared to leave and issued his demand. *Mrrow!* Lest I come back to find that Smoky had shredded Kiki's couch, I loaded him into his carrier and lugged him down the hall to the elevator.

Shortly thereafter, we arrived at the Moonshine Shack. Kiki and I kept a careful eye on the alley as we hurried from our cars to the back door and into my shop. The alarm issued another *beep-beep-beep*, warning me that I had fifteen seconds to disarm it or it would emit an all-out wail. I punched in the code and the small light changed from red to green. Having handled that pressing matter, I bent down to release Smoky from his carrier. He'd already grown impatient and started jiggling the metal door with his paw.

My cat led the way from the back room into the shop and promptly hopped up to claim his favorite spot in the front window, the spot from which he'd witnessed Cormac's murder. Through the glass, I saw that the cordon tape had been removed from Limericks, but the notice advising no one to enter without first contacting Ace remained. Three cars were parked in front of the bar. The first was Ace's Impala. The other was Marlon's SUV. The third was a small red Mitsubishi Mirage sedan.

Kiki stepped up next to me. "They're putting the thumb screws to someone over there."

While it was doubtful any torture techniques were in use, it appeared that Ace was conducting witness interviews at the bar and that she'd brought Marlon along, presumably to ensure her personal safety. The only question now was, who was being questioned and had the interrogation proved fruitful?

I wasn't left to wonder long. A few minutes later, as I

was setting out the dominoes, playing cards, and chessboard in front of my shop, the front door of the bar opened
to reveal Ace. She held the door ajar and out stepped Ashlynn. Dressed in a flowing pink sundress with her golden
hair pulled back in a big white bow, she looked as sweet
and innocent as Little Bo Peep. All she needed was a couple of sheep. But I'd seen the woman in action, attacking
her coworker on the sidewalk. This vixen had a vicious
streak. Had she unleashed it on Cormac O'Keefe after he'd
left the bar Saturday morning?

Maybe she'd determined to kill him the night she caught
him cheating, but returned to work for the week so that it
would appear as if she'd forgiven him and moved on. Or
maybe she'd come back to work so that she'd have an opportunity to get close to him, keep an eye on him and look
for an opportune moment to commit the dirty deed. But, as
Cormac's employee, wouldn't she have already been familiar with his routines? Wouldn't it have made more sense for
her to at least pretend to have been nowhere in the area if
she planned to ambush him after he left the bar for the
night? Killing Cormac, on a night when she'd worked the
late shift, put her at the crime scene only shortly before he'd
been attacked. She'd have to know she'd be implicated by
the circumstances. But maybe that was her plan. Maybe she
was clever enough to do things that a killer *shouldn't* do.
Maybe her excuse would be that no killer would be that
stupid. It was a convoluted theory, but it had a warped logic
to it.

To my surprise, once the door closed behind her, Ashlynn
stepped off the curb and aimed straight for the Moonshine
Shack. *Uh-oh.* I clutched the heavy wooden chessboard. If
she tried to attack me like she'd attacked Miranda, I'd whack
her upside the head with it. *Checkmate!*

The skin around Ashlynn's eyes crinkled ever so slightly as she walked up, as if she were assessing me. She wore the pretty shimmery pink lipstick again. I was tempted to ask about it, but I realized again that now was not the time. Instead, I gave her a nod of acknowledgment and said, "Hi."

"You remember me, right?" she said. "From Limericks?"

Not sure whether acknowledging that I recognized her was a good idea, I hedged my bets. "I think so. I mean, we were never formally introduced, but I believe I saw you at the bar once."

"You did," she insisted, the crinkles deepening around her eyes as they narrowed further. "The day you tried to deliver moonshine and Cormac turned you away."

Still unsure where this conversation might be going, I merely echoed her, in paraphrased form. "He placed an order at my grand opening, but he changed his mind."

"Guess you heard he got himself killed."

Got himself killed. She was blaming the victim. But it was uncertain whether she was doing it to assuage her guilt or because she, like Mack Clayton, thought karma had finally caught up to Cormac. "You don't think it could have been a random mugging?"

"No," she said. "Cormac gave a lot of people a lot of reasons to want him dead."

Including you.

She stared at me as she hiked a thumb over her shoulder to indicate Limericks. "The police called me in for questioning."

There seemed to be an accusation in her statement. I raised a casual shoulder. "Standard procedure, probably."

Still staring me down, she angled her head. "Any idea why they'd ask if I'd bought your moonshine?"

"My moonshine?" Rather than lie outright, I responded

with a vague phrase that was subject to interpretation. "I couldn't say." Luckily, she didn't press me to elaborate on whether I couldn't say because I didn't know or because I'd been ordered to keep my mouth shut. I forced a smile. "If you'd like to try some of my moonshine, I'd be happy to pour samples for you."

"Not today," she said. "I've got a job interview."

"Good luck," I said. "I hope you get it."

Her mouth curled up in a smile not reflected in her eyes. With that, she turned, walked back across the street, and climbed into the Mitsubishi.

Exhaling in relief, I set the chessboard down on the table and entered my shop. Kiki stood just inside the door, crouched like a ninja, wielding her spray sealant in one hand and the pointed paintbrush in the other. As always, she'd had my back.

"One false move," she said, "and that girl would've gotten it good."

I was glad there'd been no need for Kiki to defend me. Enough blood had been shed in front of my shop.

We resumed readying the shop for business. We'd just opened up when the front door opened and Heath Delaney walked in. My heart gave a little jump, and not in a good way. I remembered what Kiki had said about criminals returning to the scene of their crimes. Heath's own words came back to me, too. *That man is as cutthroat as they come.* Heath had been describing Cormac O'Keefe at the time, but did those very words now apply to the attorney before me? *Had Heath cut Cormac's throat? Had his choice of words been a premonition, one based on the dark meanderings of the attorney's mind?*

I forced another smile. "Hi, Heath. How are you?"

"Absolutely morose." He grinned and raised his empty hands. "I'm all out of moonshine."

"No worries. I can remedy that situation right away." As I met him in front of a display of Firefly moonshine, I realized this was my opportunity to determine which flavor of shine Heath had taken home from my grand opening. But I also realized if I asked him straight out what flavor he'd chosen at the party, he was likely to lie if it had been a jar of cherry shine that he'd later used to kill Cormac. I tried a sneak approach, pretending to remember what flavor he'd chosen. "What are you in the mood for? Another jar of cherry shine?"

"Cherry?" he said. "No. I got a jar of the peach flavor last time. Made the mistake of taking it to my mother's house so she could try some in her sweet tea. She loved it so much she wouldn't let me leave me with it. She plans to serve it when she hosts her Pokeno group this week."

"Another peach jar, then, since yours was confiscated?"

"Give me two," he said. "Mother's Day is coming up and Mom will be all out of the stuff after game night. Those ladies know how to have a good time."

Heath had given me the answer to what flavor of moonshine he'd left my party with, as well as a great idea. I'd offer a Mother's Day special, maybe a gift with purchase such as a lid with a built-in pour spout or an environmentally friendly reusable straw. I made a mental note to look into inexpensive promotional items I could offer on occasion as a free-with-purchase bonus.

After ringing up Heath's purchase, I asked, "Would you like your mother's jar in a gift bag?"

"Definitely," he said. "I've never mastered the fine art of gift wrap. Can't curl a ribbon to save my life."

He claims no skill with scissors, but could he cut a carotid artery with jagged glass? I pondered this possibility as I headed to the checkout counter with a jar in each hand. After setting them on the countertop, I asked, "What are you doing downtown on a Sunday? Putting in some over-time?"

"Exactly. Getting a head start on the week. I landed a new client with a high-dollar breach-of-contract case. Got my work cut out for me on this one."

I retrieved a gift bag printed with my Firefly moonshine logo from under the counter and lined it with lime-green tissue paper before placing the jar inside. After rounding up a pair of scissors and the curling ribbon, I decided to broach the subject of Cormac's murder directly and see how Heath responded. The checkout counter separated us and pro-vided a modicum of protection, and I could defend myself with the scissors if necessary.

"By the way, you were right about Cormac." I frowned and snipped a length of ribbon. "He reneged on the order he placed at my grand opening."

Heath's expression turned similarly sour. "I'm not sur-prised. That man was all kinds of crooked."

I noticed he referred to Cormac using the past-tense *was* rather than the present-tense *is*. *He must've heard the news, too.* "Shocking what happened to him, huh?"

"The murder? Not really." Heath shrugged nonchalantly, as if discussing something mundane, like the weather.

I understood that Heath didn't like Cormac, but his total lack of regard seemed crass. Then again, maybe he was merely responding with the practiced calm of a man who spent much of his time in courtrooms and negotiations. "You're not surprised?"

"Not a bit," Heath said. "The way Cormac treated peo-ple, he was asking for it."

It was the same sentiment Mack Clayton and Ashlynn had expressed, though in harsher terms.

"A detective came by my shop yesterday to see if I knew anything." As instructed, I kept the details to myself. That Cormac was killed with a broken jar of my moonshine. That I'd heard him cry out. That he'd bled out on the stoop of my shop. That the detective considered me a prime suspect. That I might have pointed to Heath as a possible person of interest. "She might swing by to see you. I understand she's talking to others in the area who've done business with Cormac. From the warning you gave me about dealing with him, I assume that includes you?"

"No," Heath said with a shake of his head. "I never did business with O'Keefe. Not unless you call suing the man 'doing business.'"

Heath had offered me a segue into fishing for information, and I wasn't about to let the opportunity pass me by. I needed to learn as much as possible about both Cormac and other potential suspects to clear my name. "You've sued him?"

"Multiple times, for multiple clients. Cormac never showed up for court, not even once. Never made full payment on the judgments entered against him, either. He'd toss a few dollars my way every once in a while, enough to keep my clients from sending a sheriff out to seize his assets. Not that it would have done any good. We tried it once. O'Keefe kept only a small amount of cash on hand at the bar and a measly balance in the bank. He leased the bar space. His only assets are the tables, chairs, and his liquor inventory. None of that is worth much. The writ wasn't worth the paper it was written on."

"Why wasn't he put out of business? Forced to close down?"

"Putting someone out of business is harder than you might think," Heath said. "Expensive, too. My clients got tired of throwing good money after bad trying to collect from O'Keefe. Eventually, I stopped even trying. I advised anyone who came to me that the best they could do is cut their losses. Short of the health department, state tax bureau, or IRS shutting the bar down, the guy was going to slide by."

"That doesn't seem fair," I said, "but it would make sense if he was killed by someone who felt they had no other recourse." *You, perhaps?*

Heath's brow furrowed as he seemed to realize he might have overshared.

To mollify him I added, "That's why the detective came to me. Cormac and my grandfather argued Friday evening. Of course, there's no way he or I killed Cormac, but she's probably just dotting her i's and crossing her t's, making sure she's considered every angle. Chances are Cormac was killed in a random robbery. Or it might have been a disgruntled customer. They've got someone in custody. It's probably him."

Heath released a loud breath. "That's a relief."

I had to wonder. Was it a relief because the police might already have the killer in custody? Or was it a relief because the police weren't on to Heath yet? I imagined it would be extremely frustrating to repeatedly beat your head against a wall, trying to get justice for clients who'd been taken by a swindler. If Heath hadn't been able to collect from Cormac, maybe he'd decided to make the man pay with his life instead.

I finished curling the ribbon, fluffed the tissue paper, and presented the bagged gift to Heath. "Ta-da!"

"Thanks, Hattie. My mom's going to love this."

"Tell her to bring her Pokeno group in for a tasting. I'll pour them extra-generous samples." I punctuated my offer with an exaggerated wink.

"Great idea. I will." With that, he left the shop, turning right down the sidewalk to head back to his office.

I watched him walk off. In the front window, Smoky stood and stared at Heath's back, too. *Does the cat know something I don't? Does he recognize Heath from the late-night attack on Cormac O'Keefe? Or is Smoky just stretching?* What I wouldn't give to be able to read that cat's mind.

Chapter Eleven

The afternoon was slow, only a trickle of tourists venturing into the shop. One of them stopped to admire my grandfather's wood sculpture of Smoky. "This little cat is so cute!"

"My grandfather whittled it for me."

"Does he sell them?"

"No," I said. "He just makes them for fun."

"Darn. I'd love a cute knickknack like that to set on my windowsill."

While Granddaddy didn't whittle for profit, maybe he ought to think about it. The little wooden figures would make great souvenirs, maybe draw even more people into the store. I'd talk to Granddaddy about it when I picked him up tomorrow morning.

My phone burst into song again. A look at the screen indicated it was my mother trying to reach me. I'd been expecting her call sooner or later. She and my father still had the print version of the local Sunday newspaper delivered. Having grown up without two nickels to rub together, Mom was a copious coupon clipper. She never ventured to the grocery store without her circulars and divided organizer in tow. She hadn't paid full price for paper towels, toilet paper, or a cleaning product in her life. My more lighthearted father skipped the ads to enjoy the sports page and comics. Even so, I realized the news of Cormac O'Keefe's murder would make the front page and was unlikely to go unnoticed.

I took a breath to ready myself and jabbed the button to accept the call. "Hi, Mom," I said in my most cheerful everything's-okay-here tone.

"A man was murdered on Market Street!" she shrieked. "He owned that Irish pub right across from your store!"

"I heard." I didn't dare tell her I'd nearly been a witness to the killing, that I'd been mere feet away from the killer, separated only by window glass, my cat, and jars of moonshine when the attack took place. I didn't tell her the victim's neck had been slashed with a broken jar of my Firefly moonshine, or that I'd held one of my promotional T-shirts to the victim's neck to stanch his bleeding. No sense sending her into an all-out stroke.

"You knew?" she cried. "And you didn't tell me?"

There were lots of things I didn't tell my mother. I didn't tell her about any man I'd dated unless the relationship lasted longer than two months. I didn't tell her when I'd planned to quit my job to open the Moonshine Shack until I'd already turned in my resignation. I didn't tell her anytime I went to the dentist or doctor or even the shopping mall or hairdresser. I didn't tell her because she'd want to know every last detail and give me her opinion, whether or not I'd asked for it. *I never asked for it.* For fashion advice I went to Kiki and Kate. For sage advice, I went to my father or Granddaddy.

Rather than worrying about everything that could go wrong, they shared my same optimistic approach that, even if some things went wrong, odds were that some would go right. Why not take a chance and see what happens?

With a sigh, I said, "I didn't tell you because I knew you'd freak out. The incident happened late at night, in the dark, way after my shop closed. I'm being extra careful. I'm moving my van to the front of the store before it gets dark. A guy is coming by tomorrow to put in security cameras, and the local police have offered to send an officer by at closing time."

"The police are providing private security now? That's unusual."

No, I thought. *That's Marlon Landers.* But no sense elaborating. She'd ask me a bunch of questions I had no answers for, at least not yet. *What are his intentions? Is he marriage material? Where is this relationship going?* "Kiki brought some self-defense spray, too," I said. "If anybody tries something, she'll douse them good."

"I'm going shopping," Mom said. "I'm going to find you a bulletproof vest. One for your grandfather and Kiki, too."

Given the manner of Cormac's death, she'd be better off shopping for a hard plastic neck brace, or maybe a turtleneck and a thick scarf. But knowing she'd find a broken jar to be a more disturbing weapon than a gun and bullet, I let it go. Eventually, I was able to calm her fears and get her off the phone.

While Kiki took advantage of the midafternoon lull to put the finishing touches on her sketch of Marlon, I used the time to restock the shelves, dust, and clean the windows. As I ran a rag in broad circles over the windowpane above him, Smoky reached up a paw, his claws out, in an attempt to snatch the rag out of my hand. I yanked the rag away and ruffled his ears. "No-no, naughty boy." He glowered at me, his green eyes at half mast.

Activity at Limericks caught my eye. A honey-haired young woman in wedge sandals, skintight jeans, and a black halter top climbed out of a convertible banana-yellow VW Beetle and walked up to the door. *That's Miranda, isn't it?* As I watched, she rapped on the door. A moment later, Marlon opened it and allowed Miranda inside. The door closed behind them, but it did nothing to stop my musings. *What is she telling them? Is Ace trying to wheedle a confession out of Miranda like she'd tried with me? There's no way Miranda could have killed Cormac, could she?* I'd only interacted with her once before, but she'd seemed polite, sweet even. Then again, maybe I was influenced by her gushing endorsement of my moonshine.

After I'd gone about my business for a half hour or so, the Latina server arrived at Limericks. As Marlon let her inside, Miranda emerged from the bar. Rather than returning to her car to leave, she stood next to the leprechaun, leaning back against the brick wall of Limericks and staring down at the screen of her phone, her thumb slowly working the screen. She could be checking her e-mails, shopping online, or swiping left and right on a dating app, looking for a replacement for Cormac. *The leprechaun statue would make a better boyfriend.* Regardless, I was less curious about what she might be doing on her phone and more curious about why she was sticking around. *Is she waiting for someone?*

Kiki took note of Miranda, too. "What's she doing?"

"I'll find out." I picked up my cleaning supplies and carried them out front under the guise of cleaning the windows from the outside. I raised my rag and waved it. "Hello, Miranda!"

She looked up from her phone and, on spotting me, gave me a wave in return. She tucked her phone into her purse and stepped forward, pausing at the curb until a couple of cars drove past before striding across the street, her long legs making quick work of the asphalt. She stopped in front of me, her French-tipped fingers wrapped around the strap of the purse hanging from her bare shoulder. "Did you hear? Cormac was killed."

"I did." I eyed her face, noting that her eyes were neither pink nor puffy. If she'd shed any tears for the man, they'd been few. "I'm sorry. I mean, I know things weren't great between you two at the end, but this still must be hard."

"It is." She blinked and wriggled her nose and mouth as she fought to keep from crying . . . *or pretended to fight.* Still, I had a hard time seeing the young woman as a killer. She'd been friendly to me at my grand opening. Even when Ashlynn had attacked her on the sidewalk in front of Limericks later that evening, Miranda had only defended herself, not launched an offensive of her own. She dropped into one of the rocking chairs and issued a shaky sigh.

"Did you leave something at Limericks?" I asked.

"Besides my dignity, you mean?" She chuckled mirthlessly. "Nothing important. Some spare clothes in case a drink spilled on me, but that's it."

Then why are you still here? It seemed rude to ask outright, so I continued to fish. "Are you hanging around to get closure, then?"

"Partly, I suppose. The police questioned me. I haven't seen Cormac or talked to him since last Sunday, so I don't have much to tell them. They said they'd let me back into the bar once they're done interviewing Isabella. I'm thinking about reopening the place."

My brows shot up to my hairline. "Really?" *Shouldn't*

she be afraid she might suffer the same fate as Cormac if she stepped into his shoes, that the killer might return to rob her and cut her throat if she refused to turn over the cash receipts? Then again, if Miranda had been the one to end Cormac's life, she'd know there was no one else to fear. Or maybe she, like the others, assumed the murder had been personal, that Cormac had been targeted because of something he'd done, and that she wouldn't be at risk. "Reopening the bar seems like a big undertaking." Miranda was young, probably in her early twenties. *Even if she'd been a stellar cocktail waitress, she wouldn't know all the ins and outs of running a bar, would she?*

"Cormac trained me to tend bar and to handle some of the management duties," she said. "He showed me how to make schedules for the staff, order supplies and liquor, and enter payments for deliveries."

"You were an assistant manager, then?"

"Not officially. He never gave me a title."

"If he didn't give you a title, please tell me he at least gave you a decent salary." *If not, she might have an additional motive for killing Cormac besides his cheating.*

She sighed softly. "No. He didn't give me a salary. Just the minimum hourly pay."

The lowest legal pay in Tennessee for workers who received tips was a measly $2.13 an hour. *If Miranda was handling administrative duties for Cormac, that would mean time away from customers and a resulting reduction in gratuities. Cormac had cost her tip income, taken advantage of her, used her.* "That wasn't fair. Handling management tasks should have entitled you to higher pay. You'd have a claim against Cormac's estate for unpaid wages."

"Maybe," she said, "but Cormac didn't have much property that I know of. He tried to hide things from me, put on like he was rich, but I was starting to figure things out. He leased the bar space, his car, and his apartment. The bar did okay, but it wasn't a big moneymaker. Anytime Cormac had some cash, he'd blow it on a beach vacation in Florida or lose it at the craps tables at the Harrah's casino over the mountains in North Carolina." In other words, he likely had a negative net worth at the time of his death. "I'm out of a job thanks to him. He owes me. That's why I'm taking over the bar."

I couldn't blame her one bit. I'd probably feel the same way in her shoes . . . though I might not feel the same way quite so soon. I might need more time to come to terms with his death. But everyone grieves in different ways and at different speeds, I supposed.

She let out a sharp breath. "I was stupid to let him treat me the way he did. He convinced me that he cared about me and that he would promote me once I proved myself. Turns out he was just a con man. A cheat, too. I thought we were exclusive, but after your grand opening, I learned that wasn't the case. He was dating one of his other servers, too. Ashlynn."

"The one you were fending off on the sidewalk?"

An embarrassed blush darkened her cheeks. "You saw that?"

"I did." In fact, everyone at my party had witnessed the catfight, but I wouldn't humiliate her further by saying so. "What happened?"

"Cormac and I went back to Limericks when we left here." She gestured to my shop windows. "Ashlynn came into the bar, saw me and Cormac together, and screamed, 'You're a dead man!'"

Whoa. "'Dead man'? Really?"

She nodded. "She went after him first, but when she couldn't get to Cormac she turned on me instead."

"That wasn't fair, either." I wondered how Ashlynn would feel when she learned that Miranda planned to reopen Limericks. *Would she be jealous of her former rival for Cormac's affections? Or would she move on? If she was Cormac's killer, would she return to seek vengeance on Miranda, too? And me?* "Do you think she carried through with her threat? Do you think she's the one who killed Cormac?"

Miranda raised her palms. "Maybe. Cormac never scheduled us to work the same shifts so I didn't know Ashlynn, but Isabella worked with her a few times. She told me Ashlynn wasn't friendly. I don't know what to think, honestly. The situation hardly seems real. I'm just trying to put it behind me and get on with my life. That's why I want to get the bar open again."

I glanced over at Limericks, noting that Ace's notice was still posted on the door. For now, the bar remained a crime scene, not a place of business. "Did the police say you can move ahead with your plans?"

"Ace said it's up to the building's owner, whether they'll allow me to lease the space. She said she's spoken with Cormac's next of kin. They haven't been in touch with him in years. Nobody seems to know if he left a will, and none of them are interested in serving as his executor. They seem to know there'd be nothing in it for them but headaches. I doubt anyone will try to stop me from taking over."

Miranda had been very forthcoming with me. I wondered if she'd been the same with Ace and whether that would hurt her case or help it. I'd been forthcoming and had only seemed to dig myself in deeper. On one hand, being straightforward made Miranda seem honest and trustworthy. On the other hand, the more information she offered, the more she appeared to have multiple motives for putting an end to Cormac O'Keefe. Not only had he cheated on her romantically, he'd also cheated her out of income and burdened her with duties well above her pay grade while offering her no remuneration in return. Moreover, the fact that she seemed so eager to take over the bar and operate it on her own could mean she'd had her eye on his business all along. Was it possible she'd asked him to show her how to handle the administrative tasks so she'd know how to manage the bar once it was hers? She had to realize Cormac hadn't exactly ingratiated himself to others. Maybe she'd realized that if he was killed, the crime could be pinned on any number of adversaries. Or maybe Miranda was exactly who she appeared to be—a hardworking young woman with ambition, much like me, but younger and more glamorous. Still, the news of Cormac's death was new. She seemed to have come to terms with his demise very quickly, though his infidelity had likely made it easier to accept.

"You know how to run the place," I said, "but do you know about corporations and contracts and stuff like that?"

"Not much," she said. "Got any advice?"

Having just gone through the process of setting up a business myself, I had oodles of information to offer her. "If you're going to run a business, you should form a corporation to protect yourself from personal liability. Change the name of the place and get a new lease. Put the utilities in the name of your new business, too. Otherwise, if you continue to run the place as Limericks, you could inadvertently take on Cormac's debts." I hadn't gotten an A in my college business law class for nothing. "You should talk to an attorney. Try Heath Delaney. His office is nearby, and he represents other businesses in the area."

Miranda pulled out her phone and opened the notes app. "Could you run through all of that again? I'm going to make a to-do list."

I repeated my advice and she typed as fast as her French-tipped thumbs could move. When she finished, she looked up at me. "You're really smart, Hattie."

I was intelligent, sure, but my education, experience, and sheer determination had carried me, too. "I studied business in college and worked in the accounting department at MoonPie for years."

"My only jobs have been serving food and drinks," Miranda said, "but I was pretty good at talking customers into appetizers and desserts. I could sometimes convince them to order call drinks rather than well drinks, too. I made more in tips as a server than a lot of my friends earned in their office jobs."

"What I'm hearing is that you've got a knack for in-person sales."

"I do." She smiled and lifted her chin proudly. "I've completed all my basics at Chattanooga State Community College and taken a couple of business classes. Basic accounting and marketing. I've got a 3.8 GPA. Made the dean's list every semester."

"Wow. I'm impressed." I felt ashamed to realize I'd judged her by her appearance and underestimated her, just like people had underestimated me at times. I should've known better than to judge a book by its French-tipped, tight-jeans-wearing blond cover.

"I think I could run a successful bar." She stared across the street at Limericks for a moment before looking at me again. "No, I know I could."

Miranda clearly had some smarts, experience, and education, and she most definitely had the determination she'd need to give the place a real go. I admired her confidence, too. "Sounds like you've got what it takes. Maybe we can do some cross-promotions that'll benefit us both."

"I'd like that," she said. "I could use a mentor. Someone to go to for business advice. Could you help me out? Woman to woman?"

"'Woman to woman' is code for 'at no charge,' isn't it?"

"See?" She grinned. "You really are smart."

We shared a laugh. "I'd be happy to help." Who was I to deny assistance to a fellow female entrepreneur? Besides, working alongside her would give me access to the bar's records and might help me figure out who had killed Cormac. The sooner his killer was identified and put behind bars, the sooner I'd be off the hook and could have that dinner with Marlon. Of course, I'd make the situation work for me, too. "I do have one condition, though."

"Name it."

"Your bar serves my moonshine exclusively. No other brand."

She didn't think twice about my demand. "Done."

She stuck out her hand and I gave it a shake, sealing our deal. The sales rep for Backwoods Bootleggers would be disappointed the next time he made a sales call at the bar and Miranda refused to buy shine from him, but I'd dare him to complain. After crashing my party, he'd convinced Cormac to carry his brand only. *Turnabout is fair play, right?*

"Speaking of my shine," I said, "how's your personal supply holding up?"

"I'm about halfway through my jar of wild blackberry," Miranda said. "I'm not sure what's left of the jar Cormac took with him."

Aha! He'd taken a jar, not a jug. That meant he might have chosen the cherry flavor. *Dare I ask outright? Would it be too obvious?* I supposed it would only be obvious to the killer why I was asking. Her response could tell me whether she was guilty or innocent. "Did Cormac choose the blackberry, too?"

"No," she said, with no detectable change in her tone or expression. "He got a jar of the cherry flavor. He said he could use it to make spiked cherry cola."

He'd chosen a jar of the cherry shine. *Hmm.* Could Cormac have been killed with the very jar he'd taken from my party? If so, it would increase the odds that his killer was someone close to him, such as a former employee like Ashlynn. If Miranda had been the one to kill him, it seemed unlikely she'd have been so forthcoming about the flavor he'd chosen. She would have probably feigned ignorance or lied outright.

"Funny," Miranda added, "the policewoman asked me the same thing. What flavor moonshine Cormac got at your party."

Feigning ignorance myself, I responded with a mere "Hmm."

Two thirtyish couples wandered up to the store. As I opened the door to let them in, I turned to Miranda. "The Shack closes at five o'clock. Should I come by the bar afterward so we can talk some more?"

"Definitely," Miranda said. "I can use your help."

"Okay. See you then." *Is she telling the truth? Has she really not seen Cormac since the night of my grand opening?* Time would tell, I supposed. But for now, my instincts were telling me she was being honest.

I followed the couples into my shop and helped them select several jars of shine. "I'm running a Mother's Day special," I said. "I can gift wrap a jar for your mother if you'd like to pick one out for her."

"What a wonderful idea!" one of the women said. "I had

no idea what I was going to get her. She already has every-thing."

The other woman reached out to a shelf. "I'll get the blue-berry flavor for my mother and apple pie for my stepmom."

I rang them up, bagged their gifts, and walked them to the door with a "Thank you! Come back soon!"

Once the door swung closed, Kiki whispered, "Dish." She gestured to the young woman still sitting on the rocker out front. "What did you and Miranda talk about out there?"

I kept my voice soft, too. "She's going to reopen Limer-icks. I gave her some business advice, and she asked me to help her out, to serve as her mentor."

Kiki frowned. "You said no, didn't you? Miranda could be the one who killed Cormac."

"It's possible," I said, "but I'm not feeling it. Besides, helping her will give me access to Limericks and informa-tion that might help me identify the killer."

"What are you thinking?" Kiki hissed as she threw her hands in the air. "You could end up dead!"

"I'll be careful," I said. "I won't let on if I figure out she's the killer."

Kiki groaned. "If Miranda kills you, I'm going to say 'I told you so.' In fact, I'll make it the theme of your eulogy."

"Understood. But you'd still take Smoky for me? Raise him right?"

"I'll take him in, but I'm going to let him run with the wrong crowd and I won't help him with his algebra home-work. He'll become a feline delinquent."

"I'll take my chances."

Chapter Twelve

Late afternoon came and, as Marlon had suggested, Kiki and I moved our cars from the small space behind my shop to street parking so that we could exit out of the front of my shop rather than the back, where we'd be more vulnerable.

Isabella emerged from Limericks and Miranda stood from the rocker in front of the Moonshine Shack. She crossed the street and spoke briefly with Ace and Marlon in front of the bar before going inside. Marlon carried a computer and monitor, which he stashed in the trunk of Ace's car. Ace yanked her notice from the door and shoved it down inside her enormous tote. *Looks like she's done with her investigation and interviews at Limericks.*

Marlon came across the street and entered the shop. "Afternoon, ladies."

I greeted him with a smile, while Kiki said, "Hey, copper."

He kept an eye out while Kiki and I closed up the shop,

and accompanied us out the front door when we'd finished, hauling Smoky in his carrier. As he headed to my car, I said, "Smoky's going home with Kiki."

"He is?" Marlon's eyes narrowed. "You're not planning on staying here at your shop alone, are you?"

"No," I reassured him. "I'm going over to Limericks. I told Miranda I'd help her with business stuff so she can get the bar up and running again."

Marlon's jaw dropped. "You did *what*?"

Kiki gave me a look of utter disdain before turning back to him. "You heard right, Marlon. Hattie offered to assist a murder suspect."

I rolled my eyes. "I'm as much a suspect as Miranda is. Probably more so."

Marlon scoffed. "Here I am, trying to keep you safe, and you're sticking your nose where it could get you killed."

My ire rose at the implication that I was taking stupid chances. "Miranda would be a fool to try anything with me. She knows I've told Kiki where I'll be."

Though Marlon's jaw flexed, the hard look in his eyes softened. "I suppose there's some truth to that. I'm coming with you, though."

Kiki looked relieved at his suggestion. "You're a good copper, Marlon."

He cut me a look before turning back to her. "If your friend is going to be such a pain in my backside, I'm not sure one dinner is going to be enough."

I couldn't argue with that, mostly because I didn't want to. If he wanted to go on more than one dinner date once this case was solved, I certainly had no objection.

Kiki slid Smoky into her backseat and took the wheel, reversing out of her spot. She unrolled her window and raised a hand, waving goodbye as she motored off.

Miranda had recounted to me earlier what she'd told Ace, but I was curious what Ashlynn and Isabella might have told the police. I asked Marlon about it as we crossed the street.

"How'd it go with Isabella and Ashlynn?" I asked. "I take it Ashlynn didn't confess?"

"Not yet, anyway," he said. "She admitted to hollering the threat when she saw Cormac and Miranda flirting, and she admitted she was the one to start the catfight. She said she was shocked to stumble upon the two of them and had a sudden emotional outburst. She even apologized to me for having to break it up, and said she was embarrassed by the way she'd acted. But as for killing her boss? No. She said she went straight home after her shift. She said she continued working at Limericks because Cormac told her Miranda had come on to him, that it was a one-sided attraction."

"She didn't fall for his lies, did she?"

"She claimed she believed what Cormac told her and that they'd reconciled, but neither Ace nor I bought her story. She was overselling it, making it sound like everything was peaches and cream. She must have sensed that we didn't believe her, because she went on to say that she needed the income. She knew she wouldn't get unemployment benefits if she quit, and she couldn't afford to take time off while she looked for another job. She said she'd put in applications at other bars and restaurants in the area, though, and had even had an interview at a new place that opened a couple of blocks from here."

"But if they'd truly reconciled, she'd have no reason to look for a new job."

"Exactly," Marlon said. "Her attempts to deflect suspicion only make her seem more guilty. Still, her behavior is only circumstantial evidence. More proof would be needed to arrest and convict her."

"What about Isabella?"

"She answered all of Ace's questions, but she really didn't know much. She's the kind of person who just keeps her head down and does her job."

"Did she know Cormac was dating both Ashlynn and Miranda?"

"She said she suspected it, but she wasn't sure. She'd never discussed the matter outright with Ashlynn. She said Ashlynn was cold to the other female staff. Could be she saw them as potential rivals."

We stepped up the curb to the front of the bar. The smiling leprechaun greeted us, though I noticed he looked worse for wear today. The top of his hat was chipped and the plaster on his right cheek was scraped. Looked like he'd taken a tumble off his tiny pedestal since the last time I'd been here. At least he hadn't lost the gold coin he was proudly holding up. I rapped on the door before calling out, "It's Hattie!"

A moment later, Miranda opened the door, a confused look on her face when she saw Marlon standing next to me.

I put a positive spin on the situation. "Officer Landers offered to stick around to make sure we stay safe."

"Oh." She looked up at Marlon. "That's very nice of you." She opened the door wide to allow us in before turning to me. "I hope you can make sense of Cormac's records. I know I can't."

The place looked much as it had the last time I'd been here, attempting to deliver Cormac's order. The lighting was dim. Chairs were turned upside down on top of the tables. The air bore a lingering smell of spilled beer mixed with pine-scented floor cleaner. The only difference was that a nearly full bottle of Backwoods Bootleggers moonshine sat on the shelf behind the bar. The previous bottle had been emptied and replaced.

Miranda led us up to the bar. The hinged bar flap was raised, allowing us easy access behind the counter. We followed her past bottles of gin, vodka, bourbon, and more, walking through an open door into a small, windowless office. Although Ace had taken Cormac's desktop computer, she'd left the printer behind. A laptop sat open on the desk, presumably Miranda's personal device. Two chairs were positioned in front of the desk. One was a rolling desk chair. The other had been brought in from the bar area.

I glanced around the room. A trash can next to the desk brimmed with fast-food wrappers and crumpled napkins. The back wall incorporated a small wall safe ensconced in cement so that it couldn't be easily removed. The safe door hung open, the interior empty. Above the safe, a screw had been forced into the mortar. A thin mirror in a lightweight frame lay on the desk next to a half empty bottle of Jack Daniel's traditional Black Label whiskey. *I suppose it's okay to drink on the job when you own a bar.* My guess was that Cormac had hung the mirror from the screw to obscure the safe behind it. I wondered what Ace had found inside.

Addressing Miranda, I pointed to the open safe. "Did you know the combination to the safe?"

"No," she said. "Cormac had only given me his computer login. I didn't even know there was a safe in the bar until I came in for my interview and saw that it had been hidden behind the mirror. I always figured Cormac locked the cash in the desk drawer until he took it to the bank for deposit."

Is she telling the truth? Maybe she'd worked everything out in advance, anticipating the questions she'd be asked and practicing her responses. The young woman was much smarter than her casual attire and copious mascara might suggest. But, again, she seemed sincere and forthcoming.

My gut told me I could trust her. "What about security cameras?"

Miranda shrugged. "Far as I know, there aren't any. I never saw a camera anywhere."

Marlon rounded up a stool and placed it in the doorway, where he could keep an eye on me and Miranda. I sat down at the desk chair and she took a seat beside me. I tapped the spacebar to bring the device to life and eyed the screen, recognizing the program immediately. QuickBooks. Before I'd opened the Moonshine Shack, I had forced myself to work through hours of online tutorials to make sure I was familiar with all of the program's functions and features.

Miranda pointed to the screen. "You know that program, right?"

"Inside out and backward. It's the same one I use at my shop." I eyed the screen, noting that the bookkeeping system had timed out. "What's the login?"

She handed me a sticky note that read:

User ID: Limericks

Password: SourMashNo.7

I mused aloud. "Why does that password sound familiar?"

Miranda pointed to the bottle of Jack Daniel's. Right there on the label were the words Sour Mash and No. 7. Looked like Cormac had kept his password close at hand.

Once I was into the system, I spent a few minutes going through the data, familiarizing myself with his accounts. I kept an eye out for an unpaid debt, unusual recurring payment, or unexpected income, anything that might provide a clue to Cormac's murder. While I'd hoped to follow a proverbial paper trail to see if Cormac's records could be a key, I soon realized the odds were against me. His bookkeeping was atrocious. It seemed a miracle he'd managed to stay in business. What paperwork remained in the pub was haphazardly strewn about and not organized in any detectable way. Most of it was invoices for liquor inventory and past-due utility bills. While Cormac seemed to have kept documentation regarding expenses and payments he'd made, his income records were spotty at best, and he'd clearly failed to input all of the relevant data, especially the cash receipts.

I fished the paperwork off the printer to determine whether it contained any financial data and, if so, whether the figures had been entered into his system and whether the documents had been scanned and stored in his electronic files. The papers included an invoice printed with the logo for Backwoods Bootleggers in red ink at the top. The invoice bore Tuesday's date as well as the name of the sales representative, Gage Tilley, the guy who'd crashed my grand opening celebration. The detail showed that Cormac had ordered six cases of twelve bottles each, for a total of seventy-two bottles. *That's a lot of moonshine. He must have decided to stock up.* The invoice showed the regular wholesale price for the case, as well as a deduction for a twenty-five percent "Exclusivity Discount."

The following page was a confirmation of sales taxes Cormac had paid via the state tax agency's online portal. I had no idea how much income a small pub like Limericks would normally bring in, but the amount of receipts he'd entered and the applicable sales tax reported seemed suspiciously low. The information on the electric bill indicated he'd paid the preceding bill's balance after the due date but during the grace period, tendering payment on the last possible date before he would have incurred a penalty. I checked his computer. The information he'd input into his bookkeeping system indicated he'd paid the electric bill in cash.

For better or worse, following the paper trail took little time. I used the system to create summary reports and sent them to the printer. The device whirred to life and spit out the pages. Once the machine went quiet, I retrieved the documents and handed them to Miranda. I waited while she perused the reports.

After giving them a cursory review, she asked, "What am I looking at here?"

I went over the reports with her. "These statements provide monthly comparisons," I said. "As you can see, the net income varies widely from month to month and follows a suspicious pattern. Cormac paid his liquor suppliers in cash. He knew they'd keep records of sales to Limericks and he'd want to make sure he got a tax deduction for the expense, so he had to make sure he reported enough cash receipts to cover his alcohol purchases. In the months where he bought little inventory, he reported much less cash income."

Miranda frowned. "He was fudging his records?"

"Sure looks that way."

"The distributors insisted on cash payments," she said. "I paid them with money from the register a few times when Cormac wasn't here to accept a delivery himself. That's what he'd told me to do."

I cringed. Transacting business in such a slapdash way went against everything my Accounting 101 professor had taught the class about proper recordkeeping. "My guess is that the liquor distributors considered Cormac a credit risk and put him on a cash-only basis for failure to pay in full or on time."

Miranda mused aloud. "I wonder if I'll have to pay cash, too, or if they'll give me credit. I don't have a lot of money or any collateral to get a loan."

"The more you distinguish yourself from Limericks and

Cormac O'Keefe," I said, "the more likely they are to let you buy on credit."

"Makes sense," she said.

I closed out of the program and swiveled the chair to face her. "The next steps would be to get your corporation set up and to open a new bookkeeping account. I can help you set up your new system and show you all the functions."

"Perfect. I'll give the attorney a call tomorrow and see when he can fit me in."

We gathered our things while Marlon returned his stool to the other side of the bar. After we exited Limericks, Miranda turned and locked the door. "I'll be in touch soon."

Marlon walked me to my car across the street. I peppered him with questions as we made our way. "What did you and Ace find in the safe?"

"Not much," he said. "A small stash of cash. Assorted bills and several rolls of coins. About a hundred dollars total."

"Saturday's start up funds." Though many people were using debit and credit cards almost exclusively these days, bars were still a predominantly cash business. A lot of cash seemed to be unaccounted for. "What about the rest of the money? Friday's cash receipts?"

"If there was any more, we haven't found it yet. There was none on Cormac's person or in his car. None at his apartment, either."

I gestured at the bar. "Is Cormac's car out back?"

"It was," Marlon said. "Ace had it towed to the police impound lot yesterday."

Where are the rest of Friday's cash receipts? Had Cormac been carrying the cash with him? Did the person who killed Cormac take the money from him? If so, did that make it more likely that the killer had been a random rob-

ber rather than an employee, Mack, Heath, or Damien? Another question crossed my mind. "If Miranda didn't know about the safe, how did y'all get into it? Did Ashlynn or Isabella know the combination?"

"No," Marlon said. "The crime scene team opened it yesterday. They've got all kinds of gadgets at their disposal. There's something called a black box that can be used to reprogram an electronic safe. Takes them no time at all to get one open."

Shoot. Now he had me wondering just how secure the money in my safe was. "Miranda told me that Cormac took a jar of cherry moonshine when he left my grand opening party."

"She told Ace the same thing," Marlon said. "She said she doesn't know what happened to it because shortly thereafter Ashlynn came into the bar and attacked her. Miranda said she hadn't been back to the bar since—until today, of course."

"Did Ace believe her?"

"Ace doesn't believe anything anyone says unless and until it's supported by irrefutable evidence."

I supposed it was only natural for a detective to be skeptical of everyone. After all, suspects probably tried to mislead her.

We stopped at my car and Marlon gave me a serious look. "Be careful, Hattie. Okay?"

Part of me was warmed by his concern, but another part of me heated at the repeated implication that I wasn't being cautious. Nevertheless, I said, "Don't worry. I will."

As I drove off, I mulled things over. I'd have liked to think that the missing cash pointed to a random robbery and Miranda's innocence. It was possible, however, that she'd believed her boss owed her, especially after she'd found out he hadn't been faithful to her. She'd know his routines. She could very well have shown up in his rear parking lot after closing time, knowing he'd have taken cash with him from the bar. She could have demanded the cash from Cormac before breaking the jar of moonshine and slashing him with it. Or maybe he'd refused to hand it over and she'd cut him, prying the cash out of his hands as he lay dying on my stoop.

Problem was, the scenario would have required a chase, with Cormac running from his rear parking area, around the end of his building, and into the street. While I'd been willing to believe Cormac might have run from another would-be robber, or even from Ashlynn, would he have run from Miranda? Especially if she was armed only with a jar of my moonshine? It seemed doubtful. Then again, maybe she'd had another weapon on her but decided to cut him with a broken jar of my shine in order to frame me. Still, the circumstances seemed awfully complicated and would require a great deal of coordination on her part, handling both a gun or knife and a jar of shine. Though possible, it appeared highly unlikely things had transpired in this manner.

I was driving out of the riverfront area a couple of minutes later when a delicious smell wafted through my van's vents. *Yum! What is that?* I rolled the window down to determine where the aroma was coming from.

That's it. The source of the smell was Bar Celona, a tapas bar that had opened a few months back. Kiki and I had talked about trying the place but had yet to get around to it. *Tonight's the night.* I'd grab some food to go. The least I could do was get some dinner for my best friend when she was putting my cat and me up in her condo.

There was a private paid parking lot across the street,

but with street parking being both free and readily available at this time on a Sunday evening it sat empty. I eased my van into a spot at the curb. I hopped down and, happily ignoring the meter, went inside.

A spicy scent and the strains of flamenco music met me at the door, as did a handsome waiter with olive skin, slick black hair, and the whisper of a mustache on his upper lip. Behind the bar was a doppelganger three decades older, whom I took to be the waiter's father or uncle. *Must be a family-owned business.*

"Bienvenido," the server said with a strong Spanish accent. "Just one tonight?"

"I don't need a table," I replied. "I'm here for carryout."

"Certainly." He directed me to take a seat at the bar and handed me a menu to look over. He held out a hand to indicate the older man behind the counter. "Our maître d' will take your order once you're ready."

The older man stepped over. "First time here?"

"It is."

"I'd be happy to make some recommendations."

"Please," I said. "Recommend away."

After listening to the man's suggestions and mulling over the choices, I opted for the patatas bravas, the tortilla Española, and the garlic mushrooms, adding an order of paella as well. As I waited for the order, I texted Kiki. On my way with dinner.

She replied with a smiley face emoji and a question. What are we eating?

For fun, I responded with the flamenco dancer emoji and the word Guess.

Kiki responded with a confused face emoji. We're eating a dancer? Have you turned to cannibalism?

To ease her concerns that I'd be coming home with a

to-go order of human flesh, I replied **Tapas**. She sent a thumbs-up followed by a gif of a Scooby-Doo hungrily rubbing his tummy.

I listened to the servers and bartender chat in Spanish and attempted to translate their conversation in my mind. Unfortunately, the two years of Spanish I'd taken back in high school hadn't stuck with me. I recognized *cerveza* as beer, *mesa* as table, and *cinco* as the number five, but that's as far as I got.

The waiter brought my food in white bags and I traded the sacks for my credit card. Once the slip had been presented and signed, I told the server *gracias* and *adiós*. At least I remembered the words for *thank you* and *goodbye*.

Chapter Thirteen

An hour later, Kiki and I were lounging on her couch with our tummies full of tapas when our phones pinged simultaneously with incoming texts. I checked my screen while Kiki did the same. The text was from Kate's husband, Parker. All it said was It's time.

The two of us leaped from the couch, searching for our shoes. Once we'd found them and put them on, we were out the door, down the stairs, and seated in Kiki's Mini Cooper in a matter of seconds. On the way to the hospital, we made a quick stop at a grocery store for a flowering plant to brighten Kate's hospital room. Unlike many couples who wanted to know their baby's sex and hosted gender reveal parties, Kate and Parker had decided to wait until the birth to learn whether they'd have a boy or a girl. Hedging our bets, we bought our friend both a potted pink azalea and a blue hydrangea.

We found both Kate's and Parker's parents in the waiting room on the maternity floor, their expressions alight with anticipation. The baby would be the first grandchild for all of them, and was sure to be spoiled rotten not only by its grandparents but by its Auntie Kiki and Auntie Hattie, too. Parker ventured up the hall to give us a quick update. "It'll be anytime now."

Though Kiki and I would gladly stay through the night for our friend, I had to admit that after missing so much sleep already this weekend, I hoped the birth wouldn't take long. Besides, I couldn't wait to meet the baby, to see whether it looked like Kate or Parker, and to have something happy and cute to think about rather than Cormac O'Keefe's murder.

Thankfully, the baby wasn't a procrastinator. A mere twenty minutes later, Parker came down the hall again, a huge smile on his face. "It's a boy!"

Those of us waiting erupted in cheers.

Parker gave us some quick stats. "He's twenty inches long and weighs eight pounds."

"Eight pounds?" I repeated. "That's only half Smoky's size."

Parker gaped. "You should send your cat to Weight Watchers."

The proud papa pulled up a short video clip on his phone and showed it all around. The baby was red, completely bald, and screaming at the top of his little lungs. He looked like an alien whose skin didn't quite fit right. Nevertheless, the crowd proclaimed him "Precious!" "Adorable!" and "The cutest baby ever!" No doubt once he had a couple days to overcome the trauma of being birthed, these sentiments would actually be true.

A half hour later, once things had settled down and the grandparents had gotten the first glimpse of their grandchild, Kiki and I were allowed a brief moment to congratulate our friend. Kate's blond hair was mussed and her cheeks were pink from exertion, yet she glowed as she cradled her chubby pink treasure in her arms. When she saw the flowering plants we'd brought, she gave us a big smile. "You two are the best!"

Kiki stepped up beside the bed and looked down at the baby. "Who do we have here?"

Kate beamed. "Dalton Prescott Pardue."

Kiki bobbed her head. "Good choice. With a pretentious name like that, he'll get into Harvard for sure. Of course, he'll probably get punched a lot, too." Kiki leaned in to look into the baby's little face. "Hey, Dalton," she cooed. "I'm Kiki. I'll be your favorite auntie."

"Hey!" I put my hands on my hips. "You don't know that. Maybe I'll be his favorite."

Kiki played with Dalton's tiny hand. "Not a chance. Look, I've already got him wrapped around my finger." The baby had instinctively wrapped his little fingers around her pinkie.

I stepped up and took his other hand in mine. He wrapped his itty-bitty fingers around my index finger. It felt like the time I'd held a canary at a petting zoo. "I'm Hattie," I told him. "Once you're big enough, we're going to chase fireflies together. And when you turn twenty-one, I'll give you your first taste of moonshine."

Kate laughed. "Let's not get ahead of ourselves. He hasn't even had his first bottle yet."

After oohing and ahhing over the baby and snapping dozens of pics of us holding him, we bade the growing family goodbye.

Kate took his noodle-like arm and waved his hand like a puppeteer, much like I sometimes did with my cat. "Bye-bye, aunties! Come see me again soon!"

* * *

Kiki had already left for a freelance graphic art gig Monday morning when I fed Smoky and sat down at her table with a cup of coffee and a plain bagel slathered with creamy peanut butter. I was fresh from the shower, my dark curls twisted up in a towel atop my head like a terry-cloth beehive. As I sipped from the mug, I checked my phone. A text had come in from Miranda. Got an appointment with Heath Delaney tomorrow at 10:00. Any chance you can come with me?

I was flattered she wanted me to come along. It was nice to be considered capable. My thumbs moved over the screen as I texted her back. Sure. Meet you at Limericks beforehand to discuss bookkeeping system? 8:00?

She responded with a thumbs-up.

I licked errant peanut butter from my fingers, polished off my coffee, and proceeded to get ready for my day. Smoky did the same, splaying his claws out like jazz hands and cleaning between his toes.

Invigorated by the caffeine, I decided to take a second look at Cormac's accounting records to see if there might be something I'd missed. Using the user ID and password Miranda had given me yesterday, I logged into his online bookkeeping software. I'd focused on his recent transactions when I'd been at Limericks with Miranda the day before, but maybe an older entry would provide a clue.

I'd worked my way back to early the preceding year when a single transaction in the amount of $615 caught my eye. The payee was a company called Hiddenvision. The name rang a bell. Kiki and I had come across its products when searching for an affordable security system for my shop. The

business specialized in concealed camera equipment. I
hadn't wanted a concealed system, though. I wanted mine to
be visible, where it would act as a deterrent to would-be
criminals. *Had Cormac bought a concealed camera system
for Limericks?*

If the cameras were hidden, it would explain why Miranda wasn't aware of them. If Miranda didn't know about
the cameras, maybe the police didn't, either. I knew I should
pass the information on to Ace, but I also wondered what
might be revealed by the camera footage. I slumped back
in my seat, debating what to do. Curiosity quickly got the
best of me. I sat up and returned my fingers to the keyboard, justifying my decision on the grounds that I should
attempt to verify if, in fact, there was a hidden camera system at Limericks before potentially wasting Ace's time.
Besides, there might be something in the footage that
would exonerate me and implicate the actual guilty party. I
had a right to seek evidence to defend myself, and I'd be
doing the detective a favor if I could point her in the right
direction.

Knowing people sometimes used the same login and
password for multiple accounts, I gave it a shot. I logged
into the Hiddenvision monitoring system and entered the
username Limericks and the password SourMashNo.7.
Sure enough, an account popped up. The account data indicated Cormac had purchased two cameras and prepaid
for three years of cloud storage for the video feeds. The
package he'd purchased would retain footage for four
weeks before it would be deleted. The page included a link
to the footage.

I leaned in to the screen, my pulse pounding in my ears.
Two questions popped into my mind. *What might I find?*
and *Where should I start?* I remembered Miranda telling

me that after she and Cormac had returned to Limericks after attending my grand opening, Ashlynn had walked into the bar, seen the two of them together, and screamed, *You're a dead man!* The security footage would let me know if she was telling the truth.

After familiarizing myself with the site's functions, I brought up the video footage from the preceding Sunday evening. Unfortunately, while the system had two interior cameras, there were no exterior devices. But I'd see what I could glean from watching what had taken place inside the bar. *What time had Cormac and Miranda left my shop? Eight-thirty, maybe?* I selected the feed from the camera designated in the system as *BAR CAM*, and started the clip at eight p.m. Although the camera was positioned over the cash register, the lens offered a wide-angle view of the entire bar. Isabella appeared to be single-handedly holding down the fort. I forwarded through the footage at four times actual speed until the front door opened and Cormac and Miranda entered. Miranda carried her jar of wild blackberry shine carefully, one hand on the lid, the other supporting the bottom. Cormac's jar of cherry shine hung loosely from his hand, as he gripped the aluminum lid with his fingers. As Miranda headed behind the bar to the stockroom, Cormac slid his jar of moonshine onto the counter next to the cash register, circled around the bar, and picked up the television remote. He aimed it at the large screen TV mounted on the side wall, turning the program from a news station to ESPN.

A man stepped up to the bar and placed an order. After scooping ice into a lowball glass, Cormac grabbed a bottle of scotch from the shelf behind him and poured its remaining contents into the glass. It was barely enough to wet the ice cubes. He held up a finger to signal the man that he'd be right back and headed for the stockroom, passing Miranda, who was on her way out. Miranda spotted the jar of cherry shine next to the register, picked it up, and slid it onto the shelf behind the bar next to the bottle of Backwoods Bootleggers moonshine. *If that's the jar that was used to kill O'Keefe, Miranda would have an explanation for why her prints were on it.* In other words, she'd have plausible deniability. Still, I didn't know whether Cormac's jar of cherry shine was the one used to kill him. Cormac had been able to snatch his complimentary jar off a shelf in my shop the night of my grand opening without my knowledge. The Ken doll frat boy had stolen a jar of shine without me noticing, too. Maybe they weren't the only ones who'd taken moonshine without me knowing.

On the screen, Cormac came out of the back room with a full bottle of scotch to replace the one he'd emptied. As he unscrewed the cap and poured another finger of scotch into the man's glass, Miranda joined Isabella in tending to the patrons at the tables. With it being a Sunday evening, there were few people in the place. In the periphery of the video, the front door opened and in walked Ashlynn. Gage Tilley followed her, lugging the jug of Granddaddy's Ole-Timey Corn Liquor he'd taken away from my party. Miranda waited at the bar, watching Cormac fix drinks for the customers at her tables. When he set them on her tray, she smiled, leaned over the bar, and pecked him on the cheek.

Although the camera recorded no sound, it was evident from the way Ashlynn's mouth came open and the snap of the customers' heads in her direction that she'd issued nothing short of a banshee war cry. Her mouth flapped. While I couldn't read lips, from the enraged expression on her face it seemed entirely possible she'd threatened to end Cormac's life, that she'd hollered *You're a dead man* as Miranda claimed. Ashlynn charged the bar like an offensive lineman vying for an MVP award. As she reached the counter, she swung her arm, fingers splayed, and swiped at Cormac in an attempt to scratch his eyes out. Cormac jerked back, jostling the bottles on the shelves behind him. Unable to get to Cormac, Ashlynn pivoted and set her sights on a more accessible target. *Miranda.* I had to hand it to Miranda. She had quick reflexes. She raised a loose fist and managed to deflect the backhanded slap Ashlynn aimed at her cheek. Rather than intervene, Cormac cowered behind the bar. Meanwhile, Gage Tilley stood stock-still in the middle of the room, stunned by what he was witnessing.

Over the next few seconds, Ashlynn slapped and clawed at Miranda, while Miranda attempted to shield herself and evade her attacker. Tilley ditched his jug of corn liquor on a table and attempted to intercede, but when Ashlynn landed a solid slap on his cheek, he reflexively stepped aside, raising a hand to his face. Miranda turned to run and Ashlynn seized the moment, reaching out to grab her by the hair. Yanking Miranda by her honey-hued mane, Ashlynn dragged her out the door. Tilley could be seen hollering at Cormac and pointing out the door, imploring Cormac to stop the brawl. Cormac merely shrugged. If there'd been a camera outside, it would have shown Marlon rushing over from my grand opening to pull the two women apart.

I paused the feed. *Had Ashlynn been serious? Or had her death threat been mere bluster?* I relaxed back on the sofa to ponder the matter. *You're a dead man* was the kind of hyperbole someone would blurt out when overcome with emotion. Maybe Ashlynn settled down once she had some time to think about things. Then again, maybe her fury festered and she came back for Cormac Friday night, made it look like a robbery. *Let's see what the camera recorded at closing the night Cormac was killed.* I leaned in again and plugged in the date and time parameters. A fresh feed popped up, starting at one a.m. Saturday morning. Cormac stood behind the bar, loading glasses into a dishwasher situated under the counter. Only a handful of customers sat at the tables.

The front door opened, and Gage Tilley strode in wearing his usual pocketed cargo pants and red Backwoods Bootleggers uniform shirt. After a quick visit to the men's room, he approached the bar with a jovial smile. He said something to Cormac, who in turn called out to Ashlynn. Once again, she was wearing a peasant blouse with elasticized wrists. She looked their way and gave a nod. Cormac dried his hands on the bar towel hanging over his shoulder and lifted the bar flap to let Tilley through. Tilley followed Cormac behind the bar to his office at the other end. Cormac opened the door and the two disappeared inside. A couple of minutes later, Tilley emerged, leaving the office door open behind him. He took long, quick strides behind the bar and had nearly reached the pass-through when he suddenly stopped and dropped down next to the shelves of glasses under the bar, his back to the camera. His elbows and shoulders moved, and he stood again. He circled around through the bar flap and strode to the door in a half dozen long steps. He seemed to be in a hurry. Given the late hour, maybe he just wanted to get home. Heck, I was exhausted working only until nine in the evening. I couldn't imagine working bar hours, not arriving home until three or four in the morning.

Tilley pushed the door open and stalked out into the dark night. Through the open doorway, I caught a glimpse of the words *MOONSHINE SHACK* glowing on my shop across the street. Curious, I dragged the timeline back to watch the footage again. *What was Tilley doing when he bent down behind the bar? Had he dropped something and gone to pick it up? Maybe his car keys or some pocket change?* Though I watched the feed a second time, with Tilley's back to the camera, obscuring the view, I couldn't tell.

A few minutes after Tilley left, the five frat boys who'd been in my shop came into the bar. With the Moonshine Shack closed at this late hour, I supposed they felt comfortable returning to this stretch of Market Street. Or maybe they'd bar-hopped their way around the area and were now making their way back to their frat house. Rather than take seats at a table, they bellied up to the bar, sliding onto stools. Cormac lifted his chin in casual acknowledgment as if he recognized the boys. He stepped over, pulled the towel from his shoulder to wipe down the bar top in front of them, and flipped it back over his shoulder before taking their order. The Ken doll placed his order first, signifying he was top dog in their pack. The others nodded and flapped their mouths.

Judging from the fact that Cormac grabbed the bottle of Backwoods Bootleggers moonshine off the shelf, the boys must have ordered moonshine and, judging from the fact that he demanded payment up front, Cormac must not have trusted these boys not to drink and dash. He was smarter than me in that regard. Cormac set the bottle down to make change for them. The financial transaction complete, he proceeded to fill their drink order. He filled five highball glasses with ice and lined the glasses up in front of the boys. After pouring a jigger of moonshine in each glass, he used the soda gun to add cola, the bubbles forming a foamy head.

For the next few minutes, the boys drank and joked around. The moonshine thief turned backward on his stool

and eyed Ashlynn as she moved about the room. He used
his elbow to nudge Short-'n'-Stocky, who was sitting next
to him, and angled his head to indicate the curvy server. As
she approached the bar with a tray of empty glasses, he
reached out and grabbed her by the arm. He said something
to her, an inappropriate proposition no doubt. She pulled
out of his grip and said something back. Once she'd passed
the boys, she rolled her eyes and pressed her lips together,
clearly annoyed. She wasn't the only one annoyed, either.
Cormac had seen the interaction from the other end of the
counter. He sailed down the bar and snapped at the Ken
doll. The kid raised his palms in innocence and appeared
to issue an apology. His buddies laughed, much as they had
when leaving my store with their contraband moonshine.
Once Cormac turned his back, the boy made a lewd motion
with his hand, a stupid move on his part as the back of the
bar was lined with mirrors. Cormac whipped back around
and pointed at the door. The boys downed the remainder of
their drinks and hustled en masse to the door. The Ken doll
cast a glance back before heading out, his narrowed eyes
sending daggers in Cormac's direction. *If looks could kill.*

I watched the rest of the video to see if it would provide
more clues. Unfortunately, it didn't. The other customers
finished their drinks and left. None paid special attention
to Cormac or the cash register. Soon, it was closing time.
While Cormac loaded dirty glasses into the under-counter
dishwasher, Ashlynn and Isabella wiped down the tables
and placed the chairs atop them. Isabella took off, but Ashlynn remained to sweep and mop the floor. When she finished, she called out to Cormac, who stood behind the bar,
restocking the shelves with bottles he'd rounded up from
the storeroom. She raised a hand in goodbye as she passed
out of the bar and into the back room, but as soon as she

was out of his sight, she rotated her hand and curled back all of her fingers but the middle one, flipping him the bird. *Doesn't quite look like she'd forgiven him, after all.* Ashlynn gathered her purse from her locker and went out the back door by herself. Cormac didn't even have the decency to see her safely to her car. *What had she and Miranda seen in him?*

Alone in the bar, Cormac turned the key on top of the cash register and pushed a button to open the drawer. He counted bills out onto the counter, stacking them by denomination, before separating out enough to begin business the following day. He turned back to the register, tapped a few keys, and printed out a paper tape. He read the tape, placed it on the counter next to the cash, and proceeded to count the cash a second time. He hesitated for a moment when he finished, standing still as if in thought. *Had he noticed a discrepancy between the amount of cash that should be on hand versus the actual amount in the till?* It wouldn't be unusual for the count to be off by a little. Humans were prone to error, especially when rushed, and the bar would have been busy that night. Perhaps the amount of the variance had been big enough to give him pause.

Lifting the divided drawer tray, he retrieved a business-sized envelope from underneath it, slid the majority of the bills inside, and tucked the envelope into the back pocket of his jeans. He went to his office and placed the small amount of cash he'd separated out into the safe.

He returned to the bar, reached under it with both hands, and pulled out a plastic bin filled with empty liquor bottles that had been haphazardly tossed into it. He carried the bin to the stockroom and set it on the floor by the back door. After punching in a code on the keypad to activate his alarm, he picked the recycling bin up again and left through the back door, alone. Through the open doorway, I got a glimpse of a sporty blue car, presumably Cormac's. The side of a large rolling recycling bin was visible, too. But no other person appeared on the screen. If whoever attacked Cormac was out there waiting for him, they'd had the sense to stay out of sight. The door swung slowly shut, blocking any view to the outside. *If only we could see what happened on the other side of that door.*

The images on the screen remained unchanging now, though the timer at the bottom told me that time continued to pass. I sped up the feed until the crime scene technicians entered the front door shortly after four a.m. to collect evidence and secure the scene. I stopped the feed and stared at the unmoving image. That was when I noticed a critical detail. *Cormac's jar of Firefly cherry moonshine was no longer on the shelf.* It had been moved, but when? And to where? *Could it have been in the recycle bin Cormac carried out?* I reversed the feed to the point where he pulled the bin out from under the counter and paused the screen, taking a close look, but with the bottles being so jumbled, it was impossible to tell if the jar of cherry shine was among them. It didn't appear to be on top, but it could have been buried under the others. By then, it was nearly time for me to get ready for work. I didn't have time to track the jar. *But I do have time to check one more thing . . .*

The fact that Cormac had hesitated after looking at the cash register tape and counting the bills told me that he might have realized something was off, that the figures didn't reconcile. I remembered my suspicion from when I'd gone to Limericks to deliver the moonshine. I'd thought I might have seen Ashlynn pilfering from the till. *Time to find out if I saw what I thought I did.*

I started the feed just after five o'clock last Monday.

Cormac and Ashlynn were going through the usual motions, opening the bar. In I came, rolling the dolly, the man I now knew as Damien Sirakov on my heels. I slowed the speed to one-quarter real time and focused on Ashlynn. Sure enough, just after she straightened the bottle on the shelf, she folded some bills and surreptitiously slid them up her sleeve, making them disappear. *Abracadabra!*

Could Cormac have realized Ashlynn was stealing from him? Could she have still been out back when he left the bar? Could the two have had a violent confrontation? Could this information exonerate me?

Chapter Fourteen

I retrieved my purse, pulled Ace's business card from it, and dialed her direct number. After identifying myself, I said, "I saw some things on the Limericks security camera feed."

She paused a moment. "How do you know the place has cameras, and how did you access the feed?"

Uh-oh. I guess I wasn't supposed to know about the video cameras. But I couldn't help it if I'd stumbled across the information, could I? I told her how I'd found the entry in Cormac's bookkeeping records from when he'd bought the system. "I tried the same login and got lucky."

"Have you told anyone else about the cameras?"

"No."

"Don't. Or else you'll find yourself in hot water for interfering with a police investigation. Concealing or tampering with evidence is a crime, you know. A felony."

The thought that I could end up behind bars like Damien

Sirakov made me feel queasy and panicked. "But I didn't tamper with evidence! I didn't conceal anything, either." Heck, I'd been the one to initiate this call. "I'm only trying to help."

"Maybe. But would we be talking right now if the footage had implicated *you*?"

I had no idea what to say to that. She'd thrown me totally off kilter. *Would I have called if something on the feed made me look guilty?* I knew I was innocent and that I wasn't obligated to offer evidence against myself. I also wouldn't have wanted to send the police on a wild-goose chase, especially if the wild goose they were chasing was me. Still, her question had sent me down a rabbit hole of self-reflection.

Rather than wait for me to sort out the goose and rabbit, she said, "Go on. What did you see?"

"Ashlynn pilfering from the till."

"Oh, yeah?"

"You can see it for yourself. Just after five o'clock last Monday, when I went to Limericks to make my delivery." I mentioned Gage Tilley, too, how he'd bent down behind the bar. "He might have dropped something, but I couldn't tell for certain."

"He didn't drop anything," she said. "He tied his shoe."

"He did?"

"Look at his left sneaker when he comes out of Cormac's office. It was untied."

She's already watched the footage. I should have known she'd be one step ahead of me. I pulled up the video from the night of Cormac's murder and watched it once more. Again, Tilley emerged from Cormac's office on the screen. Sure enough, the laces on his left shoe were undone, posing a tripping hazard. I watched as, once again, he bent down and his arms and shoulders moved. The motions seemed consistent with a shoe being tied. When he circled around the bar and his feet became visible again, the shoe was now tied. Looked like Tilley was a dead end, but at least the information I'd fed her about Ashlynn's theft seemed new. I also told her about the guys from Mu Sigma. "The ones in the video are the same ones who were in my shop just before I closed for the night, the ones I told you about earlier."

"You sure about that? Mu Sigma is a big fraternity. Those boys are all around the riverfront area on the weekends, dressed in those shirts."

"I'm one hundred percent sure. I recognize the one who swiped the shine from my store. I know because he has hair like a Ken doll. He uses an excessive amount of styling product. You couldn't get through that hair with a jackhammer. The short and stocky one sitting next to him at the bar is the one who knocked over the jars in my store."

She seemed to be thinking aloud. "The boys might have had the jar of your shine with them then."

"They could have. I noticed Cormac's jar of cherry moonshine isn't on the shelf anymore, either." When she paused, I realized she hadn't noticed this detail yet. I supposed I had a better eye when it came to spotting my moonshine.

"We need to follow that jar. I'll track down that sales rep, too. He might have heard or seen something that night that could be helpful."

"The guy you're looking for is Gage Tilley. His name and his telephone extension are on the recent invoice from Backwoods Bootleggers."

"There you go again, teacher's pet." With that, she ended the call. I hoped my assistance had earned me some brownie points or, better yet, gotten me off the hook.

* * *

Granddaddy was waiting in front of the Singing River Retirement Home late that morning when Smoky and I went to pick him up. As I pulled to a stop, he brandished his cane and hollered, "Anybody comes for us, I'm ready!"

I groaned. Benjamin Hayes had once been a formidable force, but those days were far behind him. With his sharp claws and pointed fangs, Smoky was more fearsome than my grandfather. Granddaddy was more likely to get hurt himself if he tried to defend himself or me. But there was no point in arguing with him. Any backtalk and he'd threaten to put me over his knee. It was likely to snap his brittle leg bones in two.

Granddaddy hobbled forward, opened the passenger door, and climbed in.

"No scooter today?" I asked.

"No need," he said. "My physical therapist has been working on my balance. A few more sessions and I'll be square dancing around your shop."

I doubted he'd be doing the do-si-do anytime soon, but I was glad he was feeling more confident on his feet.

As we drove to the Moonshine Shack, I asked my grandfather how he knew about Cormac's death. I'd planned to tell him today, but someone had apparently beat me to it.

Granddaddy said, "Your father filled me in over supper yesterday. Looks like things caught up with that Cormac fella. You can't do people wrong without consequences."

"That's true. But he didn't deserve to die."

"No, he didn't. Someone took things too far." He tsked in disapproval. "But that's the odds. The more people you mess with, the more likely you are to mess with the wrong one."

He had a point. His comment about odds also got me thinking. Miranda had mentioned that Cormac liked to gamble at the casino in North Carolina. Could Cormac have made some bets locally that he failed to pay up on? Maybe a bookie had sent goons after Cormac to collect. But why would professional kneecap breakers kill Cormac with a jar of my shine? A gun would have been less messy and run less risk of leaving fingerprints. *Hmm* . . . Could it be possible that the goon had come into the Moonshine Shack before or after visiting Cormac at Limericks? Maybe he was one of the customers who'd bought cherry shine with cash. Maybe he'd left the jar in his car and, when he'd come back to whack Cormac, he'd realized the glass would make an easy improvised weapon that would be much less noisy than a gunshot. Or maybe he'd simply been sipping the shine straight from the jar and Cormac had said something that made the killer lose his temper.

Another related thought crossed my mind. With my grandfather sitting out in front of the Moonshine Shack all week, he might have spotted someone suspicious without realizing it at the time. Maybe he'd seen a goon or two come to the bar to warn Cormac that his debt had come due.

As I slowed for a red light, I asked, "Did you notice anybody coming or going from Limericks last week who looked angry?"

"Besides you?"

Cheese and grits. It was a good thing Detective Pearce hadn't interviewed my grandfather. I'd probably be behind bars right now. "Yes, Granddaddy. Besides me."

He looked up in thought. "I saw that young man with the light-colored hair who came to your grand opening. The one wearing glasses and a hearing aid."

Only one person fit that description, though the "hearing aid" had actually been a wireless Bluetooth earpiece. "Heath Delaney?"

Granddaddy shrugged. "Never learned his name. Can't

say which day it was that he went into Limericks, either, but it was around half past five when he left the bar. I remember because right after you came outside and told me my dinner was ready."

A mini fridge and a microwave had been in the back room when I'd rented my shop, and I'd since put them to good use. I'd filled the fridge with drinks, snacks, and simple meals like cooked pasta and vegetable stew that could be easily warmed in the microwave. Heating up leftovers was cheaper and more convenient than ordering takeout for dinner every day. "How could you tell Heath was angry?"

"Because he kicked over that leprechaun statue by the front door. Left the little guy lying there on the sidewalk and stormed off. Didn't seem right to take things out on the fairy. Whatever had made the man angry, the leprechaun had nothing to do with it."

No wonder the little statue had been chipped and scraped. I was even more eager now to attend Miranda's meeting with Heath tomorrow. If the guy had killed Cormac, maybe he'd say something that would give it away while we discussed the bar. My mind went back to the death glare Heath had locked on the side of Cormac's face as they stood at my sample table during my grand opening. Heath had seemed relatively calm and collected, but perhaps it was a practiced calm. While Heath hadn't appeared overly emotional that night, it seemed clear he had a lot of animosity bottled up inside him just waiting to be uncapped. *Did he unbottle that rage in front of my shop last Friday?*

Immediately after we entered the shop and I'd disabled the alarm, I went to the front door and opened it to see if my security cameras and panic button had been delivered.

They had. Relief surged through me. I picked up the package and brought it inside.

Granddaddy gestured to them. "Whatcha got there?"

"Security cameras and an alarm," I said. "Kiki's got a friend coming by later to install the cameras."

"What's that gonna cost you?" he asked, knowing my funds were stretched.

"A case of moonshine."

He bobbed his head. "Best currency there is."

Luckily, I could install the simple panic button myself. All I had to do was plug the speaker into the wall and install the battery in the tiny handheld device. I proceeded to do just that. I slid the button into my pocket. Over the course of the morning, I found myself sticking my hand in my pocket and running my thumb over the gadget to assure myself it was there and ready for action if needed.

The Moonshine Shack had been open for a couple of hours when a familiar *clop-clop-clop* met my ears. Through the glass, I saw Marlon ride up. He slid down from the saddle and tied Charlotte's reins to one of the porch posts. He murmured sweet nothings to her and ran a loving hand down her neck and back. *Lucky horse.* Marlon looked up and caught me watching him. I raised a hand in greeting.

The bells on the door tinkled as he stepped inside. "Hey, Hattie." He turned to my grandfather, who'd taken a seat atop one of my stools and was hard at work, whittling away on a small chunk of wood, the shavings falling to his feet, where Smoky sat, batting at them. "How you doing today, Ben?"

Granddaddy scowled at him. "I plead the fifth."

"Goodness gracious, Granddaddy," I scolded. "Marlon's not asking you to incriminate yourself. He's just asking you how you're doing."

"How I am is none of his business." My grandfather

slashed at the wood in his hand with his little tool, sending a shaving flying through the air.

I wagged a finger at him. "You're acting like a child."

Proving my point, he stuck out his tongue at me and kept right on whittling.

Fortunately, Marlon seemed unfazed. "I'll win you over yet, Ben."

My grandfather huffed. "We'll see about that."

Marlon returned his attention to me. "Your call to Ace kept me busy this morning. She had me review the footage with her."

"Why didn't you tell me the bar had security cameras? I only found out when I was going through the bookkeeping records."

His expression tightened. "I'm walking a fine line, Hattie. I believe in you, but I answer to Ace."

"Understood." It wasn't fair for me to press him, to put him in an awkward position.

Luckily for me, he volunteered some information on his own. "That said, since you've already seen the security camera video and talked to Ace about it, we can discuss it without incurring her wrath."

"Good." The last thing I wanted was to get Marlon in trouble with his superiors.

"The crime scene technicians discovered the cameras on Saturday. Cormac hadn't put a shortcut to the cloud storage site on his computer. He probably didn't want to clue anyone in that he was secretly watching them. But Ace found the web address in his browsing history."

"Why would Cormac choose a concealed system? Isn't it better to have the cameras visible so they'll act as a deterrent?"

"Generally, yes," he agreed. "My guess is that Cormac

was more concerned about his staff stealing from him than he was about a robbery. With hidden cameras, he could keep a clandestine eye on his employees. He probably placed the one directly above the cash register so he could see if anyone was skimming from the till. It was made to look like a smoke alarm. Same for the one in the back room. He'd probably chosen to position it over the employees' lockers so he could see what they were putting in and taking out."

Given the prevalence of employee theft in many establishments, I supposed I couldn't blame him. Besides the cash in the register, the stockroom would be full of liquor, some of it quite valuable. An employee might be tempted to filch a bottle or two. It seemed ironic that Cormac had worried about his staff stealing cash or liquor from him when he'd been the one to use Miranda to her financial detriment. I supposed his lack of trust was projection. He knew he couldn't be trusted, so therefore he didn't trust others.

Marlon continued. "After you called Ace this morning, she had me look at the camera footage and track the jar of cherry moonshine Cormac got at your party. The darn thing got moved about a hundred times over the course of the week. It started out next to the other moonshine, where Miranda put it. When Cormac arrived at the bar on Tuesday, he took it down from the shelf and stuck it in a cabinet underneath. Ashlynn brought it back out later that night. On Wednesday, another bartender moved it over to the shelf where they keep the limoncello and Grand Marnier and other fruit-flavored liqueurs. Isabella moved it again on Thursday when she was dusting the shelves before the bar opened. She put it by the bottles of schnapps, but not until she tried some of it herself."

I groaned. "So all of their prints could be on the jar."

"They are, in fact. Plus some prints that haven't been matched yet."

"The killer's?"

"Maybe, but not necessarily. Could be the prints belong to someone who touched the jar while it sat on the shelf of your shop. For all we know at this point, the killer could have been wearing gloves and left no prints at all."

"But all the prints on the cherry shine mean the jar used to kill Cormac was the one that had been in his bar." After all, Ashlynn had never been in my store, so she couldn't have left her prints on another jar. "That narrows things down."

"It does," he agreed, "but only so far." Marlon wrapped up his move-by-move replay. "Last time we saw the jar for sure was on Thursday evening. Ashlynn fixed herself a shot and slid it under the bar."

"Did she put it in the recycling bin?"

"I can't say for certain, but it looks that way. It appeared to be nearly empty, and we didn't find the jar under the shelf. Friday was a busy night and Cormac emptied several other bottles that he put in the bin. They could have easily obscured the shine jar."

"If the jar was in the recycling bin," I mused aloud, "and Cormac took the recycling outside as he left, anyone could have had access to the jar." That meant Miranda, Ashlynn, Isabella, Heath, Mack, and Damien were all still in play, as were the boys from Mu Sigma. It could also mean a random person wandering down the alley might have spotted the envelope of cash tucked into Cormac's back pocket, grabbed the jar from the bin to use as a weapon, and chased him out of the alley and around to the street. Though it was plausible, I had to wonder about the choice of weapon. *Wouldn't it have been smarter to grab a bottle with a longer neck that*

could be more easily wielded? Then again, maybe the attacker had simply reached into the bin and grabbed the first
bottle they touched.

Marlon agreed with my assessment. "You're right. The
video didn't narrow down the list of potential suspects. It
did show us something quite interesting, though."

Granddaddy looked up from his whittling. "What was it?"

After the rude treatment my grandfather had given him,
Marlon could have accused my grandfather of eavesdrop-
ping, but he didn't. Rather, he included the old man in the
conversation. "Ashlynn. She slid an extra forty or fifty bucks
up her sleeve every shift."

"That often?" I said. "I'm surprised Cormac didn't notice. Seems he would have reviewed the security camera
footage on occasion."

"She was sneaky about it," Marlon said. "If you hadn't
pointed it out to Ace, we wouldn't have known. We had to
watch really close. She always wore those loose long-sleeved
flowered shirts with the elastic around the wrists that held the
bills in place. I think Ace called them 'bumpkin blouses.'"

"The term is 'peasant blouse.'"

Marlon chuckled. "Yeah. I suppose that's a better name.
I don't know squat about women's clothing. Anyway, Ashlynn didn't steal every time she was at the register, of
course. She looked for opportune moments. I missed her
doing it the first few times, but once I caught on to her little
trick I went back and reviewed the footage again. She had
a tell. Before she'd take the cash, she'd reach up to straighten
a bottle on a shelf. What she was really doing was checking
the mirror to make sure nobody was watching her. She was
so sly, someone could've been standing right next to her
and not noticed."

"Do you think Cormac might have realized she was stealing from him?"

Granddaddy held his whittling tool aloft and chimed in. "Maybe she was afraid he'd report it to the police, so she killed him."

"I had that same thought," Marlon said, "but there's nothing in the footage to suggest Cormac caught her in the act. If the till came up short after each of her shifts, he might have put two and two together, realized she was up to something. She might have been out back when he left Limericks on Friday, maybe making a phone call from her car, or waiting there for some other reason. He could have seen her removing the stolen cash from her sleeve, or maybe he saw some fall out. Things could have escalated, gotten physical. Who knows?" He lifted his shoulders. "Without a video recording, we can't say."

I wasn't generally in favor of Big Brother–type surveillance, but I had to admit that had there been an outdoor camera in the alleyway behind Limericks, Cormac's murder might have been solved by now.

In light of the fact that the boys from Mu Sigma appeared in the video, I figured maybe it was okay for me to ask about them. "What about the frat boys?"

"Ace and I spoke with three of them," Marlon said. "They claimed they headed back to the frat house once they left Limericks. They identified the boy with the hair gel who hit on Ashlynn as Tristan. The one who knocked over the moonshine in your shop is named Dane. Their friends said the two of them split off about halfway back. Tristan and Dane told the other boys they were going to check out a party somewhere."

The Ken doll and Short-'n'-Stocky hadn't returned to

the frat house with their friends. *Had they truly gone to a
party? Or had they returned to Limericks instead, to get
back at the bartender who'd told them to get lost?* "You
said you spoke to their friends. I'm assuming Tristan and
Dane won't talk?"

"Not a word," he said. "They've lawyered up."

"Does that mean they're guilty?"

"No, it means they're *wealthy*." He chuckled mirthlessly.
"They already had defense attorneys on retainer. They've
both got a prior record for the same incident. They were
arrested their freshman year of college for vandalism and
assault."

"Assault?" I straightened reflexively. Vandalism was one
thing. Property could be repaired or replaced. But physi-
cally hurting another human being crossed a line. If they'd
been physical with someone before, they could do it again.

"They pleaded guilty to shooting members of a rival frat
with paintball guns. Ambushed them in the backyard of
their frat house. The boys were sitting ducks."

"But people pay to play paintball. It's a game." Or maybe
a sport.

"Tell that to the boys they shot at point-blank range.
Those poor kids were covered in round, red welts. Looked
like they suffered from some type of oversized chicken
pox. Tristan and Dane claimed it was merely a prank
against a frat they had a friendly rivalry with, and that they
didn't mean to hurt anyone." Marlon shrugged, seeming to
acknowledge that it could be true. "The victims just wanted
to move on and forget about it. Tristan and Dane worked
out a plea deal with the district attorney's office. They
pleaded guilty to vandalism and the assault charge was
dropped. They paid a small fine with their parents' money
and went on their merry way."

"The boys could be Cormac's killers, then. If they'd been impulsive and violent before, they might have done it again."

"Could be. Since they won't talk, Ace can't rule them out."

I glanced out the window, eyeing the bar, willing its walls to speak to me. On seeing the leprechaun statue, I remembered what my grandfather had told me on the drive to the shop this morning. I turned to him. "Tell Marlon what you told me about Heath."

My grandfather frowned, but at least he spoke directly to Marlon. "I saw him come out of Limericks around five thirty one evening last week. He kicked the leprechaun over when he left."

"Oh, yeah?"

"Yeah."

Marlon nodded. "I'll pass that along to Ace." His returned his attention to me and his face tightened. "Damien Sirakov will be released today. If he knows what's good for him, he'll hightail it out of town and never show his face around here again." I felt my hopes rise until he added, "Problem is, that man doesn't know what's good for him."

I let out a weary sigh. "Good thing my security cameras will be installed today."

"Glad to hear it. You can't be too careful."

Even so, while a camera could record footage of events, it couldn't stop a killer in his tracks. But at least it would provide irrefutable evidence if Damien attacked me in my shop.

Granddaddy grabbed his cane and circled around the counter. "What's this feller look like? I'll sit out front and keep an eye out for him."

"Damien's white with dark hair," I said. "He's got a tattoo of a black bear on the side of his neck." I pointed to my own neck to show him where to look.

"A bear, you say?" my grandfather replied. "That ought to make him easy to spot."

"If you see him, press this. It'll set off an audible alarm." I placed the remote in my granddad's gnarled hand.

As Granddaddy headed out to a rocker, I waved a hand for Marlon to follow me to the back room. I pointed to a new bucket I'd bought on my last grocery run and brought with me to the shop. "That's a clean bucket for Charlotte. I thought it might come in handy if she gets thirsty."

His upper lip quirked in a grin. "You trying to give me a reason to stop by your shop?"

Darn. I've been too obvious, haven't I? "I just care about animals, that's all. Summer's coming soon, and Granddaddy says *The Old Farmer's Almanac* is predicting an especially hot one."

Though Marlon still fought the grin, he let me slide. "This was very thoughtful of you. The bucket will come in handy, too. Until O'Keefe's killer is caught, Charlotte and I will be swinging by as often as we can. I've asked the other patrol officers to do the same."

A tingly warmth spread through me. "Thank you, Marlon."

He filled the bucket at the sink and I followed along as he carried it out the front door, where he set it down in front of Charlotte. He patted her shoulder as she lowered her head and took a drink.

"Look, Mommy!" cried a young girl who was coming up the street with her mother. "A horsey!" She looked up and tugged on the hem of her mother's shirt. "Can we pet her?"

The mother eyed Marlon as they approached. "Would it be okay if my daughter pets your horse?"

"Sure," Marlon replied. "Charlotte would love it."

Just as the child reached her, Charlotte lifted her head

from the bucket, her long chin dripping. The horse turned her head toward the girl, who giggled in glee. "She's dripping on me!"

Marlon smiled and crouched down to put himself at the little girl's level. "Want to sit in the saddle?"

The girl looked up her mother. "Can I? Pleeease?"

How could her mother not give in? "All right, honey," she said. "Hang on real tight, though, okay?"

The girl smiled a gap-toothed grin. "I will!"

Marlon scooped the child up and placed her on the saddle. Her short legs came nowhere near reaching the edge of the saddle, let alone the stirrups. Keeping one hand around the girl lest she slide off, Marlon patted the metal saddle horn with the other. "Hang on to the horn. It'll help you stay balanced."

While the girl wrapped her tiny hands around the saddle horn, her mother whipped out her cell phone. "Mind if I take a pic of the three of you?"

"Not at all." Smiling, Marlon turned his head one way, then the other. "Just make sure you get my good side."

As if he has a bad side.

The woman snapped a series of photos, including one of her little girl wearing Marlon's aviator sunglasses. I found myself feeling jealous of a four-year-old.

When the photo shoot was over, the woman glanced my way. "Moonshine?"

"Yep," I said. "I've got blueberry, blackberry, peach, and apple pie, among others."

Marlon chimed in like an unpaid spokesperson. "My favorite's the cinnamon."

Sensing interest, I summoned a smile and said, "Moonshine would make mother's day out a lot more fun."

The woman laughed. "Now you're talking."

Marlon begged off to get back on his beat. Meanwhile, the mother brought her daughter into the shop. The girl said, "Hi, kitty!" to Smoky on her way in. He gave her only a slow blink in return before returning his attention to the street. Ten minutes later, the woman left the shop with three jars of moonshine to share with the moms of her playgroup on their next night off.

Granddaddy stopped the mother and daughter outside with a lift of his cane. "Hold on right quick. Got something for ya." He held out a small wood carving in the shape of a horse.

The little girl took it from him. "It looks just like Charlotte!"

Her mother prompted her. "What do you say?"

"Thank you!" the girl said with adorable exuberance. "I love it!"

Once the mother and daughter had gone, I stepped outside and told my grandfather that he might have another moneymaking opportunity on his hands. Or, more precisely, *in* his hands. "One of my weekend customers asked about the cat you whittled for me, and you saw how thrilled that little girl was. Your pieces would make great souvenirs. If you'd like to, we could sell them in the shop."

"Not a bad idea." He ran his tiny tool over the chunk of wood, releasing a thin strip of curled wood, which fell to the concrete at his feet. "Social security doesn't get a person too far. I suppose I could use the extra cash."

"What would you do with it?" My grandfather was a man of simple tastes. He'd probably spend it on socks.

To my surprise, he said, "I've had my eye on a cup holder and sun canopy for my scooter. I might get me some of those blue lights that go underneath, too."

"Gonna pimp your ride, huh?"

"If that means the same as souping up my wheels, then sure."

The conversation got me thinking about money. Curious what Ashlynn might have done with the ill-gotten gains she'd stolen from Cormac, I went back inside, logged into my computer, and searched for her on Facebook and other social media. If she had posted something about being crushed by overwhelming student loan debt, unpaid medical bills, or a similar personal financial problem, I might have been able to muster some sympathy for her. But such was not the case. Rather, she'd posted a seemingly never-ending series of selfies in her *brand-new bikini!*, with her *brand-new Dolce & Gabbana bag!*, or sitting on her *brand-new chaise!*, watching her *brand-new big-screen TV!* She'd spent a small fortune on personal maintenance as well, posting pics of herself after visiting the hair salon and getting facials and microblading for her eyebrows. She'd even posted a close-up pic of her lips after she'd bought a *brand new iridescent lipstick!* I wished she'd noted the name of the makeup brand and color so I could go buy a stick for myself.

I wondered if Cormac had ever performed a search like I had and come across these posts. Heck, her conspicuous consumption constituted a virtual admission of guilt. If he'd seen these pics, surely he'd have questioned how she could afford so many luxuries.

Chapter Fifteen

As the minutes ticked by, I lingered near the front door, looking up and down the street for any sign of Damien Sirakov. Out front, Granddaddy kept an eye out, too, halting his whittling any time a dark-haired Caucasian man approached and resuming his work only when he'd assured himself the man had no bear tattoo on his neck.

A few minutes after three o'clock, a guy with brown skin and short dreadlocks approached the store carrying a toolbox. I stepped out front to greet him.

"Are you Hattie?" he asked.

"Sure am. You must be Kiki's friend from the theater." I shook his hand. "I can't thank you enough for helping me out with the security cameras."

"Any friend of Kiki's is a friend of mine. Especially when that friend is offering a free case of moonshine."

I introduced him to my grandfather and led him inside. As he placed his toolbox on the counter, I rounded up the cameras. He opened the boxes and spent a few minutes reading over the installation instructions and specifications before getting to work. In no time, he had the cameras installed and had schooled me in their functions.

After retrieving a cardboard box from the back room, I gestured to the shelves. "Which flavors would you like? I've got six different kinds."

"Let's make it easy," he said. "Give me two of each."

"That ought to hold you for a while, huh?"

He snorted affably. "Clearly, you've never been to a cast party on closing night."

As I packed the case, Granddaddy came into the store, grabbed a jug of his Ole-Timey Corn Liquor, and held it out. "Take a jug of my stuff, too. It's my thank-you for keeping my granddaughter safe."

"I'm happy to help," the man said. "But I'm also happy to take that jug off your hands."

There was no way the guy could carry his toolbox, the earthenware jug, and the case of moonshine all at once, so I carried the box out to his car. Granddaddy followed us out. After we bade the man goodbye, I glanced up and down the street. No sign of a criminal with a badly designed bear tattoo on his neck. Good

Granddaddy resumed his guard position in the rocking chair outside, while I went back into the store. A fiftyish couple both wearing UTC T-shirts walked inside.

"Hi there!" I called. "Welcome to the Moonshine Shack."

We engaged in idle chitchat as they sampled the flavors. They'd come to town from Shelbyville for the weekend to visit their son, who was a sophomore in college. The two had decided to stay an extra day to enjoy the city on their own while he returned to classes. UTC alumni and parents could be another big market for me. I made a mental note to promote my moonshine on parents' weekend this autumn. What hot toddy wouldn't be made better with a dash of my moonshine?

The couple chose two jars of my shine. After ringing up their purchase, I held out their bag. "I hope to see you again this fall when you're back in town for parents' weekend."

The woman took the bag, giving me a nod in return. "You can count on it."

I saw them to the door before returning to the counter. The security cameras had come with a red window decal that read *SECURITY CAMERA IN USE*. I figured it couldn't hurt to put the sticker on the glass of the front door. The warning could act as a deterrent to thieves.

After gathering a rag and a bottle of glass cleaner, I picked up the decal and carried everything outside to find my grandfather asleep in the rocking chair. The sound of him sawing logs filled the air. *ZZZZZZZZZ*. So much for him serving as my sentry. But I wasn't about to wake him up. He could be a big grump when his naps were interrupted. Besides, what were the odds that Damien Sirakov would actually come here? If he'd killed Cormac, he'd have to know that returning to the scene of the crime would only make him look guiltier. Surely his attorney had told him the best thing he could do was lie low and behave himself.

Turning my back to the street, I spritzed glass cleaner on the front door and wiped the surface dry with the rag. Tucking the bottle of glass cleaner under my arm, I peeled the backing off the decal and carefully affixed it over the door handle, where it couldn't be missed. *Perfect*.

I went back inside my shop and returned the cleaning supplies to the back room. I grabbed a few jars of moonshine to replace the jars I'd packed for Kiki's friend. I had my back to the door, replenishing the display, when I heard the sound of footsteps and the door of my shop opening behind me.

I whipped around to find myself face-to-face with the black bear tattoo. The image looked even more comical up close, and all I could think was that I didn't deserve to be killed by someone with such bad taste in body art. My heart rate rocketed into overdrive as I forced myself to look up into Damien Sirakov's face. It was a wonder I didn't drop the jar of apple pie moonshine clutched in my hands. The door swung shut behind him, sealing us in the shop alone together. *This creep sure is stealthy.* If not for his criminal tendencies, he could go to work for the FBI or CIA.

Smoky stood from his spot in the window, arched his back, and hissed. Immediately thereafter, another hiss sounded, this one a furious male voice coming from Damien. "It was you, wasn't it? Where do you get off pinning a murder rap on me?"

I was too frightened to speak. My vocal cords were frozen. All I could do was shake my head in a vain attempt to deflect Sirakov's accusation. I shifted the jar of shine into my left hand and eased my right into the hip pocket of my overalls, searching for my panic button so I could sound the alarm and summon help. But my search was in vain, my pocket was empty. *Argh!* I'd given the remote to my grandfather earlier, and now he sat snoring away out front, oblivious to the fact that I could shortly join Cormac in the hereafter.

Keeping my head facing Damien, I cut my eyes toward the windows, hoping I could signal someone on the sidewalk that I was in trouble. Unfortunately, the passersby were amused by my snoozing grandfather and too busy eyeing him to notice the confrontation taking place in here. One man glanced up for a brief instant, but I supposed from his perspective it probably looking like I was merely chatting with a potential customer.

"It was either you or one of the waitresses at Limericks!" Damien barked, evidently emboldened to be louder now that we were out of earshot of anyone else.

Finally finding my voice, I squeaked out, "What are you talking about?"

He raised an arm and gesticulated wildly. "I got arrested on a bum credit card rap, and then the cops started asking me if I'd killed the bartender from Limericks. I figured one of the waitresses from the bar might have fingered me, but then I remembered you were there the last time I got thrown out. One of you girls must have did it."

Being called a "girl" was irritating, but the slight was the least of my worries at the moment. I swallowed hard, forcing down the lump of terror in my throat. I repositioned the jar of shine in my hands, holding it at the ready. Given that one of my jars had been used to kill a man, I knew it could make a good weapon in a pinch. "Cormac had already filed complaints against you with the police. Even if I had said nothing, you would've still been a suspect."

The fury burning in his eyes eased slightly as he mulled over my words.

Sensing I might get somewhere, I went on. "Besides, you're only one of a long list of suspects. I'm a person of interest myself."

Damien looked me up and down. His upper lip quirked. "They think *you* might have killed O'Keefe?"

I nodded, insulted by the insinuation that I was weak but not about to argue the point. "Cormac and I had an argument about an order of moonshine. Cormac later called the cops and claimed my grandfather had threatened him with a knife. They think I might have taken revenge on Cormac for the call." I gestured to Granddaddy, who'd lolled to one side in the chair out front and threatened to fall out.

Damien's eyes looked to the window and he barked a laugh. "Cormac was scared of that old coot?"

Though Damien had a valid point, my ire rose on my grandfather's behalf. It was one thing to insult me. It was another to insult the patriarch of my family, the man without whom I wouldn't be standing in my very own moonshine shop. *Call my granddaddy an old coot, will you?* Fortunately, my infuriation fueled my courage. I tucked the jar of shine under my arm and pointed a finger in his face. "I don't appreciate you coming in here and chewing me out when it's you that's got yourself in this predicament." I jabbed the finger and he jerked his head back to keep from being poked in the eye. "You were at a parking lot not far from here right around the time Cormac was killed. You admitted it to the police." I jabbed again, and again he jerked his head back. "Stop blaming me for your problems and get out of my store!" I moved my finger to point to the door. "Now!"

He raised his palms in surrender and cast me a hopeful look. "What about those samples you offered? Can I get them now?"

"Not now!" I hollered, brandishing the jar as if poised to crack his skull with it. "Not ever!"

He backed away. "Okay! Okay! Don't get your itty-bitty panties in a wad!"

It gave me no small sense of satisfaction to stalk after him as he yanked open the door and scurried off with a wary look over his shoulder. He clearly hadn't expected me to go off on him like that. Heck, neither had I. But I was glad I did. It felt good to stick up for myself. I stepped into the open doorway and fought the urge to hurl the jar after him. *Why waste good moonshine on a guy like him?*

As soon as Damien had gone, I took a deep calming breath and put a hand on my grandfather's shoulder, shaking him gently. "Granddaddy? Wake up."

"Huh? Whuh?" He righted himself and scrubbed a hand over his face. As expected, he was grumpy. "What in the world are you shaking me for? I was only resting my eyes."

Despite his crabbiness, I didn't have the heart to tell him that he'd fallen fast asleep and failed to protect me. Thank goodness I hadn't been hurt or he'd have never forgiven himself. I settled for, "You were leaning over. I didn't want you to fall out of the rocker, that's all."

He scowled but said nothing more.

"How about some iced tea?" A drink would wipe the frown off his face, and maybe the caffeine would help him stay awake.

He grunted. "I suppose I wouldn't say no to a glass."

I went back inside and fixed him a tall glass of iced tea with a slice of lemon from the mini fridge. I added the smallest dash of his ole-timey moonshine and carried it out to him. "Here you go."

He dipped his head in gratitude and accepted the glass.

I flopped down in the other rocking chair and texted Marlon. Just had a visit from Damien.

While I'd expected Marlon to text me back, evidently he'd decided not to take the time to do it. Less than two minutes later, he came cantering up the street on Charlotte, her usual *clop-clop* instead a faster-paced *cloppity-clop-cloppity-clop.* Lest he spill the beans about Damien, I hurried to the curb, angled my head to indicate my grandpa, and made a discreet *zip-your-lip* motion with my fingers. Marlon looked confused but said nothing.

Granddaddy took a sip of his tea and snarled, "Back so soon, Officer Landers?"

Seemingly unsure what to say, Marlon looked from me to my grandfather and simply replied with "Yep."

As he slid down from his horse, I stepped closer and spoke soft enough that my granddad couldn't hear. "I'm fine. I told Damien to take a hike and he did."

Marlon arched a brow, clearly impressed. "You scared him off? Wish I'd seen that."

I swept my hand to invite him into the store. "You could come inside and watch the footage from my new security camera."

"Let's do it." Once again, he tied Charlotte to the post.

Lest my grandfather follow us inside, I said, "We'll be right back."

Granddaddy used his cane to lever himself to a stand. "I'll keep Officer Landers's horse company. I've got no problem with her." He hobbled over and patted Charlotte's neck.

Inside the store, Marlon gathered next to me while I replayed the footage on my computer. The screen showed Damien stepping inside while my back was turned. My face contorted in terror when I turned around but, a moment later, I stabbed my finger at him. Unbeknownst to me until now, I'd taken small steps toward Damien as I'd jabbed, and he'd backed away. I'd been even more forceful than I realized.

Marlon let loose a whistle, impressed. "You showed him, Hattie. Maybe you should join the force."

I beamed. "I'm having too much fun with the 'Shine Shack to switch careers."

As I turned off the feed, Marlon asked, "Why didn't you hit your panic button?"

A wry expression claimed my face. "I'd given it to my

grandfather. He was supposed to keep watch out front. The plan went awry when he took an impromptu nap."

His gaze locked on my face, Marlon released a long breath. "Damien Sirakov could come back. Keep that button in your own pocket from now on."

"I will."

Chapter Sixteen

As Marlon and Charlotte rode away, a knocking sound caught my ear. The mail carrier rapped on the door of Limericks across the street. In his hand he held a large manila envelope. The rectangular green card affixed to the back of it told me it was certified mail—in other words, something important. Maybe even something that could tell us who had killed Cormac.

"I'll be right back," I told Granddad. As the mail carrier began to head off, I jogged across the street, raised a hand, and called, "Wait!"

He turned and scrutinized me as I approached. "You work at Limericks?"

While I didn't want to lie, I did want to save Miranda a trip to the post office, assist Ace in any way I could, and avoid delays in solving the murder. "I'm in partnership with the new owner." Okay, so it wasn't exactly the truth. But it wasn't a flat-out falsehood, either. *A mentorship is a form of partnership, isn't it?*

The mail carrier eyed me, seemed to decide either that I looked trustworthy or that he simply wanted to get the mail off his hands, and shrugged. He detached the green card from the back of the envelope and held it out to me, along with a pen. I took the pen, signed my name on the card, and handed both back to him. In turn, he handed me the envelope. "Have a nice day."

"You, too." I carried the envelope back across the street to my shop and sat down in the rocker again.

"Whatcha got there?" Granddaddy asked.

"I'm not sure."

The item was addressed to Cormac O'Keefe. The return address indicated that it had been sent by the Tennessee Board of Professional Responsibility. *What the heck is that?* I whipped out my phone and performed a quick Internet search. The board's website indicated that it was established under the auspices of the state supreme court to enforce ethical standards on attorneys. The agency had the power to impose sanctions on lawyers who'd violated their professional code of behavior, including suspension from practice or disbarment. *Why would the board be in touch with Cormac?* He hadn't been an attorney. But he had gone head to head with one, multiple times. *Had Cormac filed a complaint against Heath?*

I knew that federal mail was taken seriously. It was one thing to accept delivery of a piece of mail, but it was another thing entirely to open something addressed to another person, dead or not. I'd seen people steam mail open on television and the movies, but I suspected they made it look much easier than it really was. Besides, I had neither a teapot nor a steam iron at the shop, as well as no inclination to serve jail time for mail tampering. I stepped out from under the porch and held the envelope up to the sun to see if I could see through it and read the contents. No such luck. The envelope was opaque.

I debated texting Marlon, but his shift had ended by now and the guy had already put in a lot of overtime. Besides, the situation could earn me more brownie points with Ace. I gave her a call and told her about the envelope.

"Keep it handy," she said. "I'll be right over."

We ended the call, and I sold a jug of Granddaddy's Ole-Timey Corn Liquor to a businessman in a suit looking for a retirement gift for a golf buddy. Shortly thereafter, Pearce's white Chevy Impala pulled to the curb in front of my shop. She climbed out, looking as impeccably professional as she had before. Today, she sported a plum-colored pantsuit along with her signature copper jewelry.

I met her at the door with the mail.

"Hand it over," she said, wasting no time. She held out her hand and I gave her the envelope. She perused the addressee and sender information on the front before turning the envelope over, running a finger under the flap to loosen it, and withdrawing the contents.

The stapled document looked to be three to five pages long. She ran her eyes over each page, flipping them as she finished each one.

I nearly wriggled with curiosity. "Come on," I cajoled her. "Throw me a bone. What does it say?"

She lifted her eyes from the page to look at me. "Let's just say Cormac has filed a grievance against an attorney."

"I'd already determined that myself."

She gave me a wry smile. "I figured as much. Googled the board, did you?"

Busted. "Is the attorney Heath Delaney?"

She slid the paperwork back into the envelope. "You got your bone. That's all I'm saying."

Telling me what I already knew could hardly be called a bone. "Have you spoken with Heath yet?" I asked. "Are you going to talk to him again?"

"That's none of your business," Pearce said firmly.

"You won't tell me? Even after all the help I gave you?"

Alas, Detective Pearce was immune to the guilt trip. "I appreciate your help, Ms. Hayes, but it doesn't entitle you to confidential information."

I huffed and crossed my arms over my chest. Though I could understand her sharing information on a need-to-know basis only, I needed to know! My curiosity wouldn't be satisfied otherwise. But if the detective wouldn't tell me, maybe the board or Heath would. Maybe I could wrestle some information out of the attorney tomorrow, when Miranda and I went to meet with him. "What about the distributor from Backwoods Bootleggers? Did you talk to him?"

"I did," she said. "He confirmed that Ashlynn told Cormac he was 'a dead man.' He said she was completely out of control."

Again, she'd only told me something I had already determined on my own. After all, I'd seen the footage on the video from Limericks. I decided not to press my luck further.

Ace showed her first sign of conciliation. "Marlon told me Sirakov came to see you."

"He was just angry," I said. "The instant I showed some backbone, he made a hasty retreat."

"He could be planning to return. Stay alert, and give us a call if he shows his face. We can arrest him again."

"I will."

* * *

The remainder of Monday was uneventful. Marlon and Charlotte *clop-clopped* by several times. Marlon would stop his horse with a "whoa," lower his head to peek into the shop, and wait for me to give him a wave and a thumbs-up to let him know everything was okay before moving on. Several police cruisers eased slowly past during the day, and I waved to the officers at the wheel as well. But Damien Sirakov didn't return, and no one else came to my shop in an attempt to put an end to me.

Granddaddy whittled four pieces, two sleeping cats and two head-tossing horses, no doubt inspired by Smoky and Charlotte. I cleared a space on a shelf for his whittled wares and printed out a small sign on cardstock that read *WHIT-TLED CRITTERS $7.* By the end of the day, we'd sold half his stock.

After another fitful night's sleep in which I was pursued by bumbling black bears and belching Labrador retrievers, I was up with the sun Tuesday morning. Somehow, I felt simultaneously exhausted and eager for the meeting with Heath Delaney. If Ace wouldn't tell me much, maybe I could weasel some information out of Heath myself, determine whether he should remain on the list of potential suspects or be eliminated. My guess was that he was still a person of interest or she would have told me otherwise.

Smoky seemed confused and irritated by the alarm going off on my phone. He'd grown accustomed to our later schedule. He scowled before rolling over to face away from me. I reached out and ruffled the fur on the back of his neck. "You'll have to stay here today, boy. I've got an early meeting."

He responded with a low growl that told me he didn't give a rat's behind about my plans and to stop bugging him when he was trying to go back to sleep. He was just as grumpy as my granddad when his slumber was interrupted.

After showering, dressing, and fixing my hair and makeup, I downed a quick piece of toast with coffee and headed out.

I kept a keen eye out for creeps as I approached my shop. Fortunately, there were none in sight. All I saw were a trio of college girls with backpacks walking to the nearby coffee shop and a few of my fellow shop owners preparing for the day. I turned down the alleyway, parked behind the Moonshine Shack, and quickly made my way into the stockroom. After disabling the alarm, I made my way through the salesroom of my shop and exited through the front door, turning back to lock it.

Rather than risk my life jaywalking through morning rush-hour traffic on Market Street, I made my way down to the corner and crossed with the traffic light. As I approached Limericks, I spotted Miranda coming up the block from the other direction. A computer bag hung from her shoulder, along with a purse, and she held a cardboard coffee cup in each hand. She smiled, raised one of the cups in greeting, and called out, "Good morning!" She was a few minutes early, a sign of her work ethic.

I returned Miranda's smile. "Ready to delve into the exciting and adventurous world of double-entry bookkeeping?"

She groaned in jest. "Not at all. That's why I brought some liquid motivation." She raised the other cup as she held the first one out to me. "I took a guess and figured you might like a caramel macchiato."

"Who in their right mind doesn't?" I took the warm cup from her and inhaled the delicious aroma before thanking her for her thoughtful gesture and sharing some moonshine trivia. "Back in the day, some people used to start their morning with what they called a 'coffee lace,' a shot of moonshine in a cup of coffee."

"Seems counterproductive," Miranda replied. "The effect of the moonshine would cancel out the effect of the caffeine."

"I didn't say the people were smart. I just said that they did it."

She laughed. "Maybe I can offer a coffee lace in my bar. Made with your moonshine, of course." She reached into her purse, dug out her keys, and unlocked the door to Limericks. After we entered, she punched in a code to disarm the alarm. "Good news," she said. "I spoke with the landlord. They're willing to give me a new lease. They're also going to change the locks."

"Good. That'll keep you safer." With new locks and keys, she could better control access to the bar. I pointed to the keypad for the security system. "It can't hurt to change the alarm code, too, just in case. If there's not a manual in the office, you can probably find instructions online that'll tell you how to do it."

She pulled her cell phone from her purse and snapped a pic to note the make and model number of the alarm system. I followed her around the bar to what had been Cormac's office and would now be hers. The bottle of Jack Daniel's, the printer, and the assorted paperwork remained on the desktop, but at least we'd left the documents in an orderly stack.

This time, Miranda took a seat in the desk chair while I dropped into the seat next to the desk. She pulled her laptop from her computer bag, plugged it in, and turned it on. While we waited for her computer to boot up, I took another big sip of my coffee.

After she'd logged into her computer, Miranda pulled a notebook and pen out of her tote bag and readied them to take notes. "Where should we start?"

"First, we need to establish an account for your business. Have you decided on a name?"

"I have," she said. "I'm going to rename the bar The Tipperary Tavern. My corporation will be Tipperary Tavern, Incorporated."

"I love it!" I said. "You decided to stick with the Irish pub theme, then?"

"Seemed like the best thing to do," she said. "I don't have enough money to redecorate the bar. Besides, the place has quite a few regular customers. An Irish pub appeals to a wide demographic. We get all kinds of people in here. Some come to watch the sports on the big-screen TV. Others come to play darts or pool. Businesspeople come by after work. We even get some bikers and college kids, though there's other bars that cater more specifically to those crowds. Plus, there's not another Irish pub in the area."

She was smart not to make a lot of changes off the bat and risk losing the existing customer base. She might be only partway through her studies, but she certainly had a head for business. Her observations and intuition would get her far.

Her phone, which was lying on the desktop, pinged with an incoming text. I glanced over at it, noting that the message read SHIPMENT COST. Before I could read more, she pushed the button on the side of the phone to darken the screen and slid the device into her purse. She tossed a smile my way. "Don't you just hate notifications popping up all the time?"

"They can certainly be disruptive," I agreed. The immediate communication capabilities of cell phones were both a blessing and a curse.

I showed her how to set up an online bookkeeping account in the name of Tipperary Tavern, Inc. "The nice thing about using the online program is that you don't have to worry about losing data if your computer crashes." We set up the accounts her tavern would need. Bar receipts. Payroll. Supplies. Rent. Utilities. Internet and cable. Income tax. Sales tax. Liquor inventory.

"Speaking of inventory," Miranda said, "will I need to determine the value of the alcohol and mixers that are still on hand?"

"Because you haven't paid for the inventory yourself," I said, "you won't get a tax deduction for the value, and you won't need to input the information into your accounting data. But it would be a good idea to make a list of the bottles in the bar and the stockroom, just in case one of Cormac's creditors asserts some type of claim to his remaining assets. That's something we should ask Heath Delaney about during our meeting later."

"I've been thinking about that," Miranda said, "about the people Cormac ripped off. I know he owed several hundred dollars to the man who owns the barbecue place."

"Mack Clayton?"

"Yes, that's the guy. Limericks was packed on St. Patrick's Day, and the catered dinner was a big hit with the customers. Cormac didn't pay the full bill. Mr. Clayton came by a couple of times trying to collect, but Cormac kept saying that the restaurant had shorted the order and refused to pay him. Things got ugly the last time Mr. Clayton was here."

My skin began to prickle. "Ugly how?"

"The two of them got into a shouting match. Cormac threatened to call the police if Mr. Clayton didn't leave. Mr. Clayton said if Cormac wasn't going to pay him, he'd find a way to put Limericks out of business for good. He turned over a barstool on his way out. But who could blame him? Cormac was acting like a total jerk."

I recalled what Heath Delaney had told me when he'd come by my shop, how it could be difficult and expensive to put someone out of business. *Hmm.* Of course, that assumed the person was using legal means to try to put the other one out of business. Would the delay and cost of going to court make a person start thinking about other ways to put someone out of business for good, like putting an end to the person's life?

Before I could ponder the idea too much, Miranda went on. "I want to do the right thing," she said. "I figured once I bring in enough profit, I'll pay the bill to the Smoky Mountains Smokehouse."

"I'm sure Mack would appreciate that."

We turned our attention back to the bookkeeping program. I spent the next half hour showing her how to set up accounts, enter data, and prepare reports. In light of the fact that she already knew some bookkeeping basics, as well as the fact that she was a quick learner, we covered a lot of ground in a short time.

When we'd gone over the essentials, I closed the program, ending our tutorial. "You can always call me with questions." I checked the time on my phone. A half hour remained before we'd have to leave for the meeting with the attorney. Might as well put the time to use. "Why don't we start on the inventory?"

"Okay." She put her fingers to her keyboard and pulled up the Excel program. "I'll start a spreadsheet."

"A spreadsheet." I put a hand over my heart. "It's so nice to connect with another number nerd."

She laughed as she typed in a name for the file. She picked up her laptop and carried it into the stockroom. I followed along behind her. After a brief discussion, we decided that I should call out the names and quantities of the liquor while she entered them in her spreadsheet. She perched on a barstool in the corner and sat her computer on her lap.

I eyed the shelves, deciding where to start. While most of the bottles had been removed from the cardboard cases in which they had been delivered, there were intact cases of some of the more popular liquors on the shelves, waiting to be opened.

I started at the far end, where the gin was stored. "Three bottles Bombay Sapphire gin, seven-hundred-and-fifty-milliliter size. Two bottles Tanqueray, one point seven five liters."

Miranda's fingers flew over her keyboard as I recited the brand names and quantities on hand. She occasionally lifted a finger and said "hold up" while her data input caught up with my mouth. We went through gin, vermouth, vodka, amaretto, whiskey, and rum before reaching the moonshine section. Only four bottles of Backwoods Bootleggers sat on the shelf. Where were all the other bottles of shine? According to the invoice I'd found on the printer last Sunday, Cormac had ordered six cases, for a total of seventy-two bottles, and they'd been delivered the preceding Tuesday.

My eyes scanned the shelves. None of the cartons bore the Backwoods Bootleggers logo. I circled around to the next row. Nope. No cases of moonshine there, either. I checked a small closet at the back but found only a mop bucket, broom, and cleaning supplies. It wouldn't be unusual to lose a bottle or two to breakage or employee theft. There was even a term for these causes of missing inventory—*shrinkage*. But when over five cases of liquor were missing, it seemed clear that more than a dropped bottle or petty thievery was involved.

Miranda tilted her head in question. "Looking for something?"

"Yeah," I said. "Sixty-eight bottles of Backwoods Bootleggers moonshine."

Chapter Seventeen

I reminded Miranda of the invoice from Backwoods Bootleggers that had been on Cormac's printer. "The invoice showed he'd ordered six full cases. Any idea where the liquor might be?"

She shook her head and shrugged at the same time. "I can't imagine the bar would go through that many bottles so quickly. The bikers drink a lot of moonshine. The frat boys order a lot of it, too. But they wouldn't go through sixty-eight bottles in only three days."

Not alone, they wouldn't. But the bikers or frat boys could easily polish off the liquor if they'd held a rally or a party attended by a large group of people. The gears in my mind began to churn, cranking out possibilities. Maybe Cormac had ordered the liquor and agreed to exclusivity to get the discount, knowing he could resell the bottles to the bikers or frat boys at less than retail and make a nice profit. It would be illegal, of course. Bars were permitted to sell only poured

liquor served in a glass, not unopened bottles. But the law
didn't seem to mean much to Cormac. What's more, the tim-
ing would make sense. With the end of the spring semester
coming up soon and final exams on the horizon, all of the
frats would be hosting a last hurrah before dead week and
everyone turned to their books. Late spring was prime time
for biker rallies, too. They liked to gather before summer
came and the high temperatures made being outdoors for
prolonged periods of time miserable.

Miranda mused aloud. "Maybe Cormac didn't want them
taking up space here if they weren't going to be needed soon.
Maybe he took the other cases to his apartment." She paused
a moment before posing another possibility. "Or maybe whoever killed him took them."

"Could be." I felt a little guilty not letting Miranda know
all of the information I had about the case, but given Ace's
earlier threat about interfering with a police investigation,
I knew it was best to keep my mouth shut.

Cormac hadn't carried the cases out of the bar with him
the night he'd been killed. I'd seen the video, and the only
thing in his hands when he left was the recycling bin. But
it was possible he'd carried the cases out to his car earlier
with the intention of reselling the liquor to the bikers or frat
boys. If the cases had been in Cormac's car and intended
for the bikers, maybe the frat boys had spotted them in the
vehicle on their way back to the frat house. Maybe they'd
tried to steal them like they'd stolen the moonshine from
my store. Maybe Cormac had caught them in the act and
things had turned deadly.

Another possible scenario was that Tristan and Dane had
arranged to meet Cormac out back after the bar closed to pick
up the cases of moonshine he'd sold them on the sly. Maybe
they'd refused to pay, or gotten into a dispute over the amount

due. Maybe one of them—my guess would be Tristan the Ken doll—had grabbed the empty Firefly jar from the recycle bin to use as a weapon. Maybe he'd then chased Cormac around the building while his friend rounded up the liquor. Maybe things had gotten out of hand in front of my shop, and he'd ended up smashing the jar, turning it into a jagged-edged weapon, and killing Cormac. *But if that was the case, why weren't Tristan's fingerprints on the jar?* Because he had a criminal record for the paintball incident, his prints would be on file. *Could he have wiped his prints from the jar?*

I fished for more details to see whether my theories might have legs. "You said frat boys ordered a lot of the Backwoods Bootleggers moonshine. Were they from any particular fraternity?"

"I don't know the Greek letters," she said, "but we get a lot of boys from the one with the name that looks like it spells 'Me.'"

Mu Sigma. Maybe my musings weren't off base, after all.

As we finished the inventory of the back room, the alarm on Miranda's phone chimed to remind us it was time to leave for the meeting with Heath Delaney. We gathered up our purses from the office.

Miranda gestured to the opened bottles behind the bar as we walked past. "I'll inventory these partial bottles when I come back."

On our walk over to Heath's office, I asked whether she'd ordered a new sign for the bar.

"No," she said. "I'm thinking of painting over the one that's already hung out front. I have to watch my funds, at least until the bar starts making a profit again."

"I can relate," I told her. "I sank a lot of money into getting the Moonshine Shack ready. I'm lucky there's enough money left that I can afford to eat."

"I survive on ramen noodles, peanut butter, and off-brand cereal," she said. "I call it the part-time student diet."

I tossed her a smile. "I remember those days. Before you know it, they'll be behind you."

"I hope so," she said. "I'm taking twelve hours a semester. Between classes, studying, and work, I have no time for anything else."

"My friend Kiki is a freelance artist," I told her. "She helped me design and decorate my place."

"She did a great job. The Moonshine Shack is adorable." Her eyes brightened. "You think she'd paint my sign for me?"

"I'm sure she would." Kiki was always looking for freelance art gigs, a side hustle. "She'll give you a fair price, too."

We made small talk as we strode down the streets of Chattanooga's riverfront district. Miranda mentioned that one of the things she'd loved about working at Limericks was the repeat customers. "They're like family. They're a big reason I want to continue the business. They've told me all about their kids and jobs and spouses, and they ask about me, too. Same goes for the other staff. I'm close to most of the other servers who worked my shifts. We covered for each other, had each other's backs, you know? I always thought I'd go to work for a big company once I got my business degree, but I can't see myself doing that now. I like the small-business environment."

"Me, too." It was casual and comfortable, with fewer rules and less structure. The flexibility was great. It was also less routine. The tasks were more varied, which kept things interesting. "Have you talked to the other staff? Are they planning to work for you when you reopen the bar?"

"Most of them." Her nose quirked in disgust. "Not Ashlynn, though. I'd never hire her back. I hope I never see her again."

"I don't blame you." I mentioned the same promotional ideas that I'd suggested to Cormac the first time I'd gone to Limericks, when I'd invited him to my grand opening.

"Lasses' night is a fun idea," she said. "Maybe we could do a moonshine special on the next full moon, too."

"That's a clever concept," I said. "Wish I'd thought of it."

"I can't take all the credit," she said. "You got the ball rolling with the talk of ladies' night."

She had a point. The two of us engaging in business brainstorming sessions could be good for both of us. Our banter might make us both some bucks.

Before we knew it, we had reached the offices of Delancy and Sullivan. The receptionist held out a hand, inviting us to take seats in the foyer. "Mr. Delaney will be with you in just a moment."

As she buzzed him to let him know his ten o'clock had arrived, Miranda and I perused the magazine offerings on the coffee table. The options reflected the fact that the law firm handled primarily business matters. *Entrepreneur. Kiplinger's. Fortune. Money.* I was five paragraphs into an article on small-business retirement plans when Heath appeared in a hallway behind the reception desk.

"Good morning." He gave us a smile and angled his head to indicate the hallway. "Come on back. My assistant has the conference room ready for us."

An assistant. What I wouldn't give for a right hand. As soon as the 'Shine Shack was making enough money, I'd hire someone to help me out on a regular basis so I could focus on growing the business rather than the day-to-day details.

We followed Heath back to a small conference room in a rear corner. One window faced east, the wide river visible in the distance. The other window looked south over Market Street. A large, round table with six chairs filled the space. The circular table told me this room was for amicable client meetings, where the attorneys and the visitors were on the same side, both literally and metaphorically.

We sat down and all three of us readied our legal pads and pens.

Heath started things off by sliding some paperwork across the desk to Miranda. "We drafted your corporate documents based on the information you gave my assistant on the phone. Look them over. If everything's as you'd like it, we can get them filed right away."

I used my feet to wheel my chair closer to Miranda's. She set the document down between us so I could read over the paperwork with her. It appeared to be the standard boilerplate documents for establishing and registering a for-profit corporation.

When she finished reading, she looked up. "Everything looks correct to me." She turned to me, a brow arched in question.

"Me, too," I said.

"Perfect." Heath turned around to the credenza and picked up the receiver from the in-house telephone. He punched two buttons, listened for a moment, and when he got an answer he said, "The client has approved the corporate paperwork for Tipperary Tavern. Proceed with filing."

When he hung up, Miranda asked, "How long will the filing take?"

"The documents are submitted electronically online," he said. "Processing takes four or five hours, at most. Your registration should be confirmed by the end of business this afternoon."

"Then I'm legit?" she asked. "I can open the bar as soon as the confirmation comes back?"

He nodded. "You can start slinging drinks this evening."

"Woo-hoo!" She pumped her fists.

I couldn't help but smile. I knew exactly how she felt. It was the same exhilaration I'd felt when seeing my first jar of moonshine come out of the bottling machine, the same thrill I'd felt when making my first sale in my shop to the Desperaddos motorcycle club.

The matter of the corporate registration resolved, he asked, "What questions do you have for me?"

Miranda ran through the list I'd dictated to her on Sunday, as well as several she'd come up with on her own. Heath provided her direct and succinct answers, clearly having addressed these routine inquiries dozens of times before. Miranda's final question regarded the remaining inventory. "I'd like to settle the outstanding claims against Limericks with the income generated from the sale of the liquor."

"That's not a bad idea," he said. "Better to take the bull by the horns than worry about a claim sneaking up on you. Do you have a list of Cormac's unpaid creditors?"

"There aren't a lot of them," she said. "Almost all of his suppliers had put him on a cash-only basis due to earlier late payments. But I know he owed the Smoky Mountains Smokehouse for the St. Patrick's Day catering, and my guess is he still owed something on the new dishwasher that you came to see him about last month."

Heath went to see Cormac about a dishwasher? This was news to me.

"He still owed something, all right." Heath snorted a frustrated huff of air and shook his head. "Cormac didn't pay the appliance company a single penny. He claimed the dishwasher was defective and refused to pay. He also refused to let a repairman take a look at it."

I was about to say that I'd seen Cormac put glasses in the dishwasher when I'd watched the security footage with De-

tective Pearce and Marlon, but I caught myself just in time.
I wasn't supposed to share any information I'd seen in the
video, or even the fact that the security cameras existed.

Miranda's face screwed in confusion. "Far as I can tell,
the dishwasher worked fine from the time it was installed.
We used it all the time."

"That's what I figured." Heath glowered out the window
in the direction of Limericks, two blocks away, before turning back to us. "My guess is he was trying to wear the appliance company down, get them to accept pennies on the
dollar for a fully functioning machine. He told them they
could come remove it, but he knew they wouldn't want to
do that. A used machine is worth only a fraction of new."
He grunted. "That man always had some ulterior motive,
some kind of sleazy game plan to screw over anyone who
dealt with him."

Miranda scoffed. "Tell me about it. Do you know how
much he owed the appliance company?"

"Forty-five hundred dollars. I'm sure they'd work with you
and accept installment payments if you can't pay the full
amount due in a lump sum. As far as Mack Clayton, he'd be
thrilled to get paid." Heath's eyes cut to me for a brief instant
before returning to Miranda. "Mack was furious when
O'Keefe stiffed him. He wouldn't stop talking about it at the
chamber of commerce meeting that was held at the end of
March. He called for a boycott of Limericks and proposed
forming an agreement among the owners of other bars and
restaurants in the riverfront area to offer drinks at cost until
Limericks went under. He said they'd make up any losses in
increased market share when the pub went out of business. I
had to advise against it, though. Those types of agreements
constitute price fixing, and the participants would risk stiff
penalties for an antitrust violation."

I couldn't blame Mack for being upset that O'Keefe had stiffed him, but wanting to run Limericks out of business entirely seemed like a big, bold move. I also wondered about Heath's motives in telling us these details about Mack Clayton. Did he sense that I'd become suspicious of him, and was he trying to deflect my suspicions elsewhere?

Miranda wrapped things up by asking Heath if he could take a look at her lease when she got it from the landlord later today.

"I'd be happy to," he said with a smile.

Our business concluded, he escorted us back to the foyer. "It was nice talking with you ladies. I have no doubt you two will be the next big successes on the riverfront."

Miranda and I had made it outside and down the block when I patted the front pocket of my overalls. "Uh-oh. I think I left my phone at Heath's office." I was faking. My phone was in my purse. But I had a matter I wanted to discuss with him in private.

"Want me to go back with you?" she asked.

"Nah." I motioned her ahead. "No sense wasting your time. We'll catch up later."

With that, she headed onward and I did an about-face.

Back at the law office, I fed the same story to the receptionist. "I think I left my phone in Heath's office." She buzzed him and sent me back to his space.

I entered through the open door and pretended to look around for my phone, feeling around the chair and bending down to look under his desk.

"Any luck?" he asked.

"No." I raised a finger. "Wait. I think I might have put it in my purse this morning instead of my pocket." I unzipped my purse and slapped my palm to my forehead in mock self-punishment. "There it is! I must look so stupid."

He gave me a smile. "No worries. It happens to the best of us."

I tilted my head. "Can I ask you something?"

"Of course. It's how I make my living."

"Were you notified about a complaint Cormac filed against you with the Board of Professional Responsibility?"

He went rigid. "You know about that?"

Ace must not have told him how she'd learned of the complaint. Again, she'd held her cards close to her vest.

"It was only a guess," I told Heath. "I signed for certified mail the board had sent to Limericks." I cringed as if in self-rebuke. "Given that you'd warned me about Cormac at my grand opening and mentioned the lawsuits later, I figured the mail might address a complaint he'd lodged against you."

He shifted in his chair, as if uncomfortable. "It did. His complaint was entirely baseless. He alleged I slandered him when I went to the bar and accused him of defrauding the appliance company. He claimed it was a false statement and that some of his customers overheard me make the accusation. He said the sales rep from Backwoods Bootleggers heard my statements, too. He listed the man as a potential witness."

"Gage Tilley?"

"Yes. You know him?"

"He attended my grand opening," I said. "Uninvited, I might add."

"The allegations are ridiculous. Cormac and I spoke privately in his office, and I don't even recall the sales rep being in the bar at the time. Cormac's complaint was nothing more than a nuisance case. He probably hoped I'd offer him some money to dismiss it."

"You're not alone," I said. "Cormac accused my grandfather of slandering him, too. My granddad was warning tourists not to go to Limericks because the owner was a crook."

Heath's chest heaved. "O'Keefe was creative in his tactics. I'll give him that. Effective, too. I lost a potential client over that complaint. A big one. Construction company. Their CEO called the board to check my standing and was told a complaint was pending against me. They yanked their retainer and went elsewhere." His voice rose and so did he, lifting a few inches out of his seat as his hands fisted on the table. "O'Keefe cost me at least forty grand in annual billings over a bald-faced lie!"

My nerves buzzed on seeing the attorney lose his cool. My grandfather had told me that Heath had kicked the leprechaun statue at Limericks and left the little man lying damaged in the dust, but now that I'd seen Heath lose his temper for myself, my suspicions rose. My guess was that Heath had gone to Limericks after he'd learned of the complaint Cormac had lodged with the board and that he'd kicked the statue on leaving. *But had he gone back last Friday night to get the satisfaction he'd not gotten earlier? Was Heath the one who had killed Cormac O'Keefe?* I feared that the thoughts that were running through my mind were as obvious as if they were running across an LED board on my forehead.

Heath studied me for a moment before seeming to loosen up. "Sorry." He raised his palms. "I pride myself on my ethics. I tend to get a little incensed when my integrity is questioned."

"Rightfully so," I said, hoping to appease him. "Integrity is important. If Cormac O'Keefe had any, he might be alive today."

Chapter Eighteen

After picking up Granddaddy at Singing River, I swung by the Smoky Mountains Smokehouse. My mission was twofold. One, procure information. Two, procure potato salad. Unfortunately, while I was given a pint of the latter, I was given little of the former.

Mack wasn't working the counter when Granddaddy and I went inside, and I was forced to place my order with the middle-aged woman at the register. I decided to push the issue. "Any chance I can get a word with Mack?" I asked. "He's been putting our moonshine in his special shine sauce and I need to see how his supply is holding up."

She stepped back and pushed open the swinging door to the kitchen, releasing a waft of warm molasses, onions, and peppers. "Mack? You got a minute? The woman from the 'Shine Shack is here, wants to talk about your sauce."

Although Mack came out from the kitchen, he wore oven mitts on both hands and a harried expression on his face. I'd caught him as they were preparing for the lunch rush.

"Sorry to bother you at such a busy time," I said, "but I figured while I was here getting lunch I'd see if you needed more shine."

"Still got a full jug from my last order."

No surprise there. It had only been three days since I'd delivered two jugs to him.

He glanced back into the kitchen, where the sounds of utensils clanging, a fryer sizzling, and the kitchen staff calling to one another came through the door. *I'd better make this fast.*

"Let me know when you get low," I said. "By the way, it's too bad your boycott didn't work out."

His head spun back around and his eyes flashed in alarm, but he said nothing.

"Against Limericks?" I prodded. "Heath Delaney mentioned it during an appointment I had with him this morning." To make sure it didn't sound like the lawyer had spoken out of turn, I added, "He said you brought up the idea of a boycott at a chamber of commerce meeting."

"I did," Mack admitted. "Delaney said it wouldn't fly." He glanced away again before returning his focus to me. His eyes appeared softer now, the crinkles in the corners gone. "I feel kind of bad about it now. You know, in light of what's happened."

Granddaddy grunted. "What goes around comes around."

There's that sentiment again. As much as I'd like to believe completely in karma, to see everyone get their due, I didn't fully trust the sentiment. *What goes around comes around* might apply to the spinning teacups at Disneyland or the Tilt-A-Whirl at the county fair, but some scumbags seemed to escape their just deserts in life. They went around without ever coming around.

Voices came from behind us as a group of customers entered the restaurant. It would be rude to keep Mack from his work any longer. Besides, the odds of me learning anything new were minimal. I bade him goodbye and we carried our bags of food out to my van. Still, I had to wonder. Had that look I'd seen in Mack's eyes when his head swung around been surprise? Or had it been guilt?

When we arrived at the Moonshine Shack, I texted Marlon. I know I owe you dinner, but we've got extra BBQ at the shop if you haven't had lunch yet.

A text came back immediately. On my way.

I fixed Granddaddy a paper plate and settled him in a rocker. Marlon arrived and tied Charlotte to the post out front. "Howdy, Ben."

My grandfather scowled up at him. "Come to collect your granny fee?"

"What's that?"

"A bribe," I told him. "Moonshiners paid what they called a 'granny fee' to law enforcement back in the day to be let go." I turned to my grandfather. "A lunch invitation is not a bribe. It's called being polite and mannerly. You should try it sometime."

He merely harrumphed.

Marlon joined me at the chess table. "Bribe or not, this meal is a nice surprise."

"Speaking of surprises," I said, "Miranda and I had one at Limericks this morning."

As he filled his plate, I told him what I'd discovered—or more precisely, what I had *not* discovered. "At least five cases of Backwoods Bootleggers moonshine are missing from the bar. I don't know if they have anything to do with Cormac's murder, but it caught my attention. Miranda said she doesn't know anything about them. Any chance they were in his apartment or car?"

"Assume for the sake of this conversation that we didn't find the missing cases of moonshine, or that we didn't find all of them. What's your theory?"

"I'm thinking Cormac might have been buying the bottles from the distributor under the exclusivity discount, and then reselling them at a markup to some of his customers. It would be a win-win. He'd make a profit and they'd get the bottles at far less than the retail price the liquor stores charge. Miranda had told me that the bikers and the boys of Mu Sigma seemed to be especially partial to the brand. Cormac might have sold the bottles to them."

"A frat or biker gang could go through a lot of bottles," he mused in apparent agreement. "Maybe the boys or the bikers got in a squabble over the pricing and that's how Cormac ended up with a severed artery."

He pulled out his phone. "I'm going to fill Ace in on this development." He placed a call to her, repeated what I'd told him, and ended the conversation, exchanging his phone for a fork and digging into the potato salad. "She wants to talk to you. She's on her way."

We chatted over lunch and were finishing up when Ace's Impala pulled up in front of my shop. She climbed out and came up the curb.

"Want some barbecue?" I asked. "We've got plenty."

She thanked me but declined my offer. "I just finished a salad at my desk." She proceeded to ask me some questions about the time I'd spent with Miranda at the bar that morning.

I filled her in. "We set up a new bookkeeping account, and then we took inventory. That's when we realized the bottles of Backwoods moonshine that Cormac had ordered weren't on the shelves. It crossed my mind that fraternities consume a lot of alcohol."

"That's why I'll be heading to the Mu Sigma house when I leave here."

I think she's finally starting to trust me.

She turned and stared off into the distance, her jaw flexing. "It's frustrating. Frat boys commit a lot of the same crimes as gang members. Petty thievery. Vandalism. Recreational drug use and underage drinking. Assaults. But because they do it with Greek letters on their chest rather than a gang tattoo on their arm, they get only a slap on the wrist while the gang members do time or probation. It's the same with white-collar criminals. A man in a business suit can rip off thousands of dollars from the government in tax fraud, or bilk investors or customers in one way or another, and he'll get only a bill and a fine. But a blue-collar type pockets a package of hot dogs and he's hauled off in handcuffs." She sighed. "Sometimes, it feels like there's not enough justice in our 'justice system.'"

I attempted to be encouraging. "Maybe you can change that."

"I'm trying," she said. "In fact, that's why I joined the force all those years ago. It's not easy, though."

Given that we couldn't solve the larger, overarching problems today, I focused on what we could do, which was trying to put Cormac O'Keefe's killer behind bars. "What do you think about Gage Tilley being named as a witness in the defamation complaint?"

She gave me a pointed look. "You're butting into the investigation again."

"But I gave you information," I pleaded. "Don't I deserve a little quid pro quo?"

She groaned but said, "The defamation case is another thing for me to ask Gage Tilley about. Surely, he must have wondered why Cormac placed such a large order of moonshine. I'll take another look at the video, too, see what happened to the cases after Tilley delivered them."

First, they'd had to use the video to track the jar of Firefly cherry shine. Now, they'd be tracking cases of Backwoods Bootleggers. The security footage from Limericks was getting more views than that silly Baby Shark video on YouTube.

I pushed my luck and asked her what she thought about Mack Clayton's call for a boycott of Limericks and a price-fixing arrangement to push the business over the brink. They say where there's smoke, there's fire. But was there a fire where the Smoky Mountains Smokehouse was concerned?

Ace was noncommittal, but Marlon seemed to think there could be. "If Mack Clayton couldn't get his money, maybe he decided to take a pound of flesh instead."

"But wait," I said. "There's even more."

Ace issued a soft snort. "You're beginning to sound like an infomercial."

I told her about Heath's response when I brought up Cormac's slander complaint with the Board of Professional Responsibility. "He came up out of his seat. He said Cormac claimed that several customers and Gage Tilley overheard Heath's accusations, but Heath said they spoke privately in Cormac's office and he doesn't even remember Tilley being in the bar. This took place weeks ago so his memory could be hazy, I suppose. At any rate, he said he lost a big client and around forty thousand in yearly billings because of the pending complaint. You think the lost income gives Heath sufficient motive for killing Cormac?"

"People usually kill for love or money," the detective said sourly. "Cormac O'Keefe didn't inspire a lot of love."

Chapter Nineteen

Marlon took me aside before he left and chastised me. "As much as I appreciate the information you gave us today, you need to stop poking around. You might ask the wrong person the wrong question and end up getting hurt. Leave the investigating to the professionals, okay?"

I found myself conflicted again. His concern was sweet, but how could he fault me for wanting to help, especially when I wanted to clear my name? Rather than resist and start an argument, I figured it was best to agree, even if my agreement might be insincere. "All right," I said, mentally crossing my fingers. "I'll butt out."

"Good." He ran his gaze over my face, smiling softly.

I pointed down the street. "Get out of here."

Chuckling, he untied Charlotte's reins and swung himself up into the saddle. He tipped his helmet to me before giving her a "Yah!" and trotting off.

At the shop later that afternoon, I looked out front to see

my grandfather strapping a belt around both himself and the rocking chair. He pulled it up to his armpits and buckled it tight at his solar plexus. *What in the world is he doing?*

I went out front and confronted him, gesturing to the belt he'd buckled around his chest. "What's that all about?"

"You were worried about me dozing off and falling out of the chair, so I came up with a solution." He raised his arms and wriggled in the chair. "See? With this belt around me, I'm not going anywhere."

"You might be going to the funny farm," I told him. "Or adult protective services might take one look and take you into custody."

He frowned. "I put it on myself for my own good. A man ought to have a right to wear a belt if he wants to."

He had a point, but what would customers think if they saw him out here strapped to the rocking chair like an inmate convicted of a capital crime about to be zapped into oblivion? I proposed a solution to both of our problems. "How about I run the belt through the back of your overalls and buckle it behind the slats? That way it won't show and scare the customers."

"Fine with me." He raised his arms again, like a child waiting for their mommy to pull a sweater up over their head.

I reached down, unbuckled the belt, and slipped it behind his back, between his shirt and overalls. After slipping it through the slats on either side of the rocker, I pulled the belt as tight as I could behind the rocking chair and buckled it. Finished, I stepped back. "How's that?"

He wriggled some more, testing the belt. It held perfectly. "Your way's even better. The belt won't chafe my armpits this way."

Kiki zipped up in her Mini and hopped out. She wore a maroon beret and a bright yellow tunic over black-and-white-striped leggings. She looked like a cross between a mime and a taxicab.

Granddaddy waved to my friend. "Good afternoon, Koko!" he called, though he knew good and well her real name was Kiki. He enjoyed teasing her, just like he enjoyed teasing me and my siblings and cousins.

Kiki returned a tease in kind. "Good afternoon, Grand-doodle."

I stepped to the curb. "On your way over to paint the sign at Limericks?"

"Nuh-uh-uh." She wagged a finger. "You mean Tipperary Tavern."

I rocked forward on my toes. "I stand corrected."

She popped open the back hatch, and I hopped down to the pavement to help her unload her things. Inside the cargo bay sat the Radio Flyer wagon she used to haul heavy materials around when she was painting sets at the theater or doing other jobs that required lots of tools and supplies. She set the wagon on the ground, and the two of us filled it with cans of paint of various sizes. A gallon-sized can of periwinkle blue. A quart of bright red. A pint of daffodil yellow. She had paint in every color of the rainbow. She'd even brought some of the leftover firefly green glow-in-the-dark paint she'd used for the sign over my shop. She grabbed a metal bucket filled with a variety of brushes and placed that in the wagon, too.

After loading the paint supplies, she pulled out a sketch pad and showed me some quick mockups she'd designed. "Miranda texted me a pic of the current sign earlier so I could get a feel for the shape and size. What do you think of these?"

The wooden sign currently hanging on short chains over the door of the bar was a wide oval. Kiki had come up with a variety of designs for Miranda to choose from. Some were traditional, some cartoonish, some more modern. In one, she'd replaced the *T*s in *Tipperary Tavern* with shamrocks. In another, she'd replaced the *T*s with Celtic crosses. It was a lovely design in green, white, and orange, the colors of Ireland's flag.

I pointed. "That's the one I'd pick."

"Me, too," Kiki said. "We'll see what Miranda thinks."

"Do you want to borrow my stepstool to take the sign down?" I asked.

"Yes, please!"

Using the access ramp, she rolled the wagon up onto the sidewalk and parked it by my grandfather. "Babysit my paint for a minute?"

He gave her a mischievous grin. "Anything for you, Cuckoo."

She followed me back to my stockroom. As I wrangled the stepstool out from behind the broom and mop, I filled her in on my trips to the bar, the lawyer's office, and the barbecue restaurant, as well as my impromptu lunch date with Marlon and the visit from Ace. I also told her about my idea for lasses' night and Miranda's idea for the full-moon moonshine special. I finally freed the stool and headed back into the shop.

As she came along with me, Kiki chewed her lip. "As profitable as it could be for you and Miranda to host events together, it could be risky, too. After all, she might be Cormac's killer. I have to wonder if you're remaining objective about her."

Though my head told me Miranda could have murdered Cormac and had every reason to do so, my gut said Miranda was merely a young woman trying to make her way in the world. Then again, maybe I was simply feeling flattered that she'd asked for my help, treated me like a successful mentor. Maybe Miranda was a master manipulator who'd played me like a fiddle. Maybe it wasn't my gut talking but my ego. At the moment, I had no idea whom I could trust, myself included. *She'd acted a little squirrelly about that text this morning, hadn't she? The one that read* SHIPMENT COST? *Could the text have something to do with the missing moonshine?*

I stopped just inside the front door of my shop, eyed the bar across the street, and sighed, admitting Kiki had a point. Maybe I wasn't being objective about Miranda. "She was very eager to take over Cormac's business. Maybe she figured killing him would be an easy way to do it. She knew he had no close family or friends who'd raise a ruckus and get in her way." *Yep, she'd been chomping at the bit to reopen the bar.* "When she found out her corporate paperwork would be approved today, she nearly jumped for joy."

As if to emphasize my point, the neon light came on in the window across the street, announcing *OPEN*.

Kiki and I exchanged a glance.

"Let's be her first customers," I said. If nothing else, maintaining a friendly relationship with Miranda might give me access to yet more clues. On the way out the door, I grabbed a jar of blackberry moonshine to give her as an opening-day gift.

Kiki and I walked outside to find my grandfather slapping at his shoulders, trying to reach the belt buckled behind him. When that didn't work, he tried to stand. The rocking chair came with him. I set the moonshine and stepstool down and rushed over to free him from the improvised contraption.

"Sorry, Granddaddy." I cringed. "I guess you can see why I majored in business instead of engineering."

He waved it off. "I'm fine. I just need to go see a man about a dog." In other words, nature was calling.

"When you're done with the dog," I said, "keep an eye on the shop, okay? I'm going to step across the street with Kiki for a few minutes."

I retrieved the shine and stool, and Kiki grabbed the handle of her wagon. We made our way down the sidewalk and across the street with the paint cans jangling and jostling behind us. Kiki pulled the wagon inside when we reached the bar. We entered to find Isabella perched on a barstool with her round cocktail tray on her lap. Miranda stood behind the bar with a bar towel flipped back over her shoulder, just like Cormac had done when he was alive.

On seeing us belly up to the bar, Miranda pumped her palms toward the ceiling in a raise-the-roof gesture. "Wootwoot! Tipperary Tavern is in business!" She stepped forward and laid two napkins on the bar in front of us. "What can I get you lovely ladies?"

"I'll take a Lynchburg lemonade," I said, ordering a Tennessee standard.

"Hmmm." Kiki ran her eyes over the bottles behind the bar. "Make mine a southern mule."

"You got it," Miranda said.

"And you've got this," I replied, setting the blackberry shine on the bar. "It's a grand opening gift."

"Thank you!" Miranda said. "You really don't owe me a gift after all you've done for me, but I appreciate it. I'm going to hide it under the bar for now. That's where I keep my personal stash." She slid the jar under the counter, near the dishwasher, and turned to reach for the Jack Daniel's whiskey behind her. "By the way," she said over her shoulder as she pulled a highball glass off the shelf, "I'd love a jar of each of your Firefly flavors, when you've got time. A jug of the corn liquor, too."

"I'll bring them over as soon as we're done here."

"Perfect." She gave me a broad smile and cocked her head. "Can I buy them on credit?"

"Sure. I know you're good for it." Actually, I knew nothing of the sort. But I'd take a chance.

Miranda made our drinks and placed them on the napkins in front of us. When I pulled cash from my pocket, she raised a hand and refused it. "First drink is on the house."

"But we wanted to be your first customers."

"You still are," she said. "Say cheese!" She motioned Isabella over, then raised her cell phone camera, and the four of us leaned in so she could snap a selfie.

While we sipped our drinks, Kiki retrieved her sketch pad from the wagon and showed Miranda the mockups she'd created. Miranda looked each of them over carefully, flipping back and forth to compare them. She asked Isabella for her opinion. In the end, the decision was unanimous. The design with the Celtic crosses would grace the space over the door of Tipperary Tavern.

Miranda stood on tiptoe to see over the bar. When she saw all the different-colored paints in Kiki's wagon, she said, "It might be cute for you to paint a rainbow with a pot of gold on the wall over there." She pointed to a wall currently decorated with a faded framed print of an Irish coastline. She was obviously ready to put her own touch on the place.

"Consider it done," Kiki said.

I downed my drink much faster than I would have liked, but I didn't want to leave my grandfather alone at my shop for too long. I raised a hand in goodbye, wished Miranda the best of luck, and returned to my shop.

Kiki was still tied up at Tipperary Tavern when I arrived back at her condo late Tuesday evening. Because I'd had the early-morning meetings with Miranda and Heath, I'd left Smoky behind this morning rather than bringing him to the Moonshine Shack. He met me at the door in a rare show of affection.

"Missed me, didn't you, boy?" I scooped him up in my arms and cuddled him. While the little bugger stiff-armed me, a barely audible and probably involuntary purr gave him away. I kissed his furry cheek. "I know you love me, even if you won't admit it."

My phone chimed in my purse with an incoming text. I set Smoky down and pulled the device from my bag. Kate had sent a photo of her and Parker leaning over a crib where baby Dalton lay sleeping. He no longer looked like an alien whose skin didn't quite fit. In fact, he was plump and pink and perfectly adorable. The accompanying message read Guess who's home!

I sent a reply prefaced by the heart emoji, the kissy-face emoji, and the hearts-for-eyes emoji. Tell him Auntie Hattie says hello!

I'd left the remaining food from the Smoky Mountains Smokehouse in the mini fridge at the shop, but I found a frozen burrito in the back of Kiki's freezer that could serve as my dinner. It looked like it had been there since the ice age, so I figured she wouldn't miss it. I didn't check the expiration date. For one, the package was covered in thick frost I'd have to scratch through and, for two, I figured what

I didn't know couldn't hurt me. I plunked the cold bean brick down on a plate and slid it into the microwave.

While my dinner cooked, I changed out of my overalls and T-shirt and into my pajamas. A *ding* told me my gourmet delicacy was now ready. I rounded up a fork from the kitchen drawer, grabbed the plate from the microwave, and plunked down on Kiki's couch to watch sitcoms while I ate.

Despite having scalded my taste buds on microwave burritos approximately 876 times before, I once again succumbed to the bean lava, my blowing on the bite on my fork proving insufficient to reduce the temperature to an edible level. *Ow!* Muttering some choice words, I set the plate down on the coffee table to cool. A commercial came on the television, and I decided to take advantage of the break to start a load of laundry. Assuming Cormac's murder would be resolved quickly, I'd packed only a few items of clothing when I'd last been at my cabin. I was running dangerously low on clean panties. If I didn't do my laundry, I'd soon have to go commando.

I separated the clothing and dropped several dark items into Kiki's stackable washing machine, adding a cupful of liquid detergent. After closing the lid, I turned the dials to the appropriate settings and jabbed the start button. Rather than the sound of water starting to drip into the basin, all I heard was silence. I jabbed the start button again, harder this time. Still nothing. I lifted the lid, closed it, and pushed the button a third time. *Nope.* In case the problem was with the particular setting, I switched the dial from permanent press to gentle. Another punch of the button yielded the same result. I checked the plug. It was firmly in the socket. Apparently, the machine was on strike.

After pulling my now soap-coated clothing out of the washer and dropping it back into the laundry basket, I texted Kiki the cringing emoji. I think I broke your washing machine.

A reply came a minute later. Oops. Forgot to tell you. Darn thing's been busted for weeks.

That explained the pile of laundry in the corner of her bedroom. I'd just assumed she'd been either too lazy or too busy to get around to it. Looked like I'd have to either take my clothing to a Laundromat or wash it back at my cabin once I felt safe returning home.

I set my dirty laundry by the front door of her condo so I'd remember to take it down to my van in the morning. I plunked back down on her couch and returned to both my dinner and my program. As had also happened 876 times before, the lava-like bean filling of the burrito had cooled at a velocity generally attained only by submersion into liquid nitrogen. If not for the fact that the condo's thermostat read seventy-six degrees, I'd swear the thing somehow refroze. But it being nearly ten p.m. and me being me, I ate it anyway.

Chapter Twenty

Things at the shop were slow on Wednesday. Midweek meant fewer tourists. People weren't yet planning for the weekend, either, and hadn't thought of the moonshine they might want to have on hand for relaxing or entertaining. With little else to do, I was tempted to belt myself to a rocking chair out front and take a nap alongside Granddaddy. Instead, I plunked down in the chair next to him and asked him to teach me how to whittle.

"All righty." He handed me a chunk of wood and a small tool. "Now you listen, and listen good. Whittling is a fine art. You can't get in a hurry."

"Same as making moonshine."

"Exactly." He proceeded to instruct me on the finer points of wood carving. First, he reviewed the different blades and told me what they were for. There was a straight blade, a curved blade, a V-shaped chisel, and one for gouging wood. Once we'd reviewed the types of blades and the purposes of each, he showed me how to properly hold the small knives. "Careful now," he said. "You don't want to cut your finger."

I certainly didn't. There'd been enough blood spilled out here in front of my shop already.

Over the next hour, I worked on the chunk of wood, slowly transforming it into a rudimentary cat sitting on its haunches. I could see why my grandfather was so taken with the hobby. Whittling was somehow relaxing, yet took quite a bit of concentration. Focusing on something other than the murder investigation was freeing. The end result of my efforts was a catawampus cat, but he was cute even if a little cockeyed.

Around four o'clock, Kiki zipped up in her Mini, cut the engine, and hopped out.

"Look." I held up my cat. "Granddaddy taught me how to whittle. What do you think?"

She stepped over and took a look. "Nice kangaroo."

"It's a cat."

"No, it most definitely is not."

I blew her a raspberry. "Not everyone can be a professional artist."

"Obviously."

Granddaddy gestured with his knife, "You need to sand it now. Use the fine-grade paper."

I reached down to his little toolbox and fished out a small square of sandpaper.

Kiki nudged my grandfather's cowboy boot with the toe of her high-top sneaker. "You up for teaching another lesson, old man?"

He narrowed his eyes at her. "I might be if you ask nicely."

She spread her lips in a big smile. "Pretty please with sugar and sprinkles and a cherry on top?"

"All right." He reached down, grabbed another hunk of wood, and tossed it to her.

She caught the wood in one hand and dragged one of the chairs over from the game table with the other. Over the next few minutes, my grandfather went through his whittling lessons a second time. When he finished, Kiki bobbed her head. "I think I've got it."

Much to my chagrin and, as expected, she was a natural. In a mere twenty minutes, she'd carved a miniature jug of shine, complete with a tiny hole in the handle and three *X*s across the front. In comparison, my cat looked like a child had made it. She went on to whittle a firefly in flight, its wings spread out.

At five o'clock, noise across the street caught our attention. The doors to the Irish pub opened. Miranda waved a hand and called out to us. "Hey, y'all!"

We waved back, and Kiki stood. "I need to see if the paint has dried on her sign."

With that, she scurried across the street and disappeared into the bar. A few minutes later, she emerged with the sign and leaned it against the brick next to the chipped but still smiling leprechaun. She went back inside for a moment, emerging again with the stepstool she'd borrowed from me. Miranda came outside, too, and stood at the curb watching as Kiki hung the sign she'd painted for Tipperary Tavern. She posed for a photo under her sign, then took Miranda's camera and snapped one of her standing under it.

I stood and cupped my hands around my mouth. "It looks perfect!" Kiki had done a bang-up job.

My friend disappeared into the pub a final time, her Radio Flyer wagon coming along with her when she ventured out a few seconds later. Her sketch pad and my stepstool lay atop the cans of paint. She wheeled the wagon down to the corner, crossed with the light, and rolled up to the 'Shine Shack. After returning my stepstool to the storeroom, she fished some small brushes out of the bucket in her wagon. "We should paint our little sculptures."

We proceeded to do just that. I painted my kangaroo/cat gray, like my precious Smoky. Granddaddy painted his most recent horse to look like Charlotte. Kiki painted the firefly black and red on its back, and fluorescent green underneath. We blew on the paint to help it dry faster. My breath worked much better at drying the paint today than it had worked on cooling my burrito the night before.

Kiki begged off. She'd been hired to paint a mural of a team mascot at a local high school tomorrow and needed to go home and get her supplies organized. She pulled the wagon back over to her car, and I helped her load the wagon in the cargo bay. She raised her hand out the window and tapped her horn as she drove off. *Beep-beep!*

Shortly thereafter, I sold a single jar of peach shine to a woman who was on her way to meet friends for dinner at an Italian place down the block. Smoky was snoozing away in the window, so I went back outside to keep my grandfather company. Unfortunately, he was snoozing away, too. I sat down in the rocker beside him, alone with my thoughts. Being that most of my thoughts centered on a bloody murder that had taken place only three feet away from where I now sat, those thoughts didn't make good company.

A *clop-clop-clop* drew my eyes to Marlon as he rode up the street. I scurried inside and filled Charlotte's bucket with fresh water from the sink. I grabbed her some carrot sticks from the refrigerator as well. By the time I carried them out front, Marlon had her tied to the post and had taken a seat in the porch swing, one arm stretched in a curve along the back as if waiting for his lover to fill in the space. It took everything in me not to take a seat there.

I set the bucket down in front of Charlotte and she took a long drink. I held up the carrots, showing them to Marlon. "Okay if I feed her these?"

"Sure," he said. "But not too many. She's watching her weight."

I cupped the carrots in my hands as I'd been taught at summer camp all those years ago. Charlotte nuzzled my palms with her velvety chin, her whiskers tickling my skin. Once she'd crunched her way through the carrots, I ran a hand down her nose and turned to Marlon. "Got any news for me?"

He glanced at my grandfather, as if wondering whether he should share in front of him, but decided the sleeping man wasn't likely to blow the case. Still, when he spoke, he kept his voice low so as not to wake my granddad or be overheard by passersby. "The security footage showed Gage bringing only one case of liquor into Limericks last Tuesday."

"One case?" I repeated. "What happened to the other five?" I'd assumed Cormac had eventually taken them to his car or apartment, but had they never made it into the bar at all?

He raised a shoulder. "Your guess is as good as mine. Ace got in touch with him by phone, but she didn't ask him about any specifics. She wants to speak to him in person. He's based out of Memphis, but he'll be arriving in town on Friday for a couple days of sales calls. She's arranged to speak with him Friday afternoon at the station. She also had me review the video and find the footage from when Heath Delaney came to the bar to talk about the dishwasher. Tilley wasn't in Limericks at the time, though he did come by later that evening. Cormac might have gotten confused, remembered things wrong. 'Course, he could have just flat-out lied about Gage Tilley overhearing Heath disparaging him. Ace also spoke to the three boys from Mu Sigma. They said neither Tristan nor Dane told them anything about buying bottled liquor directly from Limericks, but they confirmed that Tristan is the head of their frat's party planning team. That means he's in charge of arranging for the kegs of beer to be delivered and buying the other alcohol and drinks. Could be he planned to buy the moonshine from Cormac and just didn't mention it to the other guys."

In other words, the police still had no concrete answers, but they seemed to at least be edging closer. That gave me some hope. "I hope Gage Tilley can shed some light on things. I'd like this case to be solved so I can stop worrying every time someone comes near my shop. My gut has been in knots since I found Cormac's body."

Marlon cut me some side-eye and a smile. "I'd like this case to be solved so you can take me out for that dinner you owe me."

His words caused a different sensation in my gut, one that was far more pleasant.

With a sigh, he stood and untied Charlotte. "I'd better get back out on patrol. I'll be in touch once I know more."

I hoped he'd be back in touch very soon.

As we drove away from the shop after closing on Wednesday night, my nose detected a delectable scent coming from Bar Celona. Knowing Kate and Parker had their hands full with their new bundle of joy, I decided to take some food to them. Kiki and I had loved the tapas I'd picked up at the place before. Why not take some tapas to the new parents?

I pulled up in front of the restaurant and placed a take-out order from my phone so I could keep my grandfather company in the van while the food was being prepared. I swiveled the microphone away from my mouth. "Do you want something, too, Granddaddy?"

"You choose for me," he said. "I don't even know what a tapa is."

I added an order of the patatas bravas for him. He could enjoy it as a late-night snack tonight or save it for the weekend. When I got off the phone, I said, "Tapas is essentially Spanish for appetizers."

His already wrinkled face wrinkled further as it drew inward. He pointed out the window. "You mean to tell me this here restaurant serves nothing but appetizers? No main dish?" He shook his head. "What will they think of next?"

After waiting a few minutes, I went inside to check on my order. The same middle-aged man as before was working the bar where I sat down to wait. After consulting the kitchen, he said, "It'll be just a few more minutes."

As I waited, I heard the servers and kitchen staff speaking in Spanish. It was such a pretty language, rolling off the tongue the way it did. I glanced out the window to check on my grandfather. He'd fallen asleep in the van, his wrinkled cheek squished against the window. Beyond him, head-lights flashed as a car left the paid parking lot on the other side of the street.

I shot bolt upright as a thought hit me. Damien Sirakov claimed that last Friday, around the time Cormac O'Keefe was killed, he was dealing with a dead battery in a nearby parking lot. He'd claimed that a man with a Spanish accent had helped him. Could it be true? Could one of the staff of Bar Celona have helped Damien get his battery up and running again?

"Excuse me," I said to the man. "This may sound like an odd question, but did someone who works here help a man jump-start a battery late last Friday night? A little after two o'clock?"

"Not me." He hiked a thumb toward the kitchen door. "Would you like me to check with the staff?"

"If you wouldn't mind," I said. "It's important."

The man went into the kitchen and returned a minute later with a bag containing my takeout order and a middle-aged man in a white cook's uniform. A woman with long, golden-blond hair followed them out with a tray of food in her hands, but I didn't pay her much attention. The maître d' angled his head to indicate the cook. "Benicio says he helped a man with his car battery."

I introduced myself to Benicio and told him that I ran the Moonshine Shack. "Can you tell me what the man you helped looked like?"

He lifted a shoulder. "Just like a regular guy," he said with a thick Spanish accent.

"What color was his hair?"

"Dark," he said. "Darker than mine even."

"Did you notice anything else about him?"

"He had a tattoo here." Benicio pointed to his neck. "A black animal. Maybe a panther? I couldn't tell. It wasn't good. The mouth was open like it was growling." He opened his own mouth, as if to demonstrate, even offering a growl. "Grrr."

The man he'd seen had to be Damien Sirakov. How many men with neck tattoos of an openmouthed indeterminate black beast could there be downtown at that hour, let alone a man of that description with a dead car battery?

"The police might want to talk to you," I said. "The man got into some trouble." Benicio might be able to get him out of it.

"What kind of trouble?" Benicio asked.

I figured the specifics would be best addressed by Detective Pearce. I left it at "Serious trouble."

While Benicio returned to the kitchen, I handed my credit card to the maître d' and sent a text to Detective Pearce with the relevant information while he ran it through the machine. A moment later, the detective replied with the thumbs-up emoji and, a moment after that, the phone behind the bar rang.

The maître d' picked up the receiver. "Bar Celona," he said as he returned my card. He used his shoulder to hold the phone in place as he handed me a ballpoint pen and the receipt to sign. "How may I help you?" After a short pause to listen, he looked my way and said, "Yes, she told us you might be in touch. Of course, you may come now. We close soon, but Benicio and I will wait for you."

He ended the call as I scrawled my name on the receipt. I separated the two copies and handed the restaurant's copy to him. As I did, a blonde walked up behind the bar. Our eyes met. Hers squinted slightly, as if she was trying to place me. But I didn't need to squint to remember who she was. She wore pretty pink shimmering lipstick and a loose, long-sleeved peasant blouse with elastic around the wrists. *Ashlynn.* Looked like she'd landed the job.

She grabbed a bottle of wine and walked off without greeting me. As soon as she was gone, I leaned in to the maître d' and whispered, "Check her sleeves."

He glanced her way before returning his gaze to me. "You know something?"

Rather than risk a slander lawsuit myself, I said, "Ask the detective when she arrives. She'll fill you in."

He gave me a discreet nod.

Remembering how Ashlynn had gone after Miranda, and knowing she was still a suspect in Cormac's murder, I said, "Don't tell her I said anything, okay?"

He gave me a nearly imperceptible nod. "Thank you," he said loudly. "Please come again."

I picked up my bag and went out the door. I knew I'd left a thief behind. But had I left a killer, too?

Chapter Twenty-One

After dropping my grandfather off, I motored over to Kate and Parker's house in the Chattanooga suburb of Red Bank. It was nearly ten o'clock by then. If the lights were out in the house, I wouldn't wake them. I'd bring them food another time and share the tapas with Kiki instead.

Fortunately, as I rolled up on their classic single-story, wood frame home, I discovered that the lights in the kitchen and living room were still on. *Good.* I parked in their drive-way, told Smoky I'd be back in just a minute, and grabbed the bag of food. As I made my way up the three steps to their porch, my ears detected the sound of a baby wailing inside. Looked like Dalton Prescott wasn't happy about something.

I raised a hand and rapped on the door. My ears detected the faint sound of footsteps approaching the door. There was a silent pause as Kate probably checked the peephole to see who had come to their place at this late hour. Her muffled voice came through the door. "Hattie!"

The door opened and there stood Kate in a wrinkled T-shirt and stretchy maternity pants, her tummy not having yet retreated back into place. Purple half circles underscored her eyes and her hair was a rat's nest, but she looked happier than I'd ever seen her. Motherhood clearly suited her. She gave me a sincere, if weary, smile.

"Sorry to come so late." I held up the bag. "I brought y'all some tapas from that new place downtown. I figured you could have it for dinner tomorrow." After all, it was far past dinnertime tonight.

Kate snatched the bag out of my hand, opened it, and peeked inside. "This food smells divine!" She pulled out the tortilla española and began eating it with her hands, tearing pieces off and shoving them into her mouth as fast as she could chew.

"Everything okay?" I asked.

"Yes," she said. "Just starving! All we had for dinner was saltines."

Parker peeked out of the baby's room down the hall behind her. "Hey, Hattie!" he called.

I raised a hand in hello. "I brought you dinner."

"What?" he hollered, cupping a hand around his ear, unable to hear over the baby's cries.

I pointed to the bag in Kate's hand and mimed putting food in my mouth.

Momentarily forgetting his fatherly duties, he hurried to the door, peeked into the bag, and moaned in joy. "I've never been so happy to see you!"

"Um . . . thanks?"

He, too, had bags under his eyes, and looked as if he could use a shower, a shave, and a seven-hour nap. "We haven't had a free second since we brought the baby home last night. How can something so little that sleeps all day take up so much of our time?" The smile on his face told me that despite his words, he was happy to make any sacrifice required for his little boy.

Though I'd only intended to drop off the food and go, now that I knew they were still up and could use some help, I said, "Why don't I tend to Dalton for a few minutes while you two sit down and eat like civilized people?"

Kate threw her arms around me. "You're a godsend."

While the two of them headed for their kitchen, I brought Smoky in from the van, then walked down the hall to the nursery. Dalton lay on his back in the crib, his mouth wide open and his tongue vibrating as if he were an opera star singing an aria or the lead vocalist in a screamo punk band. Maybe Dalton would grow up to be the next Luciano Pavarotti.

I reached over the top of the crib and stroked his soft cheek, much as I stroked Smoky's. At least I didn't have to worry about the baby suddenly turning his head and sinking his fangs into my hand. He didn't have any teeth yet. "Hey, sweet baby. Why are you fighting sleep? It's a good thing." Funny how children fought to stay awake and adults sought any opportunity to sneak a nap in.

Dalton seemed to like the cheek strokes, so I figured I'd see whether he enjoyed another of Smoky's favorites, the ear rub. I ran my thumb over the shell of his teeny ear. He quieted a bit and seemed to lean into my hand, just like Smoky did when I stroked his ear.

I figured I should sing the baby a lullaby, but as I mulled over my options, I realized I couldn't recall all the words to any of them. I could get as far as the diamond ring in "Hush, Little Baby," but that's about it. I opted for singing him a soft, slowed-down version of the bluegrass classic "Rocky Top." The old standard was included in the soundtrack I played at my shop, and I'd heard it at least once a day, every day, since the shop had opened. Of course, with my granny and granddaddy being bluegrass fans, I'd been hearing the song all my life.

Blinking in the dim illumination supplied by the night light, Dalton looked up at me with his unfocused, brand-new baby eyes, as if interested in this strange sound he was hearing. Thank goodness he wasn't old enough yet to real-ize what a terrible singing voice I had. As I continued to sing, his squalling diminished to hiccuping gulps and cat-like mews. His wriggling slowed, too. *What do you know?* The song was working. When I came to the part about people getting their corn from a jar, I booped Dalton gently on the nose. His blinks became longer and longer, his eyes barely opening between them. He heaved a big shuddering breath as he teetered on the edge of awake and asleep. By the end of the song, he'd succumbed to my tactics. I felt a surge of pride. *I'm pretty good at this baby stuff.*

Leaving the little guy to his sweet dreams, I went to the kitchen and found Kate and Parker at the dinette making quick work of the takeout.

Kate looked up. "You got him to sleep so soon? You must have a knack with babies."

As she took a big bite of the paella, I shrugged. "I just did the same things I do to calm Smoky down. Stroke his cheek and rub his ears. I'm pretty sure I heard Dalton purr."

She took a sip of her drink. "What's going on with the murder investigation? Is it moving along?"

"It's hard to tell," I said. "The evidence points in a lot of different directions." Of course, much of it pointed directly at me. "The Moonshine Shack is moving along nicely, though. I'm working with the woman who took over Lim-ericks. We plan to cohost some events at the bar to feature my moonshine. Ladies' night and a full-moon special, too."

"What a great idea," she said. "Be sure to let me know once they're scheduled. I could use a girls' night, especially now that I'm outnumbered two to one by boys here at home."

"Hey!" Parker cried, smiling.

"Speaking of boys," Kate said, turning back to me, "what's happening with that hunky cop?"

"Hey!" Parker cried again.

"Don't worry," Kate said. "You're still a hunk, too."

He placed his palms on his abs. "I don't know. Feels like I'm starting to develop 'dad bod.'"

A smile claimed my face. "We've got a date planned."

"Really?" she said. "When?"

"As soon as the murder investigation is over. We're going to dinner."

Parker took a sip of his drink. "What if it's never solved?" he teased. "What if it becomes a cold case?"

I brandished my fork at him. "What if you shut your mouth?"

"Well, I hope they catch the killer very soon," Kate said. "You've been in a slump."

She wasn't wrong.

A half hour later, I bade them goodbye. They deserved a moment to themselves and, heck, I was nearly as tired as Dalton. If only I had someone to stroke my cheek and rub my ears as I fell asleep.

The sound of my phone blaring "Good Old Mountain Dew" jerked me awake at the crack of dawn Thursday morning. Groaning and groggy, I reached over to the nightstand to retrieve my phone before it could wake Kiki. The screen indicated it was Ace calling. On seeing her name, my brain jolted wide awake. *She'd gone to Bar Celona with the intention of eliminating Damien Sirakov as a suspect, but had she learned something about Ashlynn while she was there? Could she be calling to tell me that she'd arrested Ashlynn last night? Could this nightmare finally be over?*

I tapped the screen to take the call, sat up, and put the phone to my ear. "Good morning," I croaked, my larynx still rusty from sleep.

Without preamble, she said, "There's a problem at your shop."

Panic seized me. *Could there be another body on the doorstep of the Moonshine Shack?* I croaked again, this time from terror. "What is it?"

"Nothing a squeegee and some glass cleaner can't handle."

While she probably intended her words to be comforting, the crime scene team had likely used the same tools to clean up after Cormac's murder, along with a mop bucket. For all I knew, she could be telling me there was, in fact, another person cut to pieces in front of my shop. "I'll be right there."

Forgoing a shower and makeup, I splashed water on my face, brushed my teeth, and leaped into a fresh pair of overalls and Firefly shine T-shirt. I opened a can of wet food for Smoky and dumped it into his bowl, not taking the time to loosen it with a fork like usual.

Kiki cracked the door to her bedroom and peeked out, her two cats peeking out around her ankles. "Something wrong?"

"Ace called. She said something happened at my shop."

Kiki's eyes went wide and so did her door. "What was it?"

"She didn't specify." I grabbed my purse and dug out my keys. "She only said it was something that could be handled with glass cleaner and a squeegee."

Kiki's wide eyes went squinty now. "What does that mean?"

"I'll let you know as soon as I find out."

"I'm going with you."

I didn't argue. For one thing, Kiki was stubborn and I knew it would do no good. For another, I could use the moral support and possibly the help, too. *All the moonshine in the world couldn't buy a friend like Kiki.*

Kiki slipped out of her pajamas and into yoga pants and a T-shirt with the swiftness and grace of a Tony Award–winning Broadway star facing a quick costume change. Smoky stood directly in front of the door, letting us know that wherever we were going, he was going, too, breakfast be darned. Rather than try to maneuver around him and risk a nip on the ankle or a swipe of claws on my calf, I scooped him into his carrier. Cat in hand, I hustled out the door and down to my van, sliding his carrier into its spot between the seats. Kiki was swept along in my wake.

I ignored the speed limits on my drive to the shop. The roads were still clear this early in the morning, and I figured if a cop pulled us over, I could play the Ace card and tell the officer I was on my way to meet the detective. Surely that would earn me immunity on any traffic infraction. Kiki held on for dear life as I took a corner too fast and my van leaned precariously to the left, the tires squealing.

I parked in back of my store, hopped out, and grabbed Smoky's carrier, scrambling to get inside. Kiki rushed in after me. After disarming the alarm at the back door in the stockroom, I set the carrier down, freed its feline inmate, and rushed into the salesroom.

The morning sun bathed the space in an odd, pink glow. I looked to the front of my shop. The window glass was rendered nearly opaque by illegible scrawls and scribbles.

Kiki stepped up beside me, her mouth gaping. "What the bloody heck is that?"

Smoky strode up to stand between us, his tail swishing. He, too, could tell something was wrong here.

Through the small, still-clean spaces, I could see two uniformed police officers standing out front alongside Ace.

Kiki said, "I'll get the cleaning supplies while you talk to the cops."

I unlocked the front door and walked out to meet Ace on the sidewalk. Flanking her were Officer Barboza and his younger partner.

Officer Barboza pointed to the windows. "Somebody doesn't like you much."

I turned around and gasped. From this side, the scribbling was legible. The foulest and ugliest of words were scrawled across the glass in a shimmery shade of pink lipstick, like glamorous graffiti. I spat out the name of the culprit as if it were a bug in my mouth. "Ashlynn." I turned to Ace. "Did you see her at Bar Celona last night?"

She shook her head. "By the time I got there, she was gone."

"Her shift ended?"

"No," Ace said. "She'd been fired. The owner found eighty dollars up her sleeve."

"Up to her old tricks, huh?" *Just as I'd suspected.*

"She'd gotten away with it before. I suppose she figured she could do it again."

I gestured at the window. "This is her lipstick."

"I figured as much," she said. "That woman has serious anger management issues and no self-control. I'm heading to her apartment to arrest her once I leave here."

Hope welled up in me. "For Cormac's murder?"

"Just this vandalism for now. But I'll see what else I can

wheedle out of her. Maybe she'll slip up and admit something."

I shifted my focus from the woman to the windows. It
was hard enough to wipe lipstick off skin. It would be a
bear to clean it off the glass. I let out a loud sigh.

"You can get started on the cleaning," Ace said as she
turned and headed to her Impala at the curb. "We've already taken all the photos we need."

With that, she climbed into her car, backed out of the
space, and drove off. The two officers followed suit, loading into their squad car and heading out.

Kiki exited my shop, cleaning rags and glass cleaner in
one hand, a bucket of soapy water and a squeegee in the
other. She ran her eyes over the windows. "Looks like you
got a visit from the potty-mouth fairy last night."

"It was Ashlynn," I said. "It had to be. That's her shade
of lipstick."

Kiki stepped closer. "It's pretty. Has a nice iridescence
to it." She turned to me. "Any idea what kind it is?"

"No," I said, "but I've been wanting to find out."

We set about cleaning the windows. After some trial and
error, we realized the best process was for me to wipe off
as much as I could with the spray cleaner and a rag, and
Kiki to follow after me with the soapy squeegee to remove
any remaining smudges. Inside the window, Smoky chased
my hand and the squeegee as if it were some sort of game,
jumping up to put his paws on the interior of the glass. *At
least one of us is finding this fun.*

We were still at it an hour later when Detective Pearce
pulled her Impala sideways across three open spaces at the
curb and lowered her window.

I stepped up to her car. "Did you get her?"

She held up an evidence bag with a black rectangular

lipstick tube inside. "I got her. She's in lockup at the station as we speak. I told her we found her DNA in the lipstick on your window. She believed me, broke down in tears, and confessed. She still doesn't know about the security cameras at Limericks. She thinks you knew her sleeve trick because you saw her steal some cash when you tried to deliver the moonshine order to Cormac. She figured you didn't tell him that you saw her steal because you were angry with him for not accepting the order." Her eyes flashed with mischief. "We're going to let her keep thinking that for now, okay?"

"Sure. Any chance she confessed to Cormac's murder?"

"Not yet," the detective said. "I'm working on it."

I gestured to the bag in her hand. "Mind telling me what kind of lipstick that is?"

"Nice shade, isn't it?"

"Very nice. I think it could work for me."

She ran her gaze over my face, assessing. "I think it could, too." She manipulated the bag so she could read the bottom of the tube. "The brand is Chantecaille. The shade is called Honeypot."

I whipped out my phone and worked my fingers. "Whoa. That lipstick retails for forty-eight dollars a tube."

Ace scoffed. "No wonder she was skimming from the till." With that, she lifted her hand from the steering wheel in a goodbye gesture, took her foot off the brake, and eased away from the curb. With any luck, she'd be back in touch with me soon with some good news.

Chapter Twenty-Two

My hopes that Ace would contact me with good news were soon dashed. In fact, when she contacted me Friday afternoon, she had only bad news to give me.

Despite a lengthy and heated interrogation, Ashlynn continued to insist she had nothing to do with Cormac's murder. Her act of vandalism at the Moonshine Shack gave the police the right to search her car and apartment, but they'd found nothing linking her to his death. *Was it too much to ask that she'd kept a diary in which she'd confessed to ending the life of her boss and boyfriend?*

What's more, Ace had learned precious little in her interview with Gage Tilley. "He told me that Cormac had ordered such a large quantity of moonshine for two reasons. The first was that he planned to start hosting a Monday Moonshine night every week. He'd hoped to draw some of your customers away, cut into your profits, maybe put you out of business."

That rat! I wondered if Cormac had gotten the idea from the lasses' night I'd proposed to him. I found myself wishing that Mack Clayton had gotten some traction with his proposed boycott of Limericks and the price-fixing scheme, after all. I'd previously thought the idea had seemed overly harsh and vengeful, but I'd been naïve, hadn't I? "What was the second reason?"

"An upcoming motorcycle rally. Tilley said that Cormac told him to leave the other five cases of moonshine outside, by the back door of Limericks. Cormac said he needed to set them aside to make sure he'd have enough on hand for the event. He planned to store them off-site somewhere. Cormac said the rally was going to involve a poker run. The bikers stop at five locations, get a card at each stop, and build a hand. Best hand at the end of the night wins some sort of prize. Anyway, Cormac said he was making arrangements with the rally organizer for Limericks to be the final stop of the poker run. He expected a large group of bikers to gather at the bar."

"Were you able to verify that information?"

"Not yet," she said. "I ran a search of Cormac's e-mails and texts, but nothing popped up when I searched for 'rally' or 'poker.' The words 'motorcycle' and 'biker' got me nothing, too."

"Do you think Cormac was lying to Tilley?"

"Hard to say," she said. "Could be Cormac was in touch with the organizer by phone, or maybe even in person. I don't see why he'd lie about it. That said, I've looked online. There's a number of rallies coming up throughout Tennessee and Georgia but none in the immediate vicinity. I don't know how far these folks travel for these poker runs, but my assumption is that they'd want their final stop to be somewhere near the rally's base location since that's where they'd have their accommodations."

In other words, Cormac's story had some loose ends remaining to be tied up. "Maybe he got crosswise with someone from the rally."

"It's possible," she said, "but I've spoken with Ashlynn, Isabella, and Miranda since I talked with Tilley, and none of them were aware that Cormac was working on a biker rally event. Seems like Cormac would have mentioned it, or that they would have overheard something."

"He might not have said anything if the details hadn't been nailed down yet," I suggested, "and if he'd had discussions on his phone in his office with his door closed, they might not be aware what was going on."

"Unfortunately," Ace said, "*if*s aren't evidence. They're conjecture. What I need are some cold, hard clues."

"There's nothing useful on his phone? Maybe a contact?"

"Nope. None of his contacts are associated with a motorcycle organization, and there were no recent calls to or from anyone involved in a rally."

I remembered Cormac's slander complaint against Heath Delaney with the Board of Professional Responsibility, how Cormac had listed Gage Tilley as a witness. I raised the matter with the detective. "What did Gage Tilley say about the slander case?"

"Not much," she replied. "He said Cormac hadn't mentioned filing a complaint and that he knew nothing whatsoever about the situation. He had no idea who Heath Delaney was, or that Cormac had even had a new dishwasher installed."

I mulled this information over. Heath Delaney was likely right when he said the slander complaint was nothing more than a nuisance case. Cormac had probably filed it as an act of retribution against the attorney, or in the hopes Heath would cough up some money for a settlement. Maybe Cormac had named Gage Tilley as a witness as a bluff. A third party like Gage Tilley who was not employed by Cormac would make a stronger witness, and thus a bigger threat, than someone on Cormac's staff.

"Did Tilley say why he was at Limericks the night Cormac was killed? If he made a large delivery earlier in the week and collected a cash payment on delivery, what reason would he have had to return to the pub so soon?"

"Tilley told me nature called. He said the only places open that late at night where he could use the facilities were bars or gas stations, and you know how gas station facilities can be. When he stopped at Limericks to use the men's room, he took advantage of the opportunity to check in with Cormac. Cormac invited him back to his office and offered him a drink. Tilley said he declined because he was on duty and driving the company truck, and it was against policy. They shot the breeze for a minute or two, but he'd had a long day and begged off to return to his hotel. He said he didn't notice anyone suspicious in the bar or hanging around outside when he left."

"Did he seem credible?"

"Hard to say. He seemed a little nervous, but that's normal. Most people get a bit jittery when being interviewed by police."

It was understandable, especially given that the case involved a major crime rather than some petty offense. Heck, I'd been nervous, too, during my initial interrogations by Officer Barboza and Ace.

Before I could respond, she added, "My mind keeps going back to the missing Backwoods Bootleggers moonshine. Those bottles have to be somewhere, and my intuition tells me if we find the Backwoods bottles, we'll find our killer."

But where in the world could those bottles be?

A customer entered the Moonshine Shack, and I concluded the conversation. I only wished we'd been able to reach some conclusions where Cormac O'Keefe's murder was concerned.

The remainder of Friday was uneventful, and Saturday proved to be equally routine. Nobody came into my shop to confront me about wrongfully fingering them for a murder, and nobody cast aspersions on my character via messages in lipstick inscribed on my shop's windows.

The open sign illuminated in the window of the Tipperary Tavern at five o'clock each afternoon, and Miranda was proving to be an industrious and responsible business owner. She came over to show me some promotional napkins she'd ordered for the full moon moonshine nights. They featured a big white moon and the name of her tavern, along with the words *Full Moon Celebration Featuring Firefly Moonshine!* She gave me a broad smile. "Remember the text that came in when you were at the bar? This was the shipment it referred to. I was pricing custom-printed napkins to see if I could afford them. I tried to hide the message so you'd be surprised."

I was surprised, all right. Of course, at the time, I'd been suspicious. "They're perfect!" I told her.

She said she'd check a calendar and get back to me with the dates on which there'd be a full moon. "I'll need lots of your shine."

"You got it!"

A trio of bikers visited the pub shortly after opening on Saturday, staying inside for about an hour. Around eight o'clock, I spotted a group of boys enter the Tipperary Tavern. All wore shirts embossed with the letters for the Mu

Sigma fraternity. None appeared to be Tristan, Dane, or any of the other three boys who'd come into my store the night Cormac had been killed. The frat boys remained in the pub when Kiki and I turned out the lights outside the Moonshine Shack and closed up for the night. Kiki's boyfriend picked her up at the curb so they could catch a late movie. She waved from the passenger seat as they drove off.

After leaving the shop, Smoky and I aimed for the cabin. It was already late evening and fully dark, and there wasn't time to wash, dry, and fold all of my laundry before bedtime tonight. Even if there had been sufficient time to handle the laundry, the thought of being in my secluded cabin alone at night with Cormac O'Keefe's killer still on the loose held little appeal. The sounds of the washer and dryer might mask the sounds of an intruder. Nonetheless, I had no choice but to make a quick run by the cabin to round up some fresh clothing. My undergarment situation had become dire. I'd put on my last clean pair of undies and socks this morning. I'd come back to the cabin in the morning to do my laundry.

My mouth spread in a wide yawn as I drove past the Bridge Liquor Outlet on the outskirts of the riverfront area, my eyes closing as my mouth opened. The store was named for its proximity to the Market Street Bridge, also known as the John Ross Bridge, a quaint blue drawbridge that connected downtown Chattanooga to the Northshore commercial area. If my yawn had been any longer, I might have missed the Backwoods Bootleggers box truck easing its way between the liquor store and the pizza place next door. *It has to be Gage Tilley's truck, doesn't it?* After all, he was the moonshine company's sales rep for the area. He was likely making a delivery.

An uneasy feeling niggled at me. Maybe it was only

because I was about to drive alone up the dark and curvy mountainside road to my secluded cabin. Or maybe there was something my subconscious wasn't telling me, something about Gage Tilley. *But what?*

"Let's see what he's up to," I told Smoky as I turned in to the adjacent pizza restaurant. Smoky rose from his haunches inside his cage, a rare expression of interest in my conversation. Or perhaps he was experiencing some sort of feline intuition and sensed the night was about to get more interesting.

Fortunately, there was an open parking space between a minivan and a crew-cab pickup truck with a camper shell on the back. My glow-in-the-dark van would be obscured from view when Gage left the liquor store.

I stuck my finger through the bars of Smoky's carrier to give him a nose boop. "I'll be right back, boy. Behave yourself."

He cast me a contemptuous look that said, *Exactly what kind of trouble do you think I can get into stuck in this cage?*

I climbed out of my van and circled around the far side of the pizza parlor on foot to peek into the alleyway. Though it was dark where I stood, the floodlights on the back corners of the liquor store bathed the area behind it in bright light. Gage climbed out of his truck and walked around to the back doors. He was too far away for me to see much and definitely too far for me to hear anything, especially with the noise coming from the pizza restaurant's kitchen and the traffic noise from the street.

Three large, overflowing dumpsters stood along the back of the alley, their lids open like gaping maws, spewing forth trash, half-eaten pieces of pizza, and random raw salad vegetables slathered in dressing. *If I can get behind the bins, I can sneak closer, unseen.* Their rancid, repulsive funk had me debating the task, but I'd already come this far. *In for a penny . . .*

I pulled the neck of my T-shirt up over my mouth and nose like a mask, which helped filter out the odor. Hunching down, I skittered forward in the shadows until I was behind the nearest bin. Slowly and silently, I eased behind the line of dumpsters, closing in on Gage Tilley. When I reached the last one, I was only a dozen feet from the rear doors of the Backwoods Bootleggers truck. I crouched down and picked up a used, sauce-stained pizza box that had fallen behind the bin. After poking a peephole in the box with the key to my van, I shielded myself from view behind the box, and watched through the hole, safely disguised as garbage.

Tilley unlocked the truck's cargo bay and opened the door on the right. Numerous cartons of Backwoods Bootleggers moonshine were stacked, two high near the back and three high farther in, closer to the cab. The cartons in the center were large, the preprinted count on the lower corner of the box indicating they each contained twelve bottles. The cartons stacked along the outside edges were smaller, the count indicating that they held only six bottles each. Large white labels had been affixed to the tops and sides of the cartons. The labels were printed with the customer's name and delivery address, as well as a bar code to allow the company to better track the inventory. To make things easier on the busy delivery drivers, the company's warehouse had printed the labels in all capital letters and a large font so that boxes could be quickly identified. If I squinted, I could read some of the labels from here. *SOUTHSIDE SPIRITS. DRINKER'S DEPOT.* Heck, one of the smaller cartons was destined for *BAR CELONA.* Maybe Tilley was headed to the tapas bar next.

Tilley reached down to release the security bar on the left door and swung it open. Three large cartons stood in a row along the back, separate from the others that had been pushed farther in. When I spotted the name on the labels, I gasped. All three read *LIMERICKS*. *Could these be the cases of liquor missing from the pub's inventory?*

Chapter Twenty-Three

Tilley stiffened and his head turned slightly, as if he might have heard my sudden intake of breath. When the night breeze carried with it only the sounds of pop music and the kitchen staff clanging pizza pans next door, he seemed to be satisfied he'd been mistaken. He pulled a manila file envelope out from between a carton and the interior wall of the truck. He opened it and removed a stack of white labels that were paper-clipped together. Sliding one of the cartons to the edge of the tailgate, he carefully affixed new labels over the stickers bearing the Limericks name, fully obscuring them.

I narrowed my eyes again. Though the replacement stickers closely resembled those on the boxes destined for other outlets, they weren't exactly the same. These stickers had sharp, squared-off corners, while the original labels had curved corners. The print was thicker, too, as if in boldface type. The size of the bar code on these labels was also different, slightly larger.

Are these labels fakes? Is Gage Tilley reselling the liquor he'd purportedly sold to Limericks? Did he kill Cormac to steal this liquor for resale, or could the two of them have been in cahoots somehow? Was I totally off base? Could Cormac have placed another order that had been canceled after he'd been killed? Maybe these cartons had been part of that order and had never been delivered. *But why not relabel them at the Backwoods Bootleggers warehouse rather than here at the delivery truck?*

I had no answers to these questions, but I did have a cell phone camera. While Tilley lowered the box to the ground, I snapped several photos of the cartons with the Limericks labels. He closed the doors to his truck and locked them again before picking up the carton at his feet and carrying it to the back door of the liquor store. His arms burdened with the heavy box, he turned sideways and used his elbow to push a doorbell-like buzzer next to the wide delivery door before taking a step back to wait.

A moment later, a woman opened the back door of the liquor store. She greeted him with a gravelly, "Hey, Tilley."

Gage lifted the carton a few inches. "Got your moonshine."

"Then I've got your cash. Come on in." She stepped back to allow Gage to enter. The door swung closed behind him.

I continued to lie in wait—or rather, to crouch in wait. My thigh and calf muscles burned, screaming for mercy. When I could take it no more, I straightened and stood, easing back so that I was fully behind the dumpster. A minute or so later, I heard the back door open again and the sound of footsteps. Crouching again, I peered through the hole in the pizza box to see Gage Tilley come out of the back door of the liquor store, several bills clutched in his hand. He cast a glance back at the door, as if making sure it was fully closed, before he pulled his wallet from his back pocket and slid the cash into it.

He climbed into his truck and started the engine, spewing exhaust in my direction. *Lovely. As if the garbage smell hadn't been enough to deal with.* The truck rumbled as it moved forward. He turned at the far end of the building. Waving the exhaust out of my face, I shifted my focus to the space between the buildings. A moment later, through the wide gap, I saw the Backwoods Bootleggers truck drive past. It paused in its acceleration for a brief moment, the brake lights illuminating. It was too dark for me to see into the cab, so I couldn't tell if Guge Tilley had fumbled the controls, but he promptly pushed the gas again and rumbled off. Maybe he'd slowed for another car or someone in the street. From my vantage point behind the building it was impossible for me to tell.

I counted to one hundred to give Gage time to put some distance between us before coming out from behind the dumpsters. As I passed the back doors to the kitchen of the pizza place, they burst open and a teenaged boy with braces and gangly limbs came out, dragging a trash bag. He stopped when he saw me, his face contorted in question.

Thankfully, my brain cells produced a quick excuse for my appearance in the private alley. "I saw a stray cat run back here," I lied, raising my palms. "No sign of him now."

He wrapped his hand around the top of the garbage bag and swung it, slinging it up on top of the pile. His task completed, he brushed his hands off and said, "He was probably chasing a mouse. We get a lot of them. Roaches, too."

I made a mental note never to order a pizza from this place and flounced down the alley.

When I circled around to the front of the building, my first thought was *uh-oh*. The pickup that had been parked next to my van was gone. The side of my van with the Fire-fly moonshine logo was in full view. But at least with the bright lights of the liquor store and pizza parlor, the glow-in-the-dark paint wasn't quite as obvious. *Had Gage Tilley noticed my van here? Was that why he'd braked? Or was it just a coincidence?*

Though my first reaction had been concern, I realized there was no real cause for alarm, right? Even if Gage Til-ley was up to something and had seen my van, both of which I wasn't even sure of, he'd just assume I was getting a pizza with family or friends. The fact that I'd be at a res-taurant not far from my shop after closing time shouldn't be surprising.

I continued to my van, climbed in, and turned to Smoky. "Did you miss me?"

He appeared to roll his eyes. I was pretty sure he knew exactly what the expression meant, too.

I pulled my phone from my pocket and composed a text to Marlon, despite his earlier admonishment that I should stop sticking my nose where it didn't belong. He might get angry, but I'd have to take that chance. What I'd just wit-nessed could be important. Just saw Gage Tilley making a delivery at Bridge Liquor Outlet. Noticed boxes in his truck bay with Limericks' name and address. He put a new label on the box before making the delivery and put the cash they gave him into his wallet. Could this mean something? I sent the text to him, along with the photos I'd taken.

After sliding my phone into the cupholder, I drove out of the parking lot and aimed for my mountain cabin. Once I'd cleared the city, I rolled the windows down to enjoy the fresh evening air. It had only been a matter of days since I'd been home, but it felt like forever. I missed sitting on the porch swing with a book in one hand and a glass of spiked lemonade in the other. I missed working in the flowerbeds and yard, trimming my granny's rosebushes and pulling off the kudzu that threatened to cover my great-grandfather's rusty old still. I missed sleeping in my own bed. *How much longer until this darn case is closed?*

My phone burst into song at full volume and vibrated so hard in the cupholder it nearly jumped out. I, too, nearly jumped out of my skin. I eyed the screen. Marlon was calling. With no traffic around on the dark, quiet road, I was able to slow to a near stop and safely jab the button to accept the call. I jabbed a second button to put him on speaker before pressing lightly on the gas again.

Marlon didn't wait for a greeting before he said, "How did you get those photos?"

He'd be none too happy to learn that I'd been hiding behind a garbage dumpster, but he'd be even less happy if I lied to him. I opted for the lesser of two evils and told him the truth. "I was behind a garbage bin in the alley."

"You followed Tilley?"

"Not exactly," I said. "I just happened to see him pull his truck behind the liquor store on my way to my cabin."

"Your cabin?" Marlon said. "Why are you going there?"

It would be too humiliating to tell him I was out of clean panties, so instead I said, "Kiki's washing machine broke. I'm just going to run by my place and get some clean clothes, then I'll head over to her condo for the night."

"Tilley didn't see you, did he? Please tell me he wasn't aware that you'd followed him."

"No," I said, "he didn't see me." I cringed as I admitted the next bit. "But there's a chance that he might have seen my van parked at the pizza place next door to the liquor store."

Marlon muttered something that could have been a curse. "Didn't I tell you not to put yourself at risk?"

"You did," I said, "and I didn't."

Marlon huffed a loud breath that told me he disagreed with my risk assessment. "Where are you now?"

"Halfway up the mountain." Headlights flashed in my rearview mirror, high beams. Looked like someone else was coming up the mountain, too. The lights disappeared as I negotiated a hairpin turn.

"Ace is on her way to the liquor store to check out the carton and see if the label that Tilley covered up means anything."

"She thinks it might?"

"She does," Marlon said. "She didn't feel that Gage Tilley's excuse for being at Limericks the night Cormac was killed made much sense. His hotel was only a few blocks away. Why not head back there if he needed to use the facilities? Besides, he'd delivered Cormac's order only a few days before. Seemed awfully soon to stop by and check in with a customer."

We'd originally suspected that Cormac had bought the discounted liquor to sell, not poured into drinks but in unopened, intact bottles. But now I wondered if Gage might be involved in some sort of scheme. *Had he been the mastermind all along?* "Something weird is going on here."

"I'm coming after you," Marlon said. "I'm on my way now. I'll escort you back to Kiki's. I don't want you up there alone at your cabin."

The thought of Marlon up at the cabin with me, just the two of us, sent a thrill up my spine. But that thrill was quickly replaced by a chill. The headlights I'd seen a moment ago were gaining on me now, and gaining fast. The speed of the vehicle was too high for these windy roads.

The vehicle was right on my tail now, the bright beams reflecting in my rearview and side mirrors. The light nearly blinded me, making it difficult to see the road ahead. The fact that the driver didn't switch to low beams told me I was in serious trouble here.

"Marlon!" I squeaked as the bright beams shone through the back windows and lit up the inside of my van. "I'm being follow—"

BANG!

Chapter Twenty-Four

The force of the impact nearly gave me whiplash and sent my van surging forward on the winding road. Any doubt I'd had about whether I'd been followed disappeared the instant the front bumper of the vehicle behind me struck the back bumper of my van. I yelped in terror.

Marlon's voice came through the speaker. "What was that noise?"

My heart, stomach, and lungs had gathered in my throat, choking me. I couldn't respond. I punched the gas and veered around a curve on two squealing wheels, the bend in the road giving me a brief reprieve as the lights angled away. I glanced back over my shoulder at my pursuer. It was a bright red truck painted with the Backwoods Bootleggers logo.

"Hattie!" Marlon hollered through the phone. "Are you okay?"

I tried to shout *Yes*, to let him know I wasn't hurt, but I

couldn't get the word out. It was just as well, because an
instant later I *wasn't* okay. An instant later, the truck pulled
to the left, rammed into my driver's-side rear quarter panel,
and sent my van spinning across the road like a top. My
seat belt pulled taut, but still I swayed right and left as the
van revolved. Smoky crouched in his carrier, his claws
scritch-scritch-scritching as he slid back and forth inside,
unable to dig into the plastic bottom of the carrier and gain
purchase as the carrier, too, slid back and forth in the van.

My mind whirled as I tried to remember what my father
had taught me to do if I ever hit ice on the road. *Turn into
the spin!* It seemed counterintuitive, but it was the quickest
way to regain traction.

By the time I could process the situation and yank the
wheel in the right direction, it was too late. This spinning top
had gone topsy-turvy, as tops tend to do when losing momen-
tum. I felt the van lean and, next thing I knew, we were upside down, then right side up, then upside down again. My
laundry flew about inside the van as if being tossed about
inside a clothes dryer. Glass joined in with the clothing as the
windshield and windows shattered from the impact. The air-
bags deployed with an explosive sound—*POOM!*—pinning
me to my seat for a second or two until they began to deflate.
Without a seat belt or airbag to hold his carrier in place, my
poor cat was tossed, too. *HISS! RROWRRR!* Smoky's carrier
ricocheted off the inside walls of the van until the force bent
it enough that it fell to pieces.

The van came to a stop roughly on its roof, the headlights illuminating the trunks of trees in the forest in front
of me as I hung upside down inside the vehicle like a vam-
pire bat. My curls bounced below my head and blood
rushed to my face, making it feel hot and swollen. I turned
around to look for my cat among the mess of clothing and

broken glass behind me. *There he is! He's alive!* Smoky's wide eyes sparked with fear.

"Come here, boy!" As I reached out for him, he jumped past me, bounced off the hood of the van, and ran off through the beams, my pink polka-dot bra wrapped around his neck. "Nooooo!" I screamed. Seconds later, Smoky disappeared into the dark woods.

While I'd been terrified a moment before, a hot rage consumed me now. *Gage Tilley will pay for this!* That sorry son of a biscuit had frightened my cat, and now I might never find my beloved pet in these woods.

I reached up one hand to leverage myself against the ceiling of my van and unfastened my seat belt, half falling, half lowering myself down. I dropped to all fours and crawled out through the broken windshield. A second set of headlights intersected the ones from my van. Looked like Tilley had crashed, too, probably in an attempt to avoid my spinning van. A towering pine was encased in his front bumper. *Is it too much to hope that he was rendered immobile by the crash?*

No such luck. He fought his airbag back and slid out of his truck as I grabbed a low branch to pull myself to a stand. In his hands was a large object with metal bars welded into a crisscross pattern, what I recognized as a four-way lug wrench. But while the tool might be intended to remove lug nuts from truck wheels, I suspected Tilley's intention now was to use the tool to remove my life from my body.

I ran into the woods in the direction that Smoky had gone so that I could scoop him up if I came across him. It was away from Gage Tilley and seemed as good a direction as any. Unfortunately, it's not easy to run quietly through the woods, especially at night. Fireflies flashed in front of me and to the sides, like airplane marshalers on a runway trying to show me the way, lighting up an escape route.

A sizzling sound came from behind me and a pinkish-orange flame lit up the woods like a portal to hell. I looked over my shoulder to see Tilley coming after me, brandishing the lug wrench in his left hand, a blazing road flare in his right.

Crackle! Pop! Rustle! Snap! Crack! The woods exploded in sound as I pushed onward, my elbows crooked and arms splayed in front of me as I shoved my way through thick brush and low limbs while trying to protect my eyes. The brush scratched my arms and face, but I hardly felt it. I reached a tall, fallen tree that had landed on a berm, leaving a couple feet of clearance underneath a stretch of its trunk. My small stature gave me an advantage, much as it had when I'd played the limbo game at childhood birthday parties. Barely breaking stride, I ducked under the tree and was on my way once again.

My eyes caught a glimpse of something light-colored up ahead. Though Smoky was too dark for me to make out, I could see my pink bra bouncing through the woods. *My cat must be moving with it.*

"Smoky!" I called. "Stop!"

With my brassiere wrapped around him, Smoky's speed was hindered. I caught up to him and reached out to grab him. But just when I thought I had him, he leaped up onto an evergreen tree in the path in front of us and scrambled up onto a limb, his claws slashing through the bark, sending pine-scented splinters cascading to the forest floor much like the shavings from my grandfather's whittling. I stretched my arms up and stood on tiptoe, but the branch was just out of reach. Smoky hunkered down on the limb, his mouth open in a fresh hiss. *HIIIIISSSSS!*

The bright light of the flare came bounding up behind me, and I took off again into the woods, making a wide circle around the tree Smoky was in. I didn't want to let my precious baby get out of my sight again.

I ran around the tree a second time, making a tighter circle, when my ears detected the sound of a siren coming up the winding road. *Thank the stars!* The siren grew louder, then softer as the squad car wound its way back and forth on the incline. But I soon realized it wasn't coming fast enough. No matter what evasive maneuvers I ran, Gage Tilley was gaining on me. My skull would be smashed to smithereens by the time Marlon found us, and Gage could easily disappear into the woods, coming out at any number of spots along the mountain where he could evade capture.

The siren was closer now, but still not close enough, the sound echoing through the woods as I approached the branch on which Smoky was perched. I looked up. His mouth was closed now, his eyes narrowed into determined slits. He'd somehow managed to free himself from my bra. The two ends had caught on a thick nub where vertical limbs had broken off the tree, the small cups hanging down.

I darted under my cat and into the forest. The thrashing I'd heard behind me suddenly stopped, and Gage issued a surprised shout. I turned to see Smoky gone from the branch and Gage wearing my bra like a sleep mask, the cups covering his eyes, the straps tangled around the tire iron, holding him back. He struggled in the straps, his flaming flare moving about like an off-color firefly caught in a spider's web. He dropped the lug wrench to the ground with a thud but seemed to forget that the road flare in his right hand was a flame. He dropped the flare, too, to free himself. Smoldering smoke arose around him for a second or two until the shooting flame managed to ignite the bed of dried winter leaves at his feet. In an instant, he was surrounded by flames and his pants were on fire from the knees down.

He panicked, screaming and stamping and slapping at his calves as if performing a pyrotechnic step dance routine. I seized the moment and darted forward, running onto the berm holding up the end of the fallen tree, and calling to my cat. "Smoky! Here!"

Smoky turned and sauntered across the downed tree toward me, swishing his tail and casting glances back at the flaming, dancing man behind him. New thrashing sounds came from the direction of the road, the loud sound telling me something big was coming. It could be Marlon, but given how crazy things had become out here, there was a decent chance it was Sasquatch. Whoever it was, they carried a high-beam flashlight.

With a final *crash, crackle, snap*, my favorite cop burst into view. He turned to meet my gaze for a microsecond before dropping his flashlight and hurling himself at the human inferno in front of him in a running dive that took him temporarily airborne. He tackled Tilley to the ground and wrapped him in a bear hug, rolling them both back and forth. The motion not only put out the flames on Tilley's clothing but extinguished the flames on the ground as well. *Thank goodness!* I'd feared the entire forest would go up in smoke. The road flare fizzled too, a spark evidencing its final gasp, but not before I saw Tilley's hand reach out for the lug wrench.

"Look out!" I shrieked to Marlon. "He's got a weapon!"

With the flare no longer burning and the beam of the flashlight aimed away from the melee, the dark night swallowed us. The sounds of struggling continued. Grunts, curses, and groans filled the air, along with an occasional *slap* or *whump* of an open or closed fist meeting flesh and the *clang* of the lug wrench meeting a tree trunk or rock. Marlon was a big, strong man, but Gage Tilley had a dangerous weapon and was fueled by pure adrenaline and desperation. There was a chance this might not end well. I wanted to help, but I feared I'd only get in the way and that my cat would run off again.

I held Smoky so tight to my chest it was a wonder the poor beast could breathe. Finally, the sounds of the struggle stopped. Unsure exactly how the fight had been resolved, I felt my stomach seize into a hard stone. While I was tempted to call Marlon's name, I didn't want to alert Gage to my location if he'd been the victor. I held my breath, waiting for some signal, some type of confirmation that Marlon had brought the murderer into submission.

The *click-click* sound of handcuffs being fastened told me everything was okay. I gulped a deep breath, and my muscles relaxed. My knees gave way and I sank onto the soft forest floor, still holding Smoky tight. A dozen fireflies lit up the night like fireworks over Marlon's head, celebrating the arrest of Cormac O'Keefe's killer.

Marlon whipped his radio from his belt. "I need an ambulance, stat." He noted the location of our vehicles. "We're in the woods, approximately fifty yards north of my cruiser." With medical assistance on the way, he turned his attention back to Tilley, reciting his rights.

With the situation now under control, I exhaled a long, shaky breath and put my hand on a tree limb to lever myself back to standing. Marlon rounded up his flashlight and aimed the beam in my direction, lighting my way to him.

I picked my way over to the men and glared down at Tilley. Smoky glared down at him, too, as if somehow understanding he'd been the cause of tonight's trouble. Marlon shined his flashlight down on the man's face. He blinked against the harsh glare.

"You killed Cormac O'Keefe," I said. "You needed a legitimate customer who'd agree to an exclusive arrangement and order large quantities of discounted liquor from you, but it was only to establish a paper trail and hide the truth, wasn't it? You kept most of the moonshine yourself, to resell at a profit and pocket the earnings." Gage must have realized that Cormac was a sleazebag who'd be happy to engage in a shady operation in return for a buck or two. "Then something went wrong."

Writhing in pain, he cried, "The guy screwed me over! We had a deal, but he demanded a bigger share. It wasn't fair! It wasn't what we'd agreed to!"

Tilley's confession made, I turned to Marlon. "I guess we can make plans for that dinner now."

He gave me a smile. "How's Friday look for ya?"

Chapter Twenty-Five

There was more thrashing and flashing of lights as two paramedics forced their way through the woods, carrying high-wattage flashlights and a bright orange stretcher. Leaning the stretcher against a tree, they bent down to assess their patient. They took a quick look at Tilley's burn wounds and grimaced. The guy was lucky his adrenaline masked some of his pain.

As the medics gingerly lifted Tilley and placed him on the stretcher, Officer Barboza picked his way toward us, a Maglite in his hand and Ace on his tail.

She glanced around, taking in the cat in my arms, the man on the stretcher, and the charred bra on the ground. "Whatever happened here must have been interesting." She turned her pointed gaze on me. "You're lucky you're alive."

I bit my lip. "I know."

She pulled a pair of latex gloves from the pocket of her pantsuit and slid her hands into them. She reached down and picked up my bra, letting it dangle by the burnt strap from her fingers. "If this case goes to trial, this bra will be exhibit A."

Barboza leaned in to check the tag. "Make that exhibit *double* A."

I felt my cheeks blaze again but this time with embarrassment rather than the heat of the road flare.

After dropping my barbecued bra into an evidence bag, Ace pointed to the paramedics, who had strapped Tilley to the stretcher and were lifting him up. She turned to Barboza. "Go with them to the hospital and keep an eye on the murder suspect."

He gave her a nod. "Yes, ma'am."

One of the medics turned to me and Marlon. "You need attention?"

"I'm okay," I said. "I've got some scratches, but I think that's it."

He aimed his flashlight at me. "Let me take a quick look to be sure. I saw the condition your van is in, the broken windows. You could have some glass embedded in your skin." He ran his flashlight over my exposed skin, taking a close look. He used tweezers to pull out several small shards of glass. "If you notice more later you can remove them yourself. Any pieces that don't come out easy a clinic can handle for you. Okay?"

I nodded.

"Let me check your chest and abdomen for signs of injury. Seat belts can save lives, but they can cause injuries, too, in bad wrecks like this." He motioned with his index finger for me to unbuckle the straps of my overalls and lift my shirt so he could take a look. Marlon, Ace, and Barboza turned their backs to give me privacy while the paramedic took a quick look at my chest, abdomen, and back. "Looks like you're good to go. But if you start feeling any neck pain, or any pain in your gut, you get yourself to a doctor right away."

"I will. Thanks."

He turned to Marlon next. While there were burn marks on his uniform, leaves and twigs in his hair, and smudges of dirt on his cheeks, he'd managed to escape major injury.

Once the medic was done with me and Marlon, I looked Smoky over carefully. Although his carrier had been tossed around, he seemed to be okay. I saw no blood on him, and he didn't react oddly when I took his paws in my hands and tested his limbs. He didn't mew or howl in pain when I palpated his tummy and sides. He merely looked annoyed, which was his normal state of expression. He'd probably used one of his nine lives, but he was no worse for wear. Marlon took him from me, carried him back to his police department SUV, and placed him inside so he'd be safe while we wrapped things up here.

Once Officer Barboza and the medical crew had taken Gage Tilley away, Ace returned her attention to me and Marlon, gesturing at the broken branches and smoldering leaves. "What exactly happened out here?"

We spent the next few minutes catching her up. I started first, elaborating on my earlier text. I told her how I'd been heading to my cabin when I'd seen the Backwoods Bootleggers truck circle behind the liquor store and decided to see if I might spot anything unusual. Of course, I had. Thus, the photos and text I'd sent to Marlon.

I gave her a sheepish shrug. "I guess Gage Tilley saw my van at the pizza place and realized I might have witnessed his exchange at the liquor store. I didn't know he was following me until I was halfway up the mountain. By then, it was too late. There's nowhere to turn off up here."

She cast a glance at Marlon. "Good thing Officer Landers was in touch with you."

"I'm glad he found me and Smoky in time." Tilley had been intent on putting an end to us, just like he'd done to Cormac.

Though he'd been a hero tonight, Marlon downplayed his contribution. "Wasn't hard to spot your van, what with it glowing in the dark. Besides, it was obvious where you went over the side. There was a trail of laundry to mark the route."

Ace handed her flashlight to Marlon, and he held it up while she snapped a few photos of the scene, including the broken limbs, the scorched earth, and the road flare and lug wrench on the ground. She rounded up the road flare for evidence and slid it into another clear plastic bag. Then she picked up the lug wrench and looked from it to me. "He could've done some real damage to you with this thing."

"He could've injured Marlon, too," I added. "We're lucky he didn't."

"You sure are," she said. "Now you can testify against him if need be."

"Is that the only reason you're glad I'm alive? So I can testify?" Okay, so I was fishing for compliments or accolades from her. But darn it, my business acumen had helped solve this case and, after everything my cat and I had been through tonight, I wanted some credit.

A grin tugged at her lips. "I'm glad you're alive because you're one smart cookie, Hattie. The world could use more of those. I thought the missing moonshine was the crux of this case, but you figured out why." She let the grin spread and reached out to give me a pat on the back. "Thanks for your help."

Together, we made our way back to the road, where Mar-

lon contacted dispatch and asked them to summon a tow
truck to haul my van away. The hood was crumpled, as if the
van were grimacing. Three of the four tires were flat and bent
at odd angles, the axles wrenched. Seeing the smashed-in top,
the glass shards sticking up from the trim, and the trail of
laundry that had been expelled through the broken windows,
I realized it was a miracle Smoky and I not only had lived
through the crash but had no broken bones.

"I hate to tell you," the detective said as she ran her eyes
over my vehicle, "but I think your van is a total loss."

I shrugged. "The most valuable thing about it was the
custom paint job."

She pointed up into a tree. "Are those the panties that
match your polka-dot bra?"

They were. They were also up too high for me to reach
them. I supposed it didn't much matter. With the burnt bra
taken into evidence, they were no longer a matched set
anyway.

I picked my way around the woods, snatching socks off a
limb here, yoga pants from a rock there, a striped shirt from
the ground behind a sapling. I found a pair of overalls hooked
around a limb, hanging like an unstuffed scarecrow. Marlon
offered to help me gather the laundry, but I declined his assistance. "It's bad enough you're seeing my unmentionables."
I certainly didn't want him touching them.

After the tow truck arrived and drove off with my van,
Ace looked from me to Marlon before waggling her fingers.
"You two go along now. Go share some moonshine or
something."

Marlon turned to me. "That's not a bad idea. You got
some up at your cabin?"

"I might have a jar or two." *Or ten. Plus a jug.*

A quarter hour later, Smoky was stretched out on the

couch, taking a nap, exhausted from the evening's crazy adventure. I'd poured double shots of shine for both Marlon and myself, one each of apple and cinnamon. I raised my glass in a toast. "To the end of a successful investigation."

He clinked his glass against mine and we both took a sip.

Now that Smoky and I were back at our cabin, safe, the import of the night's events struck me. My body started to shake uncontrollably as the adrenaline processed. The moonshine sloshed over the edge of my glass onto the floor, and my teeth began to chatter.

Marlon cast me a look, set his moonshine on the kitchen counter, and took my glass from me, as well. He set my glass on the countertop next to his before stepping forward to envelop me in a tight embrace, essentially swaddling me with his arms, attempting to quell my tremors. He held me for several minutes. When my shivering began to cease, he spoke softly into my hair. "I remember when I first met you in the alley behind your shop. I suspected you'd cause me trouble. Looks like I was right."

"Hey!" I huffed, putting a palm on his chest to push him back. "You can't blame me for anything that's happened."

"I suppose not." A mischievous gleam danced in his eyes as he gazed down at me. "Truth is, I'm looking forward to seeing what other trouble you might bring me."

Chapter Twenty-Six

Over the next few days, the full details came to light. Caught red-handed with his pants literally on fire, Gage Tilley decided to tell the truth. Maybe he hoped coming clean would bring him some good karma come sentencing time.

Gage knew Cormac had been delinquent in paying earlier invoices to Backwoods Bootleggers, and he figured it was due to cash flow issues or questionable business practices. Either way, he realized Cormac could be the perfect partner in crime for a scheme he'd devised to bilk money from the moonshine company. He knew he ran the risk of his employer catching on if he stole moonshine outright for resale, and he needed a legitimate paper trail to cover his tracks. If he could convince one of his customers to agree to make Backwoods Bootleggers their exclusive moonshine vendor, he'd have access to bottles at a discount and the paperwork to back it up. He'd then sell the excess bottles to other customers at a smaller discount, provide them with fake invoices, and split the profits with Cormac for his role in the scheme. What's more, Gage would get a bonus from Backwoods for convincing a customer to go exclusive with the company.

Of course, they knew they might need an explanation for Cormac's unusually large order. Cormac had come up with the part about hosting a regular moonshine special to compete with my shop, while Gage, noting that bikers were a big part of both Backwoods Bootleggers' and Limericks' customer bases, came up with the biker rally explanation. Tilley had fed this fictional story to Ace when she'd interviewed him. Looked like I hadn't been too far off when I'd speculated about the bikers and frat boys being potential buyers of the resale shine.

Even though Cormac would retain only a few of the bottles ordered, they'd agreed that the bar would serve Backwoods Bootleggers brand exclusively. Gage knew his regional manager sometimes performed spot inspections to make sure exclusive customers were living up to the agreement and serving only Backwoods shine. Any customers found to be carrying other brands of moonshine would lose their exclusivity discount. For this reason, it was critical to the scheme that Cormac serve no shine other than Backwoods.

Problem was, Cormac was not good at keeping his word and, being the deceitful devil he was, he realized he had Gage over a whiskey barrel. Though he'd initially agreed to accept a third of the profits from the scheme, when Gage had come to the bar that Friday night to pay Cormac his share, Cormac had insisted he be paid half of the profits instead. He wanted half of Gage's bonus, as well. He'd also insisted that Gage serve as a witness in his slander complaint against Heath Delaney, even though Gage had overhead nothing. If Gage didn't cough up the extra cash or agree to serve as a witness in the hearing, Cormac threatened to contact Backwoods and tell them what Gage had done. *I suppose it's true what they say. There's no honor among thieves.*

With Cormac blackmailing him, Gage had no choice but to pay the barkeep half of the profits he'd pocketed on the undocumented cash sales. Gage had been angry enough about Cormac reneging on their deal, but anger gave way to full-on fury when he'd left Cormac's office, spotted a jar of my Firefly moonshine under the counter in the bar as he'd bent down to tie his shoe, and believed Cormac hadn't stayed true to the exclusivity part of the deal. He'd tucked the jar into a large pocket on the side of his cargo pants, left the bar, and circled around to the back alley, where he lay in wait until Cormac closed the bar for the night and came out the back door alone.

Gage had brandished the jar and accused Cormac of violating the exclusivity clause and risking the whole scheme. When Cormac expressed no remorse, Gage took a swing at him. Cormac took off running and Gage ran after him, his fury igniting and growing hotter with each pounding step until he caught up with Cormac in front of my shop and cornered him in the doorway. By then, his rage was out of control. A *thud-tinkle-cry-thud-thud* later, and Cormac lay bleeding out on the stoop.

As Gage ran off, he saw the lights come on in front of my shop and realized someone had been in my store, most likely yours truly. When he wasn't immediately arrested, he further realized I must not have gotten a good look at Cormac's attacker. He thought he'd gotten away with his crime until Ace contacted him with questions. He knew she would have spoken with me, and that I would have been aware of the exclusivity arrangement he'd made with Cormac after crashing my grand opening celebration. After all, he'd reminded Cormac that he'd have to refuse the order he'd placed with me at my party.

When Gage spotted my glow-in-the-dark van at the pizza place next to Bridge Liquor Outlet after he'd made the undocumented cash sale there, he feared it was not a coincidence. He deduced that I suspected him of being Cormac's killer. He parked his truck out of sight and lay in wait a block away to see if and when I might emerge from the pizza restaurant. When I came from around the back of the restaurant rather than exiting through its doors, he knew I'd been spying on him. His fear and fury took hold of him again, and thus Smoky and I ended up going head over heels—or should I say headlights over wheels?—down the side of the mountain. One unsuccessful chase with a road flare and lug wrench, and here we all were, mystery solved with no increase in body count. *Phew!*

Ace went to Bridge Liquors and examined the labels on their boxes of Backwoods Bootleggers moonshine. She confirmed that the preprinted labels addressed to Limericks had been covered by bogus stickers printed with the name and address of the liquor store.

Thanks to Gage Tilley's admissions, as well as Miranda's affidavit stating that the dishwasher at the bar worked perfectly, the complaint Cormac had filed against Heath Delaney with the Board of Professional Responsibility was resolved in Heath's favor and the record of the complaint was expunged. He wouldn't get back the lucrative client he'd lost, but at least he wouldn't lose another to the baseless accusation.

Smoky and I were happy to be back in our cabin. Although it had been fun hanging out with Kiki and her cats, it felt nice to be home again. Smoky expressed his glee by flopping down on his back on the braided rug and wriggling to his heart's content several times a day.

The local news channels, who'd before shown no interest in airing a story about my shop or my family's history in the moonshine business, were now climbing over one another to interview me and my grandfather at the Moonshine Shack. I was forgiving and gracious, granting all requests. Same for the newspapers. My favorite piece was one cleverly titled "*Still* in Business" that not only covered my family's history in moonshining but also Marlon's family's history in law enforcement and how our two families seemed forever intertwined by fate. The photographer had taken a photo of me and Marlon back to back, our arms crossed over our chests, our eyes narrowed as each of us glanced back at our purported rival. With the difference in our heights, I'd had to stand atop a case of my moonshine so that my head would reach above his shoulders. I'd framed a copy of the article and photo and hung it on the wall in the Moonshine Shack, right next to the newspaper clipping about my great-grandfather's arrest by Sheriff Landers nearly a century ago. Granddaddy didn't even object. With Marlon having saved me from certain death at Tilley's hands, he decided to finally let bygones be bygones.

Thanks to the free publicity, traffic at the shop had increased more than tenfold. Not only did the customers buy jars and jugs of moonshine, but they also asked to take photos of me and Granddaddy with Smoky. There wasn't a single picture taken in which my darn cat wasn't giving me the stiff arm.

Now that the shop was well in the black, I'd posted an ad online looking for help. Over a hundred applicants had vied for the part-time positions. Interviews were scheduled in the upcoming days. I'd have my pick of employees.

Similarly, the liquor stores who'd earlier refused to carry my small-batch shine were inundated with customers searching for my homebrew. The stores placed orders at such a pace that the bottling company could barely keep up. It was a good problem to have.

My secondhand van was a total loss. The insurance company paid me next to nothing for it, but with sales taking off now, at least I could afford a new vehicle. I'd paid extra again to have my replacement van outfitted in custom firefly-green paint.

Mack Clayton placed an order for four jugs of Granddaddy's Ole-Timey Corn Liquor and proposed that the two of us join together to offer bottled shine sauce. We'd co-brand it under the name of his restaurant and my moonshine brand—Smoky Mountains Smokehouse Firefly Shine Sauce. Because I'd done the legwork on bottled products for my moonshine, I was spearheading the effort to get the sauce into production.

The shine sauce wouldn't be my only new product, either. I tinkered with the relative proportions of apple pie and cinnamon shine over the next few days and, with Marlon's input, settled on relative proportions of two-thirds apple pie and one-third cinnamon for what would be my seventh Firefly moonshine flavor, candy apple.

Granddaddy's wooden figurines flew off the shelves. Many of the shoppers who came in to buy a jar or jug of shine for themselves took home a cat, horse, squirrel, or bear for their child, grandchild, or a favorite niece or nephew. With the Chattanooga Choo-Choo Model Train Convention coming up in a couple of weeks, my grandfather had turned to whittling small steam engines and box-cars. He stockpiled them during the week for Kiki to paint while she minded the store with me on the weekends. I planned to hold some promotions in conjunction with the convention and take advantage of the large crowd to move some moonshine and spread the word about my new Firefly brand and Granddaddy's Ole-Timey Corn Liquor.

All in all, things were really looking up for me and the Moonshine Shack. But I knew better than to take things for granted. I'd keep my nose to the proverbial grindstone.

Friday night finally arrived. Kiki had agreed to run the 'Shine Shack for me so I'd be free to enjoy my much-anticipated date with Marlon. He picked me up at my cabin at seven o'clock, and we headed back down the mountain to have dinner at Bar Celona.

Though I'd feared we might not have much to talk about now that Cormac's murder case was resolved, my fears proved to be unfounded. Between Marlon telling me about the interesting and oddball things he'd seen on the job, and me sharing stories of growing up with my often outrageous grandfather, we easily filled the time while we got to know each other better. Before I knew it, we'd eaten our way through half the menu and the server was laying the bill on our table.

I reached for the ticket, but Marlon stretched out his hand and took my wrist gently to stop me. "It's on me, re-member?" I said. "As a thank-you for looking out for me and my shop."

"It's on Ace," he said. "She insisted."

"She did?"

He nodded. "Your input on the financial aspects of the

murder case were critical. She said it was the least she could do." He released my hand, leaving a warm sensation behind. "She also said to give you this." He reached into the breast pocket of his shirt, retrieved a tube of Chantecaille Honeypot lipstick, and handed it to me.

I pulled out my phone and sent a text to thank her for the wonderful meal and the lipstick. A reply came in immediately. A winky-face emoji followed by I hope you're enjoying the company, too.

I replied with a thumbs-up. When I looked up, I caught Marlon eyeing me.

He placed his napkin on the table. "Let's do this again, little filly."

My heart performed a somersault in my chest. "I'm game."

"Good. I'd like to take you on a trail ride. There's a horse path with some nice scenery just outside of town and a café that serves the best cornbread you'll ever eat. How's that sound?"

It sounded both relaxing and romantic. "I'll dig out my boots."

As we left the restaurant, Marlon said, "I'm not ready for the night to be over. Why don't we take a walk on the riverfront?"

"That sounds wonderful."

And wonderful it was. The night was dark and starry, a light breeze keeping the temperature cool and comfortable. We stopped to sit on a bench overlooking the river, and Marlon draped his arm protectively over the bench behind me. The water moved by before us, ebbing and flowing, lapping softly at the shore. After the tumultuous days we'd endured, a quiet moment to decompress was exactly what the two of us needed.

As I thought over the preceding days, I felt proud to have played a part in solving a murder mystery. The only mystery now was, where would things go from here? Would my shop continue to thrive and my moonshine business grow, or would sales decline once the murder case was no longer in the news? Would whatever was happening with me and Marlon turn into something serious, or would it be just some casual fun?

As I pondered my future, a firefly lit up in front of me, drawing a squiggle in the air before turning off his bright behind and disappearing into the night. Maybe the little bug had a point. Sometimes it's more fun not to know what the future holds. Sometimes it's fun to be kept in the dark.

ACKNOWLEDGMENTS

I'm over the moon about launching this moonshine series, and so grateful to all the wonderful folks who made it happen. I raise a glass to all of you!

Thanks to my agent, Helen Breitwieser, for championing this series.

Thanks to Michelle Vega for giving the series a home at Berkley. Thanks to my editor, Miranda Hill, for your perceptive suggestions and guidance through the revision process. Thanks to the rest of the Berkley team, including Brittanie Black, Natalie Sellars, Sarah Oberrender, and Megan Elmore, for all of your hard work in getting the book into readers' hands. The cover is adorable, and Smoky is sure to steal some hearts!

Thanks, too, to you wonderful readers who chose this book. Enjoy your time with Hattie, Smoky, and the rest of the gang at the Moonshine Shack.

Ready to find
your next great read?

Let us help.

Visit prh.com/nextread

Penguin
Random
House